Rima Rabih Bachrouch is a 14-year-old British writer. At the age of 11, she began writing *Magic McFee and the Legend of the Sorcerer,* which is her first novel. Having grown up with a wild imagination, Bachrouch would write her own short stories from a very young age. She also has other interests, which include acting and filmmaking, wildlife, nature, and the environment and Science. She hopes to one day be able to play a bigger role in tackling the global climate change challenge.

MAGIC MCFEE

and the

legend of the sorcerer

RIMA BACHROUCH

AUSTIN MACAULEY PUBLISHERS™

LONDON • CAMBRIDGE • NEW YORK • SHARJAH

ISBN 9789948803133 (Paperback)
ISBN 9789948803140 (E-Book)

Application Number: MC-10-01-7085030
Age Classification: 13+

First Published 2023
AUSTIN MACAULEY PUBLISHERS FZE
Sharjah Publishing City
P.O Box [519201]
Sharjah, UAE
www.austinmacauley.ae
+971 655 95 202

Chapter One
A New World

God, where had she put them?

"Mum, have you seen my trainers?" called Magic McFee as she descended the stairs onto the landing.

Magic was a young girl of 14 with long, dark hair and very bright, ocean blue eyes. She had a few freckles scattered across her pale face, as if someone had sprinkled chocolate flakes all over it.

"Yes, dear, I've already packed them for you."

Magic very much resembled her mother, Lauren McFee. She had the same ocean blue eyes, but instead of her hair being long and dark like her daughter's, it was shoulder-length and a very bright blonde.

"Thanks, Mum," replied Magic as she crossed the room and sat in a corner next to a pile of boxes. She began helping her mother with the packing. The house looked a mess; bundles of clothes were piled up next to the fireplace and all the velvety sofas were pushed against the wall. The rest of the space in the room was filled with cardboard boxes.

"Where's Dad?" asked Magic.

"He's in his office, talking to the company that will lend us the moving vans," replied Mrs McFee as she pressed hard on the top of a large cardboard box, trying to get it to close. Magic eyed the empty boxes with a groan and got to work.

Magic sort of noticed when the afternoon had arrived after a few hours of packing; at that moment, she sighed, in an exhausted voice, "I'm going upstairs to check if anything is left."

She crossed the room, being careful not to trip over any boxes, and started up the stairs.

The walls in the corridor upstairs were a pale yellow and looked very plain and odd, since she was used to seeing family photos hung there. She turned left and opened her bedroom door, the room inside completely empty and the curtains drawn. The walls were of a very bright, pale pink; the paint on the slanted ceiling had begun to peel. Magic exited the room when she found nothing left in there, the door snapping shut behind her just as she heard a deep, muffled honk issuing from the street outside—the van was here.

She hurried downstairs to find her father standing in the hallway, smiling broadly.

David McFee was wearing the same black overcoat and black bowler hat he wore to work every day. He had the same dark hair that Magic had but a different set of eyes—a pair of dazzling dark brown.

"Have you finished packing yet, or do you need more time?" he asked, his eyes scanning over what he could see of the house, checking how much packing they had left. He seemed satisfied.

"Yeah, we've finished," answered Magic.

"Well then, the moving van is outside," said Mr McFee.

Magic stepped over the threshold and onto the landing outside where a large, white van was waiting for them.

It took about an hour to move all their essential belongings into the van, most of them packed in cardboard shipping boxes. They stacked them neatly in rows and columns before slamming the van doors shut with an exhausted sigh.

Once all their items were settled, Mrs McFee brought out some sandwiches and orange juice on a large, round silver tray. They munched happily on the doorstep just as the sun began to dip down below the horizon, the sky turning from periwinkle to salmon orange.

"Are you excited for school?" Mr McFee asked Magic after he'd eaten his fill.

Magic's stomach knotted nervously. She hadn't given her new school much thought; she refused to think about it and get herself worked up over the pain and struggle of trying to make new friends.

"I don't know, I guess…" she replied hesitantly.

"Well, I really do hope you'll like it," sighed Mr McFee.

They swivelled the last of their orange juice and gobbled down the final bits of their sandwiches before packing up the tray. Magic stared fleetingly through the door of her house one final time, before her father locked up the front door, the keys clinking against each other.

They finally hopped into the car and made sure everything was with them, before Mr McFee turned the key in the ignition, and the car engine rumbled. Magic stared at her house as it grew smaller and further away from her, not taking her eyes off it before they turned a corner, and it vanished.

By six o'clock arrived, the sky had deepened to a clear mauve, few white flecks starting to appear, twinkling mysteriously. As Magic stared out the car window, her face in her hand, it became harder to assess the views outside. Everything came and went in dark, blurry shadows, her eyes giving up completely.

Magic laid her head against her seat and stared up at the skies. More stars had appeared since she had last inspected the night sky, and she couldn't help thinking about the future, although she knew she would regret it later when her mood dropped significantly.

Magic had no idea how she was supposed to settle in, or how long it would take her if she was going to at all. She had always cringed at the idea of *trying* to make friends, because she had always just *had* them. She wasn't exactly used to being alone all the time, and, although she was afraid to admit it to anybody but herself, she felt a slight twinge of fear in the pit of her stomach at the unknown. She had not the slightest idea of what to expect, so for now, she held her breath.

She tucked these thoughts at the back of her mind because she was well aware of the danger of letting herself think too long… the long marathons of time she spent thinking about things that worried her always left her downcast by the end of it. Instead, she tried to focus on the music her mother was happily singing along to. She smiled, and felt her eyelids becoming heavier, and heavier…

Magic's mind drifted off in a deep slumber, where her thoughts couldn't disturb her any longer—they failed to find a way to sneak into her dreams.

While she lay there sleeping peacefully in the backseat, the sky continued to fade from mauve to a beautiful, glossy black—more white flecks appeared, twinkling fiercely against the dark horizon. The moon beamed so pearly white that, despite their beauty, the stars looked like mere sparks next to it—they could not compete with the proud glow of the stunning white orb, floating high above the world.

They continued to twist and turn through the dark English neighbourhoods. It was so perfectly tranquil, it seemed like the whole city was asleep—it was night's turn to open its eyes.

The car began to slow down—the sudden change in speed caused Magic to jerk awake. Her eyes stung and watered, but she blinked back the moisture, lifting her forehead from the backseat window.

As Magic rubbed her head gently, she stared through the glass as they slowly pulled into a driveway. She leaned closer to the window eagerly, and, in the glowing rays of the headlights, she could just make out a front lawn of crispy, damp green grass. But, before she could analyse anything else, the engine cut off, the lights turned out and the car's rumbling ceased.

David McFee turned round in the front seat to face Magic, grinning. Magic sat up straight.

"Home sweet home," he murmured.

Magic smiled before there was a *click* as she tugged at the car door, and a *slam* as she heaved it shut.

Magic ran a hand through her sweaty hair, the cool evening breeze seeping through her locks and cooling the back of her neck. Her hair fluttered behind her as her gaze swept her new home.

Smooth, hard concrete made up the front porch, surrounded by the crispy green grass she had seen from the car window. Mini, darker green bushes lined the edge of the front lawn. Magic liked it so far; she was a huge fan of nature. Her heart smiled.

Two echoing slams behind her announced her parents exiting the vehicle. Magic whipped round to catch their reactions before they could get the chance to take it all in.

Magic smiled to herself as her mother squealed at the sight of the house, while her father trampled towards the front door, the grass crunching softly beneath his feet. Magic followed him, and behind her, she heard her mother doing the same.

Silently, Mr McFee fiddled with his pockets before pulling out a shiny, brass key, which he inserted into the white, wooden door. The outside walls were brick red, and the three windows Magic could see were curtained. Although simple, she liked the outside appearance.

The front door opened slowly with a low moan; Mr McFee climbed the two front steps before entering the darkness of the house and flicking on the lights.

As Magic slipped off her shoes, her eyes swept over the light pinewood panels that made up the floor, the off-white of the walls and, to her left, the dark oak of the stairs and the banister, which twirled up to the floor above.

The double doors leading to the first room on the right were lined with rippled glass windows. Magic gently shoved at them, and they gave way, revealing a cosy living room with fluffy armchairs, each of a different colour, surrounding a television that was fixed into the wall. The low coffee table matched the colour of the banisters—a warm, dark oak.

Next, she headed into the second room from the front door, which was the kitchen, merged with the dining room. First was the fridge on the right, followed by the white cupboards and dark oak countertops, and then the stove. The dining table on the right was perfectly rectangular, and the same dark oak as the countertop, the banister, and the coffee table in the living room. Magic was starting to understand the theme of the house, and quite liked the warm colours and muted tones. The dining table was able to accompany eight people, four wooden chairs on either side.

Magic's bedroom was the first on the left of the corridor upstairs; the floors kept up the light pinewood panels. Her bed was the first thing on the left, and opposite it sat a (dark oak!) dresser with a tall, narrow mirror propped up on it. She stared at her reflection, dark circles lining the bottom of her eyes, and her hair falling lank down her shoulders. Next to the dresser was her desk, and finally to the right of the desk was a white-curtained window. She drew them to reveal the grassy lawn outside, which glistened in the sparkling moonlight, and the cobbled pathway which led to her car.

Magic retrieved her pyjamas from the backpack she had taken with her, changing into them before heading downstairs for dinner.

As they chewed on pastries Mrs McFee had saved from their old house, Mrs McFee was ranting excitedly about her new kitchen space and how much more creative freedom she'd now be able to have with her cooking. Magic zoned out through the entire conversation, only tuning in when her father mentioned some guests that would be coming the next day.

"I've invited Mr Harrow and his family to come for dinner tomorrow," Mr McFee told them. "He's an old friend of mine who I'll be working alongside at my new job." He turned to Magic. "His daughter goes to your new school, Magic, so it'll be nice to get to know someone before you go there."

"Oh," said Magic, getting distracted again as she tried to picture what this girl might be like.

"That's lovely, dear. It'll be wonderful to get to know some new people in this new area…I don't know anybody in Krington…yet," Mrs McFee said thoughtfully. "And, yes, it would be nice to get to know someone from school before the start of term, wouldn't it, dear?" she addressed Magic.

"Wha…oh, yeah," muttered Magic, picking at her pastry. She didn't feel hungry anymore, just nervous. She yawned, and then decided to call it a night. She bade her parents goodnight and headed upstairs.

The bathroom was much larger than the one she had in her old house; the floor was of black marble, and there was much more shower space.

As Magic splashed water on her face and dolloped some toothpaste onto her toothbrush, her mind sighed with relief. She had been unsure as to whether she'd like her new life, but for now, she didn't mind it.

Minutes later, she flicked off her bedroom light and slumped down in bed. She had expected to be awake for a while, but she drifted off moments later.

Magic awoke the next morning to the smell of roast beef and potatoes wafting up the stairs.

"Why're you preparing *now*?" Magic asked incredulously when she entered the kitchen. "They won't be here until six!"

Mrs McFee pursed her lips. "It's good to be prepared, darl. A good first impression!"

Magic knew her mother all too well, so didn't press the matter.

None of the boxes with any of her major items had arrived yet, so she didn't have any unpacking to do. So, while chomping on a piece of toast, Magic tried to come up with ways to keep herself company. She was an only child, so she had no one to talk to or get up to mischief with.

Once finished, Magic headed upstairs. She had brought some books with her in her backpack, and decided she'd eat through one after the other by the time the Harrows arrived.

She set herself up by the window; she moved her desk chair to the windowsill at exactly the right spot for a perfect view, even though she wouldn't be looking out the window at all.

She grabbed her pile of books and kicked her feet up onto her desk, opened the first one on the pile and began to devour it.

Magic only looked up from her books to get a glass of water or visit the bathroom—reading was one of the only things she could say, with pride, that she'd be able to do for an entire day without getting bored.

Magic slotted her bookmark in and slapped the book shut when she reached page 200—it was a good place to stop, as she had reached the beginning of a new chapter. She yawned, stretched, and then stared out the window—the day had gone by too quickly for her to remember when the time had slipped away. The sky outside was a clear salmon, with streaks of red and orange. The sun had dipped down low over the horizon; it was a semi-circle-shaped orb sitting on the buildings far, far away.

Magic reckoned that the Harrows would be arriving any time soon, so she thought it an appropriate time to get ready to greet them.

She threw on a pair of jeans and a grey jumper and hoped they would suffice. Magic then pulled her hairbrush out of her backpack and straightened out in front of her bedroom mirror. She'd never given much thought to her hair, so she just brushed through it and twisted it into a plait.

Magic was just crossing over the final strands of her hair, when something she saw out of the corner of her eye caused her heart to leap out of place.

Out the window, she noticed a dark figure on the other side of the road. Its face was concealed, and it was draped in a long, black cloak. It held in one hand a long object that looked to Magic like an oddly shaped stick.

Magic hastily scrambled over to her window to get a closer look.

It was like the figure knew Magic could see it—as soon as Magic reached the windowsill, the figure looked up, and even though she couldn't see its expression, she could feel its eyes on her.

Instinctively, she ducked down below the windowsill and out of view of the glass. Her heart throbbed oddly against her chest.

What was that? What did it want? There was a very strange aura that figure emitted that had Magic on edge. What was it doing there? It definitely didn't look like any ordinary person.

Hesitantly, Magic peeked over the windowsill as little as possible so that she was only just able to get a view of the streets outside—but it was completely deserted.

She slowly stood up straight so that she was in full view of the window once again. It was like the figure hadn't been there at all. Although shaken, Magic told herself that she was probably just imagining things. No existing being could travel that fast.

Magic headed downstairs to see what her parents were up to, and walked into the kitchen to find the table completely laid, thick steam rolling off the top of the crispy brown turkey in the middle of the table. There was a large bowl of mash potatoes, another of corn, carrots and green beans, and another of Caesar salad.

In the living room, Mr McFee sat with one leg on top of the other, flicking through the television channels. He wore a simple outfit consisting of a neat pair of black trousers and white blouse.

"You look good," Magic complemented him with a grin. "Where's Mum?" she asked.

He returned her grin. "Thank you. She went upstairs a few minutes ago." He checked his wristwatch. "They should be here any moment now."

Magic took a seat on the sofa next to him. "Have you found anything interesting on there?" she asked, frowning at the television.

"Not at the moment, I've only just turned it on…" replied Mr McFee. He handed her the remote. "Here, just look through it, I'll be back, I've got to check something." He left the room.

Magic flipped from channel to channel, listening in for a few moments on each. Nothing really hooked her in, so she just watched absently when a news channel popped up.

She heard some cheerful murmur in the corridor before Mrs McFee walked into the room, sporting a bright orange dress spotted with palm-sized white flowers, with matching gems in her ears.

Just as Mrs McFee opened her mouth to say something, a muffled *ding-dong* echoed from the corridors. With an excited squeal, she glided past the rippled glass doors and down the corridor, Magic tagging along behind her.

Mr McFee came crashing down the stairs; he looked through the peephole before he clattered round with the security chain, and the door swung open.

A family of three stood on the front step of the house—in the front, a girl round the same age as Magic smiled shyly. Her chestnut hair was tied back in a low ponytail that fell down her shoulders. She sported a turquoise, knee-length dress with a pair of matching ballerina shoes. Her eyes were the exact shade of her hair—clear and calm.

Behind her to the left, the father stood—he was slightly plump, and donned a black suit and leather shoes. Magic got the impression that this family's clothing style was very simple. His black hair was greying in some places, and the kind smile he wore triggered wrinkles at his eyes.

To his right stood his wife, in a pair of smooth, black trousers, and a red silk shirt. She carried a small velvet purse in her hands, and her hair was tucked back into a neat bottom-knot—it was the precise chestnut shade of her daughter's.

"Ah, Mr Harrow! So lovely to see you here." Mr McFee beamed at the sight of them. "Why don't you come in?"

"Thank you for having us," replied Mr Harrow. His voice was deep and smooth, which reminded Magic of a businessman.

As Mr McFee shut the door behind them, Mrs Harrow hugged Mrs McFee in a warm embrace. They greeted each other in soft, quiet murmurs as their daughter slipped off her shoes.

"Hi," the daughter said to Magic timidly.

"Er—hello," Magic responded awkwardly.

"Nice to meet you, Magic," Mr Harrow greeted Magic with a smile. "This is Katie, and she'll be joining you at school next term, which starts…tomorrow?" He looked to his wife, who nodded in confirmation. Magic's stomach turned to knots at the reminder.

"Hello, Katie," Magic greeted her again with a smile. "Nice to meet you."

"Nice to meet you too," Katie replied. Magic was slightly relieved—she would at least know one person when she walked through the school gates tomorrow.

Mrs McFee led them to the dining room, where they sat and ate cheerfully.

"Oh, Lauren, you really shouldn't have," Mrs Harrow tittered. "This is really too much."

"No, no, it was nothing," Mrs McFee reassured her, waving her off. "It's lovely having you here."

Mrs Harrow pursed her lips but continued to eat.

For a short while, there was silence but for the clattering of forks and knives and the scraping of cutlery against plates. Magic wasn't very good with awkward situations, so she occasionally cringed silently in her seat, flushing down at her plate.

The food dishes were almost empty once everybody had eaten their fill; Magic set down her knife and fork and excused herself from the table as an excuse to escape the unbearable awkwardness.

She sighed in relief when she reached the corridor and hopped up the stairs towards the bathroom. She took her time up there—it was not that she didn't *like* the Harrows, it was just that beside from being a naturally awkward person, she wasn't very good with socialising, either, which made the awkwardness of it all that much more displeasing.

When Magic finally left the bathroom, she was surprised to meet Katie at the foot of the stairs.

"Er—sorry," she said awkwardly. "Where's the bathroom?"

"Oh, just over there." Magic gestured to the room she had just left, mustering a smile.

"Thank you, Magic," replied Katie. She seemed to hesitate before saying, "You've got a cool name… Magic," she enunciated the name.

Magic felt the heat rush to her cheeks—she had not expected that. "Oh—thank you, Katie."

Katie nodded and headed off towards the bathroom.

Downstairs, the parents had relocated to the living room. Magic took a seat in her usual spot at the armchair by the window and tried tuning in on both the conversations happening between the mums and the dads.

Magic absorbed some talk about work, business, and some other stuff she didn't quite understand from the dads' conversations. As for the mothers, they conversed about recipes and Katie and Magic's school.

Magic tuned out when Katie walked back into the room. Her gaze swept the armchairs, and then quietly took a seat in the one beside Magic, next to the fireplace. Magic gave her a warming smile, before Katie opened up a conversation.

"So, are you nervous for school tomorrow?" Katie asked her.

Magic's expression turned thoughtful. "Anybody would be, right? Do you know what classes we'll be in?"

"No, we usually get told about our sortings the first day we arrive. They have us line up on the front lawn, and then they take us to our classes. Our deputy headmistress tells us where to go." Katie responded. She didn't seem to be as awkward as Magic.

"Oh, that's good, I could really use some direction on the first day," Magic admitted, trying to spark some humour. Katie laughed.

"Don't worry about it. You can ask me if you need help with anything tomorrow," Katie offered kindly.

"Thanks."

They talked about the subjects that they were planning to take for GCSE, exams, and the fear of how much harder work was going to get in Year 10. Magic didn't realise how fast she'd grown up—Year 10 already? She shuddered at the thought that she'd be turning fifteen next month.

The sky outside had turned a clear jet-black, stars strewn across it with white paint, like usual. The day had passed so fast, but Magic was glad it was over. Her eyes felt drowsy, and her limbs felt like rubber. She was about to excuse herself again, when Mr Harrow flickered a glance at his wristwatch.

"Goodness gracious, is that the time?" he asked incredulously. "We should really be heading off, the kids got school tomorrow," he told Mr McFee as he got up and headed into the corridor. The women followed, and so did the girls.

"It was nice seeing you," Katie told Magic as she slipped on her shoes. "See you in school."

"Yeah—see you," Magic replied, smiling.

"Thank you for having us, dear, it really was lovely of you," Mrs Harrow thanked the McFees. "Hopefully, we'll get to see you again soon."

"Yes, for sure," replied Mr McFee.

Katie gave Magic one final smile before stepping over the threshold behind her parents. Magic waved goodbye to her, and Mr McFee gently snapped the door shut.

Magic's eyes watered as she yawned. She was barely conscious of what she was doing when she bade her parents goodnight, and headed upstairs towards her bedroom.

Once all washed and changed, she flicked her light off and tucked herself in. She yawned again as she turned over on her side and dozed off with the thoughts of school, turkey and black cloaks colliding senselessly in her mind.

Chapter Two
Creavey High

A sore itchiness in her throat woke Magic up the next morning. She was about to turn over and drift off again, before a wave of nervousness swept through her as she remembered that today was the first day she'd be starting at her new school.

She hopped out of bed and brushed her teeth, twice. Downstairs, the table was already laid—some muffins and a glass of milk waited for her. Magic assumed that her parents had already left for work. She tried to eat, but it felt like chewing rubber. Her nerves skyrocketed again.

She scarfed down as much of the food as she could, but couldn't finish; she was afraid she was going to be sick.

Upstairs, she was pickier than usual about her outfit—when she was told that they didn't have a specific uniform at this school, she was surprised, but also relieved—she felt insecure in a big, clunky blazer.

She whipped out the pair of jeans she'd worn yesterday, a red t-shirt and a plain, grey zip-up jumper. Not too head-turning, not to dull. She was not planning on attracting any attention at all today…She shivered at the thought.

Magic's parents had told her that on the first day of school, a school bus would be coming to pick her up, and this was where most of her nervousness was concentrated. To her misfortune, Magic was one of the students who lived further away from the school—so, to her utter displeasure, she realised that the bus would be full of students by the time it reached her house.

She inhaled deeply, trying to control her breathing. Magic had always been a worrier, and she figured this wasn't a great time to have a panic attack.

Her mother had told her that the bus would be here at seven forty-five and would only wait five minutes. So, to be extra careful, Magic packed up her stuff, checked and re-checked that she had everything, and made sure she was out the door by seven forty.

She strode down the concrete pathway in front of the house, and halted just before the edge of the pavement. Her car was missing from the driveway, so her parents were definitely at work. The sky was still a dull grey colour; Magic hoped that the sun was only hiding today, and was still too tired to break through the clouds.

Too quickly for her liking, she heard the low rumble of the slowing down of an engine, and a large, mustard-yellow bus turned a corner. As it slowed to a stop in front of her, her legs shook violently. Magic dug her fingers into the straps of her backpack until her knuckles turned white. How could her body betray her like this?

There was a *whoosh* as a pair of glass doors slid open. She clambered the two black steps that followed, and the driver gave her a grunt of 'good morning'. She smiled weakly at him and then made her way down the aisle.

Many curious eyes followed her as she stumbled between the crowded seats; Magic was about halfway there before a wave of whispering swept over the bus. Magic just stared at her feet, hoping and praying that she would not trip over.

To her complete relief, the entire back row of the bus was empty. She shuffled down the row towards the window, and slipped off her bag, setting it down beside her. Magic placed her face in her hand and pressed her forehead into the glass just as the engine rumbled once again and her house drifted past her as the bus took off once more.

Magic was silently grateful that no heads were turning over shoulders towards her direction; she felt as if she was about to burst into tears. That sinking feeling built up in the pit of her stomach as roads, houses and cars passed by outside in a colourful blur.

Magic's body felt numb with nervousness that she barely realised her right arm was shaking in her pocket. Her vision was slightly shaky as her forehead dug deeper into the vibrating window of the bus. She was dreading the arrival.

Magic *was* one of the people who lived furthest from the school, but that did not mean she lived *far away* from school, so she was met with even more displeasure and anxiety when the bus pulled up in the school car park a few minutes later; it was quite empty except for a few cars scattered here and there.

A bead of sweat trickled down the side of Magic's forehead as she followed the suddenly very chatty line of students filing out of the bus. She stumbled down the two steps before another *whoosh* from behind her indicated the glass doors slamming shut.

Magic fiddled nervously with her feet for a split second before the group of students took off to the left. Magic followed them automatically, unsure where she was supposed to be going.

The school building was vast and wide, made entirely of red and rust-coloured bricks—it was quite magnificent, even though Magic had not seen the front yet.

18

The only thing visible from this side was a pair of dark, grey double doors in the middle of the building with a small 'EXIT' sign above them, and rows of tall, narrow windows.

As the students walked on, Magic realised that they were headed towards the side of the school, where there was a wide alleyway that they would cross to enter the front of the school, Magic guessed. Her insides churned as they walked between the school and a wooden fence to her left, and blades of grass began to sprout in the sandy ground, before the alleyway opened up to the front field of the school.

Two lines of students stood organized in straight lines, facing the school. A teacher stood in front of each, a checklist in their hand, facing the students. The two lines were spaced far apart.

A group of kids were clustered at the far end of the grassy field. As Magic and the students approached them, they joined the group, waiting silently.

In front of this cluster of students, a teacher donning a lavender coat and holding a checklist just like every other teacher Magic had seen so far spoke to each student one by one, directing them to their new classes for the year. Slowly, the group thinned as every now and then, a student would walk towards the left line, or the right as directed by the lavender-coated woman.

While Magic waited for her turn, she took the time to assess the school sight—to her far, far left, a few circular, wooden benches were scattered here and there across the grass, hidden under what would have been the shade of the trees—the sun still hadn't decided to break through yet.

Next, Magic took in the front of the school.

First, two large, birch wood double doors attracted her attention. They were huge, about double her height, she estimated. The brick walls were lined with tall, narrow windows, the panes topped with flowerpots consisting of either rose pink or blood red peonies. The roof was a warm, clear maroon colour, the tiles made of slate.

Before Magic knew it, there was one more person left to be sorted into their class before it was her turn. As the girl in front of Magic trudged away to the line on the left, the woman with the clipboard looked up.

Magic took in her appearance, that nervous feeling building up in her once again. The lady's rectangular specs rested halfway down her nose, her face lined with a few wrinkles here and there. Magic estimated that she was in her early sixties. Her greying hair was subdued in a high bun, and a lanyard consisting of a black whistle, some keychains and a few cards dangled from her neck.

She studied Magic's face, before her thin lips broke into a smile.

"Ah, you must be…" She checked her clipboard, her bony finger tracing down a list of names. "Magic McFee! Welcome to the school, Magic. I'm sure you'll immensely enjoy your time here." She tucked the clipboard under her right shoulder and extended her arm. "I'm Miss Ross, the deputy headmistress. Nice to meet you."

Magic shook her hand and tried returning her smile. "Nice to meet you too. Thank you," she replied, her voice almost disappearing with uneasiness. It took all she had at this point to not be sick on the spot.

Miss Ross gave Magic another fleeting smile before checking her clipboard once again.

"Ah, you are in Miss Spencer's class, Magic," Miss Ross informed her, pointing to the line on the right. Magic thanked her before dragging her feet across the damp grass towards the long line of kids, staring self-consciously down at her trainers.

At the head of the line, a much younger woman with straight, blonde hair and a tight-fitting baby pink dress stood facing the students.

"Alright, is that everyone?" she called across the field towards Miss Ross. She must've gotten a nod of confirmation from the deputy headmistress, because she then turned round and headed straight towards the steps leading to the birch front doors, and her new class followed.

Magic held the heavy door out for the teacher leading her class behind her, before turning and following the other students once again.

The floor of the school was made of smooth quartz that *clitter-clattered* loudly with all the noisy footsteps the students made. The sound reverberated off the walls, along with the excited chatter of her new classmates.

As she walked along the corridor, Magic managed to get a glimpse of the other classes, which were all next door to each other on either side of the corridor, all lined up.

In each classroom, there was a colourful, checkered carpet surrounded by many smooth, birch tables (that she supposed were intended to match the front doors), with up to five wooden chairs tucked underneath them. Many bookshelves stood up against the walls, filled with books of different sizes and colours. The spaces on the walls the bookshelves had not concealed were filled with posters and drawings. Magic assumed these were the junior classes.

As she followed her classmates down the corridor, Magic's eyes continued to dart nervously round at her surroundings; some of the classrooms were completely empty, while others had their doors closed, through which Magic could see just a slither of the young students sitting at their tiny desks through the glass panel in the doors.

As she peeked continuously through the glass panels, Magic began to notice that at every door she passed, the kids inside got slightly taller—the year groups increased as they strode down the corridors. She assumed there were two classes in each year group, each situated opposite each other.

Magic could also deduce that these must be the form rooms; she could just hear the faint sound of names being called issuing from the closed doors.

Miss Spencer came to a halt three doors away from the end of the corridor. Magic wanted to lean out of the line to see what Miss Spencer was doing, but didn't dare step out of it.

Magic guessed Miss Spencer was trying to locate a key, because moments later, she paused and the door swung open. The students filed through the door as Miss Spencer held it open for them.

The classroom was completely identical to the others, except that the desks and chairs were a little larger, and were arranged in a horseshoe, the inner part facing the left side of the room, where the teacher's desk sat.

The students walked down the horseshoe of desks until the person at the front of the line reached the head of the horseshoe at the far end of the room—there was just enough seats for everybody, and, inevitably, Magic got the very edge of the other end, right next to the door.

There was a loud shuffling as the whole class sat down in unison, tucking their bags under their desks as Miss Spencer shut the door and took her seat at the front of the class.

She pulled out a drawer in her desk and shuffled round with the contents, before pulling out a sheet of paper and attaching it to the clipboard. She grabbed the pen on her desk and began calling out names.

Magic had tried not to zone out today; she wanted to avoid any embarrassment, and secure her first impression. However, she couldn't help staring at her new class out of the corner of her eye. She surveyed everyone as they randomly answered the register, wondering who she could be friends with, and who was most likely to be the class bully, popular girl, and the nerd.

"Magic?" Miss Spencer finally reached the bottom of the register. Magic was shocked but managed to cover it up well. She cheered wildly inside.

"Morning, miss," she responded. Magic had also mentally noted how the other children had responded to the register.

"Alright, then," said Miss Spencer, and she clicked her pen and set it down, before standing up and making her way to the middle of the horseshoe of desks.

"Good morning, everybody," Miss Spencer spoke with a smile. She seemed to be more relaxed and open now that she had got the register out of the way. She tucked her blonde locks back behind her shoulder and continued. "I am Miss Spencer, and I will be your form tutor for this academic year. Now, some of you may know me, but I see lots of new faces sitting here today." Her eyes swept the classroom fleetingly. "So, to the newbies, welcome to Creavey High, and to the rest of you, welcome back." She seemed like the kind of teacher that would poke fun at her students. "Now, before you head off to your classes, you need to know where you'll be going! I'm going to give you your planners as well as your timetables, which you will follow for the rest of Year 10."

She rummaged through another drawer in her desk and pulled out a stack of what looked like blue school planners and another pile of paper. She took the planners in one hand and began to distribute them across the class, before handing out the timetables, licking her thumb every now and then to separate the paper.

Today, Magic had Chemistry, English, Maths, Geography, and (she groaned) double History. The noise level in the classroom suddenly went up, but Miss Spencer silenced them immediately. She opened her mouth to say something, but a loud ringing in the corridor cut her off, followed by a loud shuffling and an outburst of chatter.

"Class dismissed! Have a lovely first day!"

Everyone scooped up their backpacks and scrambled to the door. Magic scooped up her own before she was ushered into the corridor, where she could barely move because of the crowd shoving each other. She had no idea where the Chemistry lab was located, so she decided she'd follow a group of people from her class again.

They clambered the stairs at the end of the corridor and then lined up at the first room on the left. Magic joined the end of the line and then leaned against the wall, biting her lip and staring nervously at her feet. Other doors in this corridor had gathered students as well; Magic would have to get used to the loud chatter between classes.

She couldn't help tuning in to some conversations…after all, there was a fine line between being nosy and being curious.

Magic looked up when she heard someone say, "Just do it!" to a redheaded girl with curly hair and green eyes. The girl with curly ginger hair looked just as nervous as Magic, before, to Magic's utter shock, the girl walked towards Magic, smiled at her, and said, "Hi, my name's Maria Kenfield. It's nice to meet you."

Magic's brain suddenly betrayed her, freezing. "Er—it's nice to meet you too," replied Magic, smiling back awkwardly.

Before the conversation could blossom any further, the class door opened, and a very plump man stood in the doorway beaming at the children. He wore a white, long-sleeved shirt underneath a puce waistcoat that matched his trousers. He had very little hair, which was all greying.

"Well hello there!" he boomed. "Come on in, come on in, don't just stand there, you have a class to attend!" he added, seeing their puzzled faces. Some people bit into their sleeves to stifle their snickers. Magic thought he seemed much too happy.

The room inside was what every typical school lab Magic thought would look like—rows of white lab tables, grey stools and three taps per row.

As the class settled down, the teacher introduced himself.

"Welcome to my classroom, everyone! You might have seen me round school sometimes. But, for those who don't know me, my name is Mr Clark, and I will be your new Chemistry teacher this year."

Magic enjoyed her first Chemistry lesson quite a bit; they were exploring reactivity and they were told that they were even going to do an experiment where they got to test out different metals and see what would happen to them if they were placed in different acids. For this experiment, they would need to work in groups of seven. Magic was put in a group with Maria Kenfield, a stout boy with black hair called Mark Irvine, a stuck-up girl with a thick layer of makeup on called Michelle Kurt, a girl with hazel-brown skin and black, curly hair called Chloe Smith, a blond, tall boy called Charlie Stocklin and a girl with curly, brown hair and blue eyes called Phillipa Morris.

Mr Clark said that everyone had to have a part in the experiment. Almost everyone in Magic's group worked well; unfortunately, within minutes, Michelle proved to be a very difficult person to work with.

"I honestly don't understand why we have to wear these stupid goggles anyway," she babbled in an annoyed voice. "Right, Phil?"

"Oh—yeah! Really stupid," Phillipa agreed immediately, as if Michelle had just pointed out a piece of chewing gum stuck to her foot.

"She's really thick," someone whispered in Magic's ear. She turned round, slightly shocked, to find the tall, blond-haired boy with blue eyes called Charlie grinning at her. Magic tried to grin back—she silently agreed. Michelle seemed very snobby, while Magic got the impression that Phillipa was simply one of her cronies that tagged along behind her. The thought of them made her disgusted but also cringe, which resulted in her finding the two girls' behaviour quite humorous.

Magic tried as hard as she could not to laugh throughout the lesson at Michelle's constant outbursts, occasionally shoving her face into the sleeve of her lab coat and turning away from her. Eventually, Magic decided she didn't really like Michelle.

However, when Michelle got told off, everyone in the group was laughing except Mark. He was quiet a serious boy who cared deeply about getting on with his work and knew all the answers to the questions the teachers asked. Although she was quite a kiss-up, Phillipa was just as stuck up as Michelle. She was always complaining about how everyone was doing the experiment wrong, and that Magic was the lousiest. Magic decided that she didn't like Phillipa very much either.

The only people in her group that Magic found she got along with were Charlie, Chloe and Maria. They exchanged looks during Michelle's pointless outbursts, and they also managed to do the most work.

When the second bell rang indicating the end of period one, once again everyone began scrambling out of the room. So far, she had enjoyed her first lesson despite Michelle and Phillipa's nonsense.

And, once again, Magic wandered round, trying to find the English classroom (she was too shy to ask someone for directions). She was about to resort to tailing behind her classmates again when, unexpectedly, Maria, Chloe and Charlie approached her.

"Er—hi," said Charlie awkwardly over the loud noise of chatter and footsteps, "would you maybe want to walk to English with us? I reckon you're still getting used to navigating this place."

"Er—yeah I am…sure," replied Magic, trying not to cringe back at how naturally awkward she was, though Charlie, Chloe and Maria didn't seem to think anything of it.

They walked up to the third floor. Magic assessed the crowded corridors, all the while wondering how many floors there were in this building. She tried to remember how many rows of windows she had seen when she had looked at the school out on the front lawn, but couldn't recall.

They continued walking along the crimson-carpeted floors and brick walls until they reached the end of the corridor, where there was a line of students waiting outside a large oak door with a brass knocker, talking silently to their friends.

"Where's the teacher?" asked Magic, confused. She knew that they were a few minutes late to the classroom due to the traffic in the corridors, so she had expected the teacher to be out here waiting for them.

"We don't know who it is, we've never met them," replied Charlie. "I don't know if he's inside."

"Hope they're good though. I swear, I'll be so mad if they aren't nice," said Chloe, throwing a dirty look at the oak door.

Just then, the classroom door flung open and a skinny man in striped black and green trousers, blazer, and tie appeared in the doorway. He wore his dark brown hair in a deep side parting which he had stuck down with gel and had the very ends slightly flicked up in a sort of style. The rest was cut in a fade. Magic thought this look was very unusual. His eyebrows had extremely high arches, which gave him a devilish look. But the thing that was most terrifying was the grin he wore from ear to ear, pearly white teeth bared.

The chatter in the corridor surrounding that area completely cut out.

"In, then," he cackled maliciously, and his grin widened.

Slowly and hesitantly, the children stepped into the classroom and took their seats, while Magic tried to disguise her questioning frown. Why was this teacher behaving in this manner? Magic was almost positive that he wasn't just picking fun at them, or joking round: his frightening gaze seemed so real.

It was an eerie sight; the room was dimly lit with wooden desks and benches arranged in rows. The curtains were shut, and ancient paintings were hung upon the walls, which were dark brown and had tiny golden patterns painted onto them. At the front of the room, a blackboard was hung on the wall behind the teacher's desk, which was also wooden.

Magic, Charlie, Chloe and Maria took seats next to each other in the back, taking off their bags and putting them beneath the desks.

As most people were staring round the room dumbfounded, Magic realised that the teacher hadn't entered the classroom yet. In fact, he'd completely disappeared.

Magic gave Charlie a slight poke in the arm. When he turned round questioningly, she asked, "Where's he gone? It's—" Magic checked her watch "—ten past nine. Shouldn't class have started five minutes ago?"

"I can't say I'm complaining," Charlie replied, grinning. "He doesn't exactly seem like the biggest ray of sunshine, does he?"

Magic unzipped her large backpack and took out her English textbooks. She then leaned in towards the table and glanced to her left; Charlie was staring into space and drumming his fingers onto the desk. On Magic's right, Chloe was immersed in *Romeo + Juliet,* the play lying open on the desk, elbows on the table and her face in her hands.

Another five minutes, ten minutes, fifteen minutes passed, and the teacher still hadn't turned up. The class started to get anxious and there were even outbursts like 'Where is he?', 'Is he gonna be here soon?' and 'This is getting weird!' Magic was slightly surprised. She thought everyone would take advantage of the teacher's absence to get up to some mischief.

When the noise level rose too high, a boy who was about a head taller than Magic and had jet-black hair and grey eyes got up and said, "Guys, for the love of God, could you calm down? He'll probably be here soon and we'll get in trouble for being loud."

This made people quieten down a little, but there was still a lot of murmuring going on across the room.

"D'you reckon he'll be here soon?" Chloe asked Charlie impatiently, looking up from *Romeo + Juliet* for the first time in minutes.

"No idea…" Charlie replied slowly. "He'll be here."

"Half the lesson's done, though," Chloe told him, staring anxiously at the clock above the black board.

Suddenly, Magic had an idea, though she couldn't say it was a very good one.

"Hey—" she hesitated, thinking better of it, but Charlie, Chloe and Maria were already tuning in "—d'you reckon we should go look for him? Chloe's right, half the lesson's gone, and, well, I don't know…" She regretted opening her mouth in the first place.

"Are you crazy?" gasped Maria.

"Actually, I think Magic's right. We should go look for him—it's the right thing to do. And plus, it'll be fun." Charlie said, then his expression changed. "You can stay if you want to," he added, seeing the look on Maria's face. He then got up, glanced at Magic, who nodded, and there was a tiny scrape of a bench as they slipped out of their seat and headed towards the door.

As they walked past everyone, there were cries of 'Where are you going?' and 'Have you gone nuts?'

Just as Charlie's fingers were about to brush against the brass doorknob, the door was flung open, taking Magic and Charlie with it, and they were slammed into the solidness of the brick wall.

She heard her classmates gasp as white sparks exploded in Magic's vision as the back of her head collided with the hard rock. She felt her vision collapse for one moment just as an outburst of throbs broke out, drumming against her skull.

When her vision returned, the world spun for just a moment and her classmate's terrified expressions floated into view. Magic suddenly realised that their faces seemed so high up, and a split-second later realised that she had sunk to the ground.

The white sparks in her vision evaporated immediately as Magic realised in horror that the entire class had just seen her crumble to the ground.

26

She scrambled to her feet, flushing in embarrassment as she tried not to meet anyone's eyes. She came to realise a few seconds later, however, that the students didn't seem to be looking at her. In fact, they weren't even paying attention to her at all. They weren't even looking in her direction.

Magic traced her classmate's gaze, and, to her horror, she was met with the blood-curdling face of the English teacher. He was livid.

"Have a seat, then." he demanded, his voice a furious fire blazing so fiercely there was no way of burning it out.

Chapter Three
The English Teacher

Magic was no longer concerned about her classmate's gazes. She was more worried about the teacher's.

She could feel the electric fury of his piercing glare stabbing her in the back of her head as she followed Charlie back to their seats at the back of the class.

Magic tried not to scrape the bench against the ground as she slid back into her seat, Charlie slipping in next to her, though she mentally begged for something to break the suspenseful silence.

"Now," the teacher spoke. Magic couldn't tell if he was whispering, or his natural voice was just that thin and chilling. "Allow me to introduce myself."

He raised his voice as he continued, the corners of his mouth twirling up into an awful smile.

"My name is Marcus Slay. You will call me sir, or Mr Slay. Understood?"

"Yes, Mr Slay," the class chanted back.

"While you are in my class, you are going to have to follow a certain set of rules. Everybody will abide by these rules, no matter how superior you think you are. No exceptions," Slay spat. "You will practise these rules until they become engraved into your little minds. You will treat them like *tenets*."

He marched towards the blackboard and tugged on a string that hung beside it. At his pull, a huge sheet of black paper with scruffy white writing rolled out on top of the board.

"Read through these carefully and copy them down into your books. No questions."

Bemused, the class began copying down the rules. Magic scribbled away mindlessly, unaware of what she was writing down, while wondering if she was going to hate English by the end of the school year.

It was silent for a while, except for the scratching of quills against paper. Magic's focus was constantly jeopardised by the furious electricity emanating from Slay. She could feel it even being this far away from his desk. She started to pity the people who had chosen to sit at the front.

"Because of you dawdlers, we have now wasted fifteen minutes of the lesson. Shame on you." Slay finally said after a while.

Magic could feel anger starting to bubble in the pit of her stomach. She had so much she wanted to yell back at him at that moment.

Wasted fifteen minutes of the lesson? He'd been the one who was twenty minutes late to begin with! She would not stand his hypocrisy. But she would at least work to keep her growing temper under control. She did not need to attract more attention to herself than she already had, though her angry thoughts were bursting so loud in her head that Magic was surprised Slay could not hear them.

Slay seemed to be losing his patience.

"Have you not *finished* already?"

"Yes, sir," the class chanted nervously.

"No, you certainly have not!" Slay shouted. He marched over to the blackboard and pulled another black string. Another large piece of parchment rolled out from the top of the blackboard, 'EXPECTATIONS' blazed across the top in bold, red letters.

The words tumbled out of Magic's mouth before she could stop herself.

"That's not fair! *How* were we supposed to know they were there?"

There was a long, dreadful silence.

People shuffled uncomfortably in their seats, keeping their heads down, while others fidgeted round and stared at Magic, their mouths draped open.

Magic wasn't sure whether she regretted bursting out or not—she simply waited with baited breath, taking extra care not to allow her furious expression to slip and keeping her chest high.

Slay curled his lips into that awful, scary smile. Then, he marched over to his desk, opened one of its drawers, rummaged in it for a while, and pulled out a ruler. He then walked towards Magic and shoved one end towards her, pointing it directly in front of her chin. Magic did not flinch.

"There is an idiot at the end of this ruler," he hissed.

Magic quickly rummaged through her brain, trying to find something smart to throw back at him.

"Which end?" she hissed back.

An even deadlier silence followed this. Even Magic was surprised at her own daring. She thought this was a good enough response, though she had not thought through the reaction she would get.

Without warning, Magic felt a sharp pain in her ear as she felt herself being yanked upwards, before being dragged across the classroom, stumbling. Her classmates' faces flickered by her in jagged blurs.

"Brat. Stupid brat." The unmistakably cold voice of Marcus Slay echoed in Magic's ears. It was more than livid. It was sharp, stabbing. "Learn to keep your mouth shut. I'm taking you straight to the headmaster's office. You will never speak out of turn again. Do you understand? DO YOU?" screamed Slay in anger as he walked briskly along the corridor, still pinching Magic's ear. He was walking so fast that her feet were almost dragging across floor. Her classmates' frantic whispers trailed out into the corridor after her.

Magic's ear began to throb painfully as Slay pinched it firmly between his thumb and index finger.

"Yes," Magic hissed, and then kept quiet.

They turned a corner and began walking down a dim hallway with purple-carpeted floors. The stone walls were covered in candles that were held in golden holders embroidered in tiny, intricate patterns, but other than that, the walls were completely plain.

They reached the end of the hallway and were greeted with a long staircase, made of clear quartz. Slay dragged Magic down it, until they finally reached the bottom. Two symmetrical Krosswood doors stood in front of them. Slay stepped forward and knocked ferociously. Magic's ear screamed.

After a couple of seconds, a deep voice replied, "Come in."

Slay pushed the door open and revealed a very untidy and simple but beautiful brown room. Wooden shelves carried cardboard boxes filled with overflowing leaflets and documents. There was a square tin filled with sweets placed at the corner of an antique desk, which sat in the middle of the room, sweet rappers scattered all across the wood. In between all of this, a man in his late thirties sat at the desk, sporting a beige tie with a matching suit to go with it. His thick brown hair was parted to the side. As he looked up at his visitors, Magic looked into his eyes and realised they were a similar bright blue to hers, though everything had happened so fast she could barely comprehend how she had got here.

"How can I help you, Marcus?" the man asked in a calm voice, not looking up from the papers at his desk.

"This—this dunce of a child!" Slay replied slyly, and then addressed Magic. "Think you're a smartass, eh?" he spat at her, and all of a sudden, yanked her forwards by the ear, turning desperately to the headmaster. Magic snarled and then winced as her ear screamed again.

The headmaster looked up, and a worried expression flashed across his face for the briefest moment that, had she blinked, Magic would've missed it.

"I do not appreciate you mishandling my students, Marcus."

Slay was fuming but kept quiet. He threw Magic's ear out of his grip, dissatisfied. The headmaster turned to face Magic and smiled as she tried to balance herself again.

"Good morning, Miss McFee," the headmaster greeted her when she found her balance. "Marcus, could you step outside for a minute?"

"Headmaster, please—" Slay began.

"I understand, Marcus. Please step outside." the headmaster demanded, though his tone remained calm. He and Slay exchanged a look, before Slay forced himself to step outside, and gently clicked the door shut, as if trying so hard not to let his fury slip out.

"He'll live."

The headmaster turned to Magic, and then a smile appeared on his face as if he just remembered she was there. "Well then. Where do we start? Take a seat."

Magic just noticed the little cushioned stool in front of the desk. She pulled it back and took a seat. They sat in silence and the headmaster's smile turned puzzled for a moment.

"But of course! I haven't introduced myself! I'm Mr Michael Brownlow, Headmaster of Creavey High. I hope you're having fun!" he introduced himself happily, almost like a young child's reaction to a Christmas present. Brownlow asked, "Have you made any friends yet?"

Was he really making small talk when she was supposed to be in trouble?

"Oh—um—yeah, I have. They're really nice."

"That's lovely," Brownlow replied. His expression turned slightly more serious before continuing. "Now, I do want to warn you about Mr Slay. Don't make him lose his temper. It's one of those things that are just best to avoid." He sighed.

Just then, a large burst of muffled chatter broke out in the corridors. Brownlow checked his watch.

"Well, I think you should start heading out to your break," he said. "It was lovely seeing you." He smiled. "Oh, and please remember what I told you about Slay. It's best not to get under his skin," he reminded her.

"Oh, yes. Thank you, sir," replied Magic. Brownlow nodded to her once before she left the room.

As soon as the door clicked shut behind her, Magic half expected to see Slay standing their waiting for her, like a predator to his prey. But, to her utter relief, as she climbed the stairs leading to the corridors above, she found them deserted.

Too soon, she reached the top of the staircase and headed back down the purple-carpeted corridor.

Magic was dumbfounded—*how* had she not gotten into any trouble at all? She had thought that there was absolutely no way she was going to get out of this one.

"What happened in there? Are you alright?" asked Maria anxiously when Magic had located her, Chloe and Charlie in the loud, crowded corridors. Her face was practically white.

"I'm fine, don't worry," replied Magic hastily, trying to diminish her worrying. "Brownlow just gave me a small pep talk about not getting under Slay's skin. I've got to say, I didn't expect that, especially on my first day…thought I'd get into more trouble."

Maria sighed.

"Well, let's just hope not all of our teachers are like that."

"Clark is great," said Chloe.

"I guess so."

"We should start heading out, before the bell rings," Charlie told them.

As they began making their way to the field outside, bustling round large groups of students, Maria whispered into Magic's ear, "Please be careful with Slay. He doesn't seem like the type of person you want to mess with. I just thought to let you know, so you don't get into trouble again."

"Thanks, but—" Magic responded, but cut off, trying to think of the best way to phrase this, "—but if he's going to be—*unfair*—and—*manipulative*—and—and— just *unjust*, then, well, I'm not going to just sit there and take it."

"I guess so, but…" Maria bit her lip nervously as the large birch doors came into view. "Just be aware of the *way* you respond. Just in case."

"Alright."

Charlie, Chloe, Maria and Magic stepped out onto the vast, grassy front field. Immediately, Maria's eyes swept the crowd.

"What're you looking for?" Magic asked her, surveying her expression.

"Our other fr—Oh! There they are."

Magic and the others simply followed Maria as she staggered down the small slope of grass towards a circular wooden bench in the shade of a tree where two boys sat, conversing.

"Hi, Will," Maria greeted one of the boys, throwing her backpack across the wood of the bench. "Magic, this is—"

"William Brakk," said one of the boys. Magic recognised him immediately as the boy with jet black hair that had been trying to calm the class down earlier on as he stood up. His eyes were a stunning shade of grey.

"And Thomas Wright," the other boy sitting next to Will introduced himself. "I'm in year eleven." He had an average American accent; not too harsh, not too soft. The chestnut brown of his hair was slightly lighter than the shade of his eyes. Even sitting down, it was apparent that he was at least a head taller than everyone else.

"Hey, erm—it's nice to meet you," said Magic. She fidgeted awkwardly. "My name is Magic McFee."

"That's a cool name, Magic," Will complemented her.

Magic flushed. She cursed in her head. "Oh, thanks."

"I wouldn't exactly call it cool. I think it's stupid."

A new girlish, cunning voice joined the conversation.

"Get lost, Michelle," snarled Chloe. Magic whipped round.

She was met with the big, blond head of a snickering Michelle Kurt, her eyes lined with eyeshadow and a set of thick lashes. Standing right by her, almost flanking her, was Phillipa Morris, her bright blue eyes gleaming as she twirled a finger round one of her tiny brown curls.

Michelle surveyed Chloe through narrowed eyes, her hands on her hips.

"I don't think anybody *asked* for your input, Smith, so *hold your lips*," she spat at Chloe.

"Shut up, Michelle," Charlie threw at her. "I don't recall anybody asking for yours, either."

Michelle opened her mouth to respond, but Thomas cut her off.

"Seriously, Michelle, cut it out," he snapped.

Instead, Phillipa spoke up. "Come on, Michelle, we have no business with—" he looked Magic up and down, as if she was something gross stuck to the bottom of her shoe "—with *scum*."

At this, Charlie lunged at the two of them, but Will caught him under his shoulders just in time, before Charlie could do them any harm. Michelle flinched, but immediately tried to regroup herself.

"Slow down, mate. They're not worth the aggravation," Will assured him.

"I'm going to end up strangling her if she doesn't learn to shut up," Charlie muttered under his breath.

"Language, Stocklin. Language," Michelle snickered, and she turned on her heel and strutted away. Phillipa threw them one last dirty look before following her.

"Seriously, Charlie, you've got to calm down," Chloe told him, her expression serious. Charlie slumped back down into his seat, still fuming.

Magic wasn't at all hurt by anything Michelle had said—in fact, she found that she didn't even care. She was more concerned about how her friend had reacted.

"If you show them that you're offended, or that they've gotten to you, they win. Just ignore them," Magic told Charlie, sliding in next to him. The rest nodded in agreement.

Charlie scratched the back of his head. "I guess you're right… but it's like what you said about Slay, Magic—you weren't just going to sit there, were you? You spoke up to him!"

"Ah, but this is different," replied Magic. "Slay was being *completely* unfair, while they were just teasing for no reason, which means there's no reason for you to go out of your way to acknowledge them."

There was silence between them for a few moments.

"Wow…she's got a point." Charlie finally said.

"You sound surprised," replied Magic, trying to lighten the atmosphere.

"Haha."

When the bell rang, Thomas headed towards Biology, while Magic, Maria, Chloe, Charlie and Will headed towards Maths, making their way up the outdoor staircase and into the corridor. When Magic made to turn left towards the staircase leading to the long corridors of classrooms up above, she felt a hand grab her shoulder and turned to find Charlie looking back at her.

"Maths is one of the very few classrooms that you turn right for," he told her, and he tilted his head towards a passageway on the right. "It's called the Maths wing."

"Ah, alright."

She followed him and the others down the short corridor, which was only a few metres long, before they turned left to a smaller area which revealed three oakwood panelled doors. They carried on walking until they reached the door furthest from them and joined the forming line.

"These are all Maths rooms, but you get sorted into each class depending on your ability," Will informed Magic.

Magic began to realise this when mini groups of people began to gather in front of each door. She began to wonder where she was supposed to be, and what door she was standing at.

"How do you get sorted?" she asked Will anxiously.

"It depends on the results of your previous Maths exam."

Magic breathed a sigh of relief; she had done well on her previous exam. However, she didn't quite know how high the standards were in this school.

"What class is this?" Magic asked, nodding towards the door they were standing by.

"Miss Glant—number one," Maria informed her.

"Is that—"

Maria answered Magic's question before she could ask it.

"Yes, it's the top in the year group."

"I haven't been told I'm supposed to be here, though. I haven't been told where I'm supposed to be at all."

"How much did you score on your last test?"

Magic frowned before the number popped into her head. "Ninety-four, I think."

"Oh, you're fine, then. You have to get at least eighty to be sorted into *this* class." She jutted her head at the door.

"Oh, phew."

Maria grinned at Magic. Magic grinned back, the pleasant feeling of relief washing through her. She had always been really good at all her subjects.

The noise level began to increase gradually as more students arrived in the Maths wing, and the crowds in front of the three doors thickened.

"Did you have Miss Glant last year?" Magic asked to none of them in particular.

"Yes," replied Chloe. "At the end of each year, the teachers let us know what classes we'll be in the following year. The majority of us usually remain in the same classes, only a few people change."

The sound of faint footsteps suddenly became apparent; they quickly became louder, like a crescendo, until they were fully audible. Heads began turning towards the entrance to the Maths wing, where the corridor stopped. Three figures appeared, walking swiftly towards the children. A short man with puffy grey hair stopped in front of the first oak door, a middle-aged man with ginger hair stopped at the second door, and then Magic recognised the third teacher as the woman wearing a lavender overcoat who had introduced herself as the deputy headmistress, Miss Ross, who stopped in front of the door Magic and her friends were at, carrying a pile of essays. Magic looked round and saw that the other two teachers were leading their classes into the rooms. When the rest of the wing emptied, Miss Ross addressed the Magic's class. She looked slightly flustered.

"Sorry for the delay, children. Miss Glant is very unwell, so therefore has asked me to cover your class for today."

There was slight mumbling as Miss Ross handed the essays to a nearby student and then fumbled with her lanyard until she found a thick golden key; she shoved it into the keyhole and turned it. The door clicked and opened, revealing a lovely little room.

Red velvet curtains were wide open revealing the beautiful lawn and benches below. The floor was made of timber wood and the desks were arranged in twos, except a row of three tables at the back. There was a large chalkboard at the front of the room, and a pale wooden right by it. The dark oak shelves were piled with dusty, thick books which looked as if no one had touched them for a while.

Maria, Chloe and Magic took seats next to each other at the back of the class, in the row of three. Will and Charlie took their seats in a pair directly in front of them. There was distant, loud chatter coming from other classrooms and students in the corridors making their way towards their lessons across the school. The mumbling that had occurred amongst Magic's class before entering the classroom had returned, and Miss Ross began trying to quieten everybody down, taking the essays back from the student and sitting at her place at the pale wooden desk.

"Children, I know that your Maths lesson today is slightly different because your teacher was unable to show up today, however I must ask you to behave the exact same way you do when she is teaching you. My expectations are just as high."

The mumbling quickly died down until the room was completely silent again. She pursed her lips and ruffled through a drawer in the desk. She pulled out a scruffy register attached to a clipboard along with a pen and began calling out names.

"Michelle?" began Ross.

There was snickering from the opposite side of the room before Michelle answered. "Present." Magic rolled her eyes.

"Mark?"

There was no response. Everybody turned towards the back of the room to face Mark, who had fallen asleep.

"Irvine!" exclaimed Ross. Another wave of snickering.

Mark awoke suddenly, startled.

"Oh, er—present. Sorry."

Ross continued down the list until she reached Magic.

"Magic?"

"Present, miss," replied Magic quietly.

36

Miss Ross slowly looked up to face Magic. She brought her reading glasses further down her nose so she could see Magic with her naked eyes.

"You've got a lovely name, you have," Ross told her. Heads snapped towards the back of the class, but Magic forced herself to keep her eyes on Ross.

"Er—thank you."

The class fell silent. Magic assumed that Miss Ross didn't usually give out complements, noticing the reaction of her classmates.

"I do really love it," Ross added, giving Magic a small smile. She pushed her glasses back up her nose and began calling out the remaining students on the register. Once she was finished, she opened the same wooden drawer, placed the register inside, and locked it up again.

"Now, we shall start with the lesson."

Ross stood up and walked over to the other side of the desk, pulled out another drawer and took out a small box. She placed it on the table and extracted a small piece of chalk.

"Maths," she began. "The basis of all Science, the key to the prediction of the future and the stretching of the brain."

Nobody said a word. Elizabeth Ross just had this special way of catching people's attention with just one sentence.

"Today, we will be working on Algebraic equations."

Some students groaned, while others perked up. Algebra seemed to be a very infamous subject in this class.

"Quieten down, please. I will set you some questions on the board so you can get on with some independent work. I would like you to keep the volume level to a minimum, therefore I will allow some whispering, but if it gets too loud, we will have to work in silence, so please try your best to work at an acceptable volume. I would like you to write the date and title for today, which I will write on the board."

Ross turned to face the board, firstly writing down the title 'Algebraic Equations' and the date, 'Monday, 6th September 1996.' Then, she began writing down some questions for the class to solve. Personally, Magic was alright with equations and enjoyed them on most occasions.

"If you find yourself stuck," began Miss Ross (she had already finished writing down five different equations, and Magic began to wonder how she could write so fast), still facing the board, "You can refer to the step-by-step example on page two hundred and forty-eight. If you are still stuck, ask your friends. If after asking your friends you are still unsure, only then should you raise your hand and ask me for help. You may begin."

Ross took a seat back at her desk and began marking some essays from her previous class. Magic noticed that as Ross's eyes moved from side to side, reading the essays with remarkable rapidity, her facial expressions would change slightly, from disgust, to interest, to delight.

Magic stared at the board, and then looked to either side of her to see what her friends where up to. She looked at Charlie, who shrugged his shoulders and began copying down the equations they would be solving. Magic ruffled through her brown, leather pencil case, in search of a quill or pencil she could use.

Chapter Four
The Calculator

Magic found extracted a quill from the bottom of her pencil case and began swiftly copying down the first equation, her eyes flashing up every few seconds.

She found the first few relatively easy, but as she moved on, the numbers in the calculations became more complicated and involved decimals. A calculator was forbidden (which she found rather unusual), so Magic had to do the calculations by hand. Luckily, she was quite good at multiplying decimals, so it was no difficulty for her. After a couple of minutes, it was no surprise that Magic had finished, and she raised her hand to notify the teacher.

"Miss, I—"

"Then sit and wait patiently for your classmates to finish," Miss Ross interrupted, without looking up from her now thin pile of unmarked essays. Beside her, a larger, two-foot pile of marked essays stood like a tower.

Magic began taking in her surroundings. She stared outside at the rolling hills of Krington, the happy, blue skies that smiled down at her. Her first day at school had turned out better than expected; so far, at least. She had embarrassed herself more than she would've dreamed (she flushed at the memories) in front of her new classmates, though surprisingly she found that she didn't care as much; everybody seemed to be traumatised by Slay.

Magic's short daydream came to an end. As she returned to her senses, she suddenly became aware of a slight tingling, more of a vibration, in her fingers. She looked down at them and the vibrations became stronger…as if coming from the table.

She looked round inquisitively while ringing out her fingers, thinking she may have gotten pins and needles, but as she placed her hands back on the desk the vibrating continued. In fact, she could hear it now.

She finally noticed that this odd vibrating was coming from a very unexpected object: her calculator.

The ferocity of the vibrations quickly escalated; the calculator was shaking rapidly it made a clacking noise against her desk. Magic hesitated for a split second before quickly picking it up and holding it firmly between her hands. As soon as her fingers brushed against the material, the vibrating came to a halt. Magic was about to put the calculator back down and ponder its strange behaviour, when the unexpected happened.

Numbers, on their own, began rapidly appearing and disappearing, being mixed up and jumbled, scrambled and unscrambled, on the screen of the calculator. Little beeping noises could be heard as the numbers appeared. After a couple of seconds, the numbers too came to a halt, and nothing appeared. Magic was wrong to once again consider that the strange behaviour would end here: the device had only remained clear for a split second.

Immediately after, a message appeared on the calculator! Magic, still trying to regroup herself after the bizarreness of the previous events, tried to decipher the message as quickly as she could. It read:

The worst is yet to come... I warn you... He who goes in, does not come out... past the treacherous sea, she will lie... Frozen, and unmoving...

As quickly as they appeared, the words vanished. Blinking, Magic tried to process what these words meant. 'She will lie? Who was this she? Was she OK?'

What had just *happened*? Her brain exploded with a million colliding thoughts.

Magic must've been thinking out loud, because Charlie was now staring at her, turned round in his seat, alarmed. He seemed to have also noticed that entire bizarre ordeal.

"What the hell?" he whispered to Magic, his alarmed expression now locked on the calculator.

"I... don't know," Magic replied in a whisper, equally alarmed.

The calculator trembled in her hands, but this time it wasn't due to it behaving of its own accord.

Before leaving for Geography, Charlie and Magic were contemplating on telling the rest what they had seen, but they ended up deciding to keep it to themselves: for now, at least (they were still unsure whether they had been imagining it or not); though concealing it form everybody else was proving more difficult than they had anticipated—every now and then, when the reminder of the calculator popped into their minds for whatever reason, inevitably it would appear on their faces. To make matters slightly more difficult, Maria seemed to be keeping a close eye on them, as if she knew they knew something she didn't.

Magic followed Charlie, Chloe, Maria, and Will to Geography, which was situated on the fourth floor. They climbed up another flight of crimson-carpeted stairs and entered the second door on the left, which was already standing open, waiting for them.

It was quite a different room than any Magic had seen so far. The carpeted floors were a jet-black colour (Magic was reminded of Will's hair), giving the bottom of the room almost a dark glow. The walls were blood-red, matching the open curtains. There was a white desk at the front of the room, which stood in front of a blackboard next to the door. Desks in the same bright-white colour filled the room; they looked slightly cramped, as if whoever put them inside got their measurements wrong. Maps of different parts of the world hung scattered across the walls, as well as population pyramids and labelled diagrams of rainforests. Shelves of exam papers and essays stood on the left side of the room. The layout of this class was very simple, though oddly peaceful and beautiful.

With just enough space for five in a row, Charlie, Chloe, Maria, Will, and Magic managed to fit perfectly at the very back of the classroom. It took a good couple of minutes for the class to settle in, as they had slight difficulties sliding into the cramped seats and benches. Soon after, the teacher had caught up with them.

"Good morning, everyone, welcome to your first Geography lesson," she said. Her voice was a little high-pitched and delicate. "My name is Miss Mills, and I will be your teacher for this year."

Miss Mills was quite an odd-looking lady: she looked quite older than the previous teachers, perhaps in her sixties or seventies. Her grey hair was tied to the back of her head in a neat knot. She had rectangular-shaped silver spectacles lying on top of a curvy nose, and sported a neatly cut purple and red stripy skirt, which matched her blazer, which she wore on top of a white, button-up shirt. Her trainers and tights were black, almost the same colour as the floor. Despite her old age, she didn't exactly seem frail.

"Today we shall be doing a quick quiz…nothing to worry about!" she added at the fallen look on the class' faces. "It's all stuff you learned last year! But first, I must ask somebody to hand out the new exercise books. Let's see…" She scanned the class through her specs as a few people's hands shot up. "Ah, yes, Chloe, dear, thank you."

Chloe got up with difficulty (she was sitting in the middle of the bench), stumbling as she slid through desks and chairs to reach the front of the class. Once she had retrieved the books from Miss Mills, she weaselled her way back in between the rows, handing out new, bottle-green exercise books as she went. Chloe handed Magic her exercise book with a grin, which Magic returned.

At the top of the exercise books, there were three black lines, one for the student's name, the second for the subject and the third for year group. Magic filled it in and look round at the front of the class, where Chloe was now handing out the quiz sheets. They were all easy multiple-choice questions, like 'Which out of the three factors is not considered a measure of development?' and 'What is (roughly) the population of the UK?' which Magic and her new friends whizzed through. Five minutes before the fifty-minute-long lesson came to an end, Miss Mills collected in the quiz sheets.

"Stocklin, Brakk, Kenfield, Smith, and McFee have all received full marks! Well done!" exclaimed Mills brightly, looking up from the papers and beaming at them all. The five of them exchanged grins. Miss Mills' eyes flitted to her wristwatch. "Well, have a look at that, it's the end of the lesson! Class dismissed!" she announced cheerfully, beaming at them all once more. The students left the room with the same difficulty as they came in, squeezing through the crammed desks in the room.

The school cafeteria was filled with long rows of solid white tables and benches, with two wooden ones perpendicular to them at the back of the hall, which held cups and cutlery. The area near the door was taken up by a large line of people holding trays and sliding along, piling their plates with food.

Magic took a tray and lined up with the others; she hadn't realised how hungry she was until now.

"Well, I'm exhausted!" exclaimed Maria once they finally took seats at the end of one of the white lunch tables. Magic took her seat at the very end with Charlie to her left, opposite Maria, ate quietly and listened in; she was starving. "At least we didn't get too much homework. I mean, it's typical, it's still the first day, we haven't learnt anything yet," continued Maria.

"Do you ever get tired of talking?" Charlie asked.

Maria ignored him. "So, how're you finding it here, Magic?"

Magic sipped some orange juice. "It's good. Different from what I'm used to."

"What the hell?" Charlie's gaze was suddenly fixed on a spot above Maria's shoulder.

Magic lifted her eyes for just a second to get a glimpse of what was happening just as Maria shifted round in her chair.

Two people were disputing at the back of the hall.

Oh God, thought Magic. She didn't need more twists and turns on her first day of school; it was already less normal than she would've liked. But, being the overly

42

curious type of person, she just couldn't resist listening in. Magic gasped as she recognised the two people arguing.

"I won't ask you again, Miss Harrow!" Slay was exclaiming. Although his voice was raised, he very evidently was trying to keep it down, but he seemed to be losing his patience. "I want you to come with me, I must have a word with you in my office!"

"I—told—you—NO!" Katie cried out with a tone of finality in her voice.

Mr Slay looked livid.

"Please, sir, if it's about—" Katie leant in closer and whispered something into Slay's ear "—then I'm not going anywhere!" she cried desperately.

Slay looked even more outraged than before, if possible. He stabbed one final piercing stare at Katie before sweeping from the room, leaving her looking crestfallen.

Chloe and Will had their mouths hanging open in confusion; Maria had not turned round yet. Only Charlie pulled his gaze away.

"What the *hell*?"

"Be right back," Magic excused herself.

She shuffled round the students lining up for food and made her way towards where Katie still stood, devastated.

"Hey," Magic announced her presence.

Katie looked up with glistening eyes, which widened when she realised who it was. She wiped her face frantically against her sleeve.

"Hi, Magic," she sniffled. "How's your day going?"

"I really should be asking you. Are you OK? What happened?" Magic took a swift look round to check if anybody was listening and leaned in closer. "I saw what happened with Slay," she whispered.

Katie's eyes tightened. "Yeah."

"What was that about?"

Katie hesitated and then sniffed. "It was nothing. He's just been acting strange lately."

Magic frowned. "Yeah, he *is* quite odd. Almost knocked me out today, actually."

"*What?*"

"Yeah…long story."

"Be *careful*, Magic. Seriously."

"You, too."

Katie smiled before giving Magic a quick hug.

"Are you sure you're OK?" Magic asked her anxiously.

"I'm *fine*, Magic. Take care of yourself."

"Yeah, you too. See you!"

Magic returned to her seat beside Charlie. His mouth still hung open.

"What in all of—? Do you know her?" he spluttered, bemused.

"Our parents work together. She came to my house," replied Magic casually.

"I—"

"Oh, that's good, at least you knew somebody before coming," said Maria, gathering her tray and leaving to clear it.

"Are you guys OK? You've been silent for so long you're starting to worry me," Charlie said anxiously. He addressed Chloe and Will, who sat opposite each other, exchanging looks every now and then. They had not said a word yet.

"Yeah, we're fine," replied Chloe, still staring at Will.

"Just thinking about something," Will told them. Both of them seemed distracted, lost in thought.

After they had finished eating, they headed out onto the field outside, and took seats their seats round the same round, wooden bench in the shade of the old, thick-rooted oak tree. They watched as students were fighting, laughing, and playing together.

So, Magic's day had taken a strange turn, and she was barely half way through it; she'd gotten into big trouble with a teacher, and her calculator decided it appropriate to start displaying strange messages about unexplained things.

Being only halfway through her day, Magic could only wait for how the rest of her day would go.

She felt a small poke in her side as Charlie nudged her. The others were watching younger kids goofing round.

"What?" Magic whispered to him.

"Magic, should we tell them what happened during Maths?" Charlie asked in an undertone.

Magic turned to face him and gave him a contemplating look. She thought that they might be taking this whole thing a bit *too* seriously, and perhaps overreacting to the situation. It was simply a calculator that had had a malfunction, and Charlie was treating it like they had seen a tiger lurking in the school woods.

"I mean, if you want to. But I think it's not something we need to worry about—besides, every calculator muffs itself up once in a while!" she replied. She didn't want to tell the others about the calculator and have them think she was weird for worrying about something trivial. Not that she was worrying anyway.

"OK."

Charlie threw a glance at Maria, Chloe and Will, who stared blindly at two kids wrestling each other across the grass.

"Guys…"

Charlie dove into the story of how the calculator had vibrated, how it bore a strange message, how numbers had flickered across the screen, and how it had shut off abruptly after. Every now and then, there was a shift in expression from someone.

By the end of the story, everybody was left with a thoughtful frown written across their forehead. It was silent for a few moments, and then Chloe was the first to speak.

"Well," she started slowly. "I don't think anybody could've hacked into the calculator, that's just impossible. It's likely it could've been tampered with, though. Maybe someone wanted to play a prank, so they switched out yours for a prank one, or something. I bet Michelle and Phillipa would be up for a laugh."

"Nah, they're too dim to be able to work out how to mess with that thing," Will disagreed.

"Maybe we're just overreacting," Magic interjected. No, they were definitely overreacting. All eyes turned to her. "I mean, it's not something serious. It's just a calculator acting strange. I mean, strange things have been happening all day. Like, yesterday—"

She broke off.

Magic had been about to get into the story of how she had briefly caught a glimpse of a dark, cloaked figure from her bedroom window. Its silhouette had been strange, frightening…Unhuman like…

"Yeah, what happened yesterday?" Will asked slowly.

"Oh—uh—"

Magic held her tongue for just a second. Should she tell them? She'd barely known them for a couple hours and, although she liked them very much, she wasn't sure where the limits stood when it came to confiding things in them. Although, Magic herself had shook it off when it happened, so surely there would be no harm in telling them…

"Well, basically—" Where would somebody start retelling a story like this? Magic took a deep breath and continued. "I was minding my own business in my bedroom, and I see, out of the corner of my eye, out my bedroom window, this—figure—on the street, that looked kind of—odd," Magic chose her words very carefully. "It didn't exactly look—um—" Magic swallowed, "—human."

Everybody spoke at the same time.

"Ah."

"What?"

"You're not serious!"

"Are you sure?"

"Magic, I don't think you—"

"I know, I know," Magic said quickly. What had she expected? She wasn't even entirely sure herself that it had happened. It felt like it had all been a dream. "It's just what I saw. I'm not even sure if I was imagining it or not. He—it—was holding something." As she described the appearance, the vivid image of the figure popped even clearer back into her mind. Yes, it had been holding something. An object that very much resembled a staff…

"Wait, one second," Charlie spoke. "I—sorry, Magic, this is about something else—I think I might've read something…Or maybe someone was telling me…no, it's irrelevant…never mind."

Magic didn't mind—she wasn't exactly opposed to a change of subject.

"Who told you what?" Maria asked curiously.

"Well, you know Katie, right?" asked Charlie. The rest nodded slowly.

"Well, one day—I think it was towards the end of last year—I was walking down the English corridor, and Katie had burst out of Slay's office, looking frightened out of her wits. I asked her what was going on, she just mentioned Slay interrogating her about her grandfather. About something he had, I think."

"And what, is that any of his business?" Magic blurted out angrily. "What the bloody heck does he want with her grandfather's stuff?"

"I guess not, but it seemed awfully suspicious. Like, Katie always looks terrified every time Slay tries talking to her, and when she sees him in the corridors on the way to lessons, she quickly tries to bustle away before he can even notice her. She was like that at the end of last year," Charlie informed her, a glum look on his face.

"Maybe he's after whatever her grandfather had? I bet it must be valuable, because he wouldn't make this much of a fuss about something ordinary!" Maria cried shrilly. "Honestly, if he is that concerned over her grandfather's things, why doesn't he leave the poor girl alone and speak to her parents!"

"No, he shouldn't speak to anybody at all! It's got nothing to do with him! D'you reckon her parents even know what's going on?" asked Magic.

"I don't know, the girl's super secretive and quiet, I bet she's too frightened to tell them anything," said Chloe, her expression pitiful.

"She isn't *that* quiet. When she came over to my house, she seemed really open and stuff. Really willing to have a conversation." Magic remembered how talkative Katie had been while conversing in her living room.

"Hold on," said Will, speaking for the first time in minutes. "If Slay's interfering that much about something quite private, what if whatever Katie's grandfather had was kept illegally?"

"I think you might be right!" cried Maria, while the others processed what he'd just said.

"But if it was that valuable, and kept illegally, wouldn't it be all over the news? Wouldn't someone caught her grandfather already?" asked Chloe inquisitively.

"That's a good point," began Will, "but Slay has been trying to get a hold of Katie for so long. If whatever her grandfather had was stolen or kept illegally, it would've been on the news ages ago. Everyone has probably forgotten about it…well, at least *almost* everyone…"

"People can do illegal stuff and be very good at keeping it secret, though," Magic piped in. "I mean, who knows if it even would've been on the news? Maybe nobody but Slay knows about it."

"Or maybe Slay's just got it all wrong, being the git he is," Charlie snarled. "Almost killed you and I, remember?"

"Yeah…"

Their conversation was cut short when the bell rang, signalling the end of lunchtime, and Charlie, Chloe, Maria, Will and Magic headed to History. As they approached the birch front doors, Magic stopped abruptly.

"Where's Tom?" she asked, suddenly remembering his absence.

"He's in Year 11, poor guy, they've got a huge workload so sometimes their lessons run into lunchtime."

"Oh—right."

They went back up the stairs to the third floor, where the English room was located. But, instead of stopping at the second door, they continued all the way to the end, stopping at a shabbily fitted black, wooden door with a bronze knocker shaped like an eagle. Magic had never seen so many different-looking doors in one building before.

"So, this is History?" groaned Magic, staring at the black door. She was not excited, having regretted choosing the subject for GCSE over the holiday.

"Mm-hm. It looks misleading on the outside, but it's really a decent room," Charlie assured her.

At that moment, the door gently clicked open. Magic had forgotten to wonder what the History teacher would look like.

Standing in the doorway was a man with hazel-brown, wavy hair that covered his forehead in half a fringe. He had bright, kind, twinkling brown eyes, and wore a pair of corduroy trousers with a matching blazer and brown leather shoes.

"Hello, everyone. Come in so we can get started," he welcomed them, in a deep, soothing voice. He smiled kindly as he stepped back to let the class in.

Charlie was right about the front door of the room being misleading; the inside was magnificent. Tall, narrow windows lined the ancient, brick walls that made up the room, daylight drifting inside in narrow rays, ending in light-coloured rectangles stretched across the ground. Oakwood desks sat in rows, like almost everyone class in the school, but with a nice aisle splitting the desks into two columns, presumably so the teacher could walk by and check on everyone. Magic wondered why the other classrooms didn't follow this logic. Stone brackets held up unlit torches all across the walls of the room. A large, brown cupboard stood at the back of the class, which was locked, presumably holding spare textbooks. On the left and right sides of the room, rows and rows of wooden and stone shelves held up ancient looking artifacts: things like old and worn gold coins, combs with missing fingers and dusty book covers.

Charlie, Chloe, Maria, Will, and Magic took their usual seats at the back of the classroom, Maria and Magic taking a seat in one column while Chloe, Charlie and Will sat in the other, as the teacher began to speak, standing in front of a wooden desk and chalkboard.

"Hello, everyone," he said in his kind and soothing voice. "Welcome to your first History lesson of the year. My name is Mr Lockwood and I hope you will enjoy all our future lessons and learn something new."

Magic wondered in amazement why she had groaned at the fact that she was having double History that afternoon. It had been one of the best and most interesting History lessons Magic had ever had. They were learning about the breakout of the Plague disease during 1348; they learned about all sorts of cures and remedies doctors had tried and failed. It was truly fascinating: Magic had no idea that victims died within the first twelve hours of being bitten, or that the famous nursery rhyme, 'Ring Around the Roses', was based on what happened to victims of the disease.

With three minutes left of the second half of the double lesson, meaning the end of the school day, everyone began helping restore the class to its normal state, as the lesson had got a bit hectic: some chairs had been toppled over and books fallen to the ground in the excitement of the students. Magic had never seen kids this excited during a History lesson.

"Alright everyone, our first lesson together has been wonderful—" began Lockwood, but Debbie Winningham, a girl with shoulder-length black hair, had tripped over a fallen chair, and landed on another, knocking them both to the ground. "Are you alright? Good. Now, as I was saying, this first lesson with everybody has been absolutely amazing and I am simply delighted to be your teacher for the rest of the academic year. Keep up the good work. Class dismissed."

Magic gathered her belongings and dropped them into her backpack, before slapping it onto her back and following the others down the aisle. She was at the door, about to walk out— "Magic, can I have a quick word?"

Magic stopped abruptly and turned round to face Lockwood's desk. He sat there expectantly, his fingers laced.

"Er—sure."

Magic gave Maria the I'll-meet-you-outside look, before Maria nodded, having understood. Chloe and Will had already set off down the hallway, but Charlie stood there, frozen. Maria tugged at his elbow before he threw Magic a curious look, and they left the room.

Chapter Five
Lockwood's Warning

"Don't worry, you're not in trouble," Lockwood reassured Magic just as Maria shut the door behind them. He sighed. "So, how has your first day been? Have you enjoyed it?"

"Fine, yeah," replied Magic. Had he just wanted to ask her how her day had been? She needn't have worried then—

"That's great to hear. Now—" he suddenly looked quite serious. Maybe she should have worried, after all "—I must bring to your attention the incident you had with Mr Slay this morning. Do not panic, I am not penalising you, you had every reason to be aggravated. You may have already heard this from the headmaster, but you want to avoid irritating the English teacher. I understand, Magic." Lockwood held up a hand as Magic opened her mouth to speak. "Again, I am not telling you off, I am looking out for you. Mr Slay isn't the kind of teacher you want to mess with, I'd say keep your head down and focus on your work, that way you can avoid any possible wrath that could come down on you. I have known Marcus—Mr Slay to you—for longer than you think. I know what this man is capable of—"

Magic's heart pounced. "'Capable of'? I'm sorry, sir, I'm not sure I understand."

Lockwood's eyes tightened. "Sorry, that was a bad choice of words. I meant to say I have known him for quite a while." He wore a reassuring smile, but Magic still felt uneasy. He continued. "I am not trying to turn you against him; after all, he is your teacher, but I will reiterate; don't mess with Mr Slay. If you encounter any issue with him in the future—" Lockwood wore a warmer expression "—please don't hesitate to come to me. I'm here to help."

There was a minute's pause as Magic processed what he had just said. *I have known Mr Slay for longer than you think. I know what this man is capable of.* What could this mean? Was Slay a regular English teacher who just had a bad temper, or was he more than that? Could he be dangerous? Could he—Magic stopped herself before her thoughts became too wild. She knew she was notorious for overthinking things. For now, she would trust what Lockwood said, and worry about his 'choice of words' when she had the time.

Her mind continued to buzz, but the expression on Lockwood's face brought her back to earth. Judging by his expression, he was also in deep thought. Frowning slightly, he turned to Magic, seemingly contemplating saying something.

"Er—thanks, sir," said Magic awkwardly, trying to break the silence.

Lockwood stopped frowning and smiled.

"Anytime. You can go," he said, with a finality in his voice.

"Thanks. See you."

Magic had barely grasped the doorknob before Lockwood spoke again.

"Oh, and one more thing—sorry," said Lockwood apologetically.

"Sure—no problem," replied Magic, turning back round to face him.

"Your surname is McFee?" he seemed to hesitate. "David and Lauren's daughter?" he asked, almost hopefully.

Magic gasped in shock. "You know my parents?" asked Magic quickly, her eyes widening with astonishment.

"Oh, I know them, alright. Your parents are there for me in the harshest of times."

"What did he mean?"

"He knew your *parents*?"

"Wow!"

"You're kidding!"

There were surprised outbursts from Charlie, Chloe, Maria, Will and Tom (who had joined them a few minutes before Magic finished speaking to Lockwood) as Magic informed them of what Lockwood had said; they had been waiting curiously in the corridor for her to tell them everything.

"Wait—d'you think he went to school with your parents?" asked Charlie inquisitively.

"Charlie, that's not important,' said Maria irritably, "there are more urgent matters we need to focus on here—Lockwood says he knows what Slay's capable of, which could easily mean we need to watch out. Especially you, Magic—" she turned to look at Magic and continued "—because he seems to have this sense of loathing towards you—or it could be that he was just angry, but as you said, Tom, he's always been like this. I think Lockwood's right—just don't give Slay a reason to harm you."

"H-harm me? Come on, guys, don't you think…?"

Privately, Magic thought that they may have been getting a bit carried away. What could Slay possibly do to hurt Magic? He was only her English teacher, for God's sake! Surely, they were overreacting…

"I don't know, but if Lockwood went so far as to warn you about Slay's 'capabilities', I definitely think you should look out for yourself," replied Maria anxiously. Magic thought this over, and decided Maria had a point.

"Seriously, though, how did he get employed? I mean, if he was dangerous—say he had a criminal record—Brownlow would know to watch out…" said Will, frowning in frustration.

There was a silence as everybody mulled over these thoughts. A criminal record? No, they were definitely taking this too far. Magic knew very well that if Slay had a criminal record he would not have been employed at all. She thought they were perhaps being a bit *too* cautious.

Although, she couldn't blame them—today was the first time Magic had ever been slammed into a wall and dragged down a school corridor by a teacher. She did have to say, he *did* seem a bit off…

Magic realised they were still standing cramped outside Lockwood's classroom. The hallways were completely silent; most of the students had already gone home.

"Guys, let's leave," Magic suggested, looking at everyone. They all seemed as deep in thought as she had been.

They descended the stairs, the sound of their footsteps muffled by carpet until they passed through the junior's corridor, where the *click-clack* of six pairs of feet against quartz echoed throughout the near-deserted building.

It was a breath of fresh air when Magic was finally able to step out into the fresh breeze of the field outside, after being cramped inside for so long. The front of the school was deserted, nobody outside except for the six of them.

"So…" Will began awkwardly.

"I think we should—head off," Tom announced. Magic cringed—the situation was too awkward for her liking.

"Yeah…" she said.

"See you round, Magic." Maria smiled.

"Yeah, see you," murmured Chloe, Will and Charlie.

They exited the school, passing under the curved metal sign sitting on top of the space between two brick walls that read 'CREAVEY HIGH'. Magic wondered why whoever built the school neglected a school gate.

They bade each other goodbye and parted ways on the street outside, Magic turning left, Maria turning right, and the rest crossing the street and splitting up.

Magic had barely started taking off towards her house, when the burning pain of the straps of her backpack cutting into her shoulders stabbed at her. She wiggled her fingers beneath the straps to reduce the friction and flipped her hair away from her face.

Inevitably, with nothing much to distract her, she broke into thought.

Today had been a very strange day.

"How was your first day at school, dear?" Mr McFee asked eagerly, before Magic had even put her foot over the threshold of the front door.

It had been—*interesting*. "Oh—it was great," Magic stammered.

"Ooh, you'll have to tell me all about it!" Miss McFee demanded cheerfully, as Magic took off her coat and hung it on one of the pegs behind the door, along with her jumper.

"Well, get inside, then, and tell us all about it," said Mr McFee, looking as eager as his wife.

Magic sighed and went into the dining room to find the table already laid; a huge pot of soup lay in the middle of the table, thick air wafting out of it, causing a slight humid temperature in the room. Sausages and roast that had been left over from yesterday lay on either side of the pot, along with a glass bowl full of salad sat on the edge of the table and small bowl of gravy.

"Who—?" began Magic. Her mother should have arrived home from work not too long ago, so she wouldn't have had enough time to prepare dinner. Magic's eyes flickered to her wristwatch; they didn't usually have dinner this early, either.

"I did, while your mother was away," said Mr McFee happily. "Tuck in, then."

Magic sighed again and told them all about school as they sat at the table—the huge field, the cafeteria, the teachers, (she didn't dare mention the incident with Slay), the grand walls of the school and, of course, her new friends.

"Oh—hold on—I wanted to ask you—" said Magic, for she had just remembered to ask them about Lockwood, "—my History teacher's name is Mr Lockwood, and he said he knew you."

Miss McFee dropped her cutlery, which clattered against her plate, and Mr McFee looked up excitedly.

"R-Remy teaches at your school?" asked Mr McFee softly.

"You're on first name terms?" asked Magic, surprised.

"Yes, yes—he was one of my best friends at school! Never left my side!" Exclaimed Mr McFee, his eyes glittering with glee, "If we're talking about the same person, of course."

"Wow—blimey," stammered Magic—she had not expected Lockwood to have this close a relationship with her parents—she simply thought he was an old work colleague, or someone he knew briefly through mutual friends. So, they had been close…

"I always wonder what that man's got up to! Haven't seen him in years, have we, dear?" Mr McFee cried happily. "I wonder if I could visit him some time?"

"Yeah, that would be nice," said Magic. A warm feeling was growing inside her; so the school hadn't really been so scary and unfamiliar after all.

Magic put down her cutlery. "Well, I'm off to bed," she announced.

Miss McFee stared at her wristwatch. "It's six thirty!"

"Well—I thought I'd read a little before sleep," Magic said awkwardly.

"OK, n-n-night, dear," said Miss McFee, stifling a yawn.

Magic trudged up the stairs, her feet as heavy as dumbbells. She hadn't really been planning to read—she had so much on her mind that she needed a quiet space to go to, and just *think*.

So, even though the sky outside hadn't yet deepened to that calming marine blue, Magic changed into her pyjamas, brushed her teeth and got ready for bed.

Her thoughts couldn't wait any longer—they burst through her mind as she flicked off the light and hopped into bed, tucking herself in.

The best way she could describe her first day at school was hectic. She had thought she could get away with lurking in the shadows and not attracting any attention, but today had proven wrong. She had managed to talk to more people than she thought she would, and made somewhat friends, if she may—that, however, was only the bright side of it.

Was it even legal for a teacher to physically hurt a student like Slay had to Magic? She didn't care that he had hurt her—it was more the idea that was frightening. The idea that a teacher was so violent towards a student he didn't even know yet. Magic could only shudder at the thought of how he treated his students he knew so well…

On a brighter note, it turned out that Lockwood did really know Magic's parents—he didn't just know them, but had an established relationship with them. And if Lockwood had gone as far as to warn her about Slay, who was supposedly a fellow colleague, he didn't seem to have a very good relationship with Slay, either.

I know what this man is capable of.

She had a feeling that that hadn't just been a 'bad choice of words'. Oh!

And the calculator! That *had* been strange, though Magic had tried to shake it off as a manufacturing flaw. It definitely wasn't as major a fluctuation in her day as her incident with Slay had been. Though, oddly, the more the day had went on, the stranger she had found its behaviour…

Magic's eyes widened in the darkness as she suddenly had an idea.

Lockwood had been one of her father's greatest friends—she didn't want to involve anybody unnecessary, but she felt like she had no other option.

She didn't know what possessed her in the moment, but she made the random—and some may argue *irrational*—decision that she would tell Lockwood about the calculator. She didn't know what came over her in that moment, but her gut suddenly poked at her, begging her to do so. Oh, and her gut also spontaneously decided that Magic should tell Lockwood about the figure, too. Even though she didn't think it important at first, completely trivial. So, in the morning, she would do just that.

It's strange how humans work, sometimes.

Chapter Six
Blood and Baffle

"Yesterday, I asked my parents about Lockwood, and they were so surprised… get this—he was my dad's best friend at school! He said he never left his side!"

"You're kidding!" exclaimed Will.

Charlie, Chloe, Maria, Will and Magic (since he was in Year 11, Tom's class had headed in earlier) sat at their circular wooden bench on the front field, waiting for the morning bell to ring. Magic had been heading towards Lockwood's classroom, and stopped to tell them about what she had decided the night before.

"Wow! Magic, that's amazing! Do you realise what this means? I hope he can cover for us if we end up murdering Slay…" said Charlie, while everybody laughed.

"Anyway… Maria, what lessons have we got today?" asked Magic, dreading the answer.

"Art, Maths, P.E, History ("Yes!" everybody cried) and double English (everybody groaned)," replied Maria, consoling her timetable.

"I swear, if Slay gives us a hard time I'm dropping English…" said Charlie thoughtfully.

"You can't drop English, Charlie, that's compulsory," cried Maria shrilly, throwing him a stern look.

"Well, I give up! Maybe I can try to waste time, give Slay a good taste of his own medicine…"

Charlie stopped conspiring against Slay with a few more disapproving looks from Maria.

Magic sighed and got up.

Charlie flashed a look of mingled curiosity and confusion at her. "Where're you off to?" he asked.

"I've got to go to Lockwood's, remember?" she reminded him.

"Oh—yeah—right. See you in Art."

"Yeah, see you."

Magic waved goodbye before she turned on her heel and headed for the birchwood front doors. She walked down the junior's corridor, climbed the familiar steps up towards the third floor and jogged all the way to the end, where the black, shabbily fitted door with the bronze eagle knocker sat shut. She hesitated for a second before knocking gently with one knuckle.

There was a moment's silence before a muffled, soothing voice spoke from behind the door. "Come in."

Magic gently grasped the doorknob between her fingers and twisted it. Inside, Lockwood set down his quill and looked up from the pieces of parchment that lay scattered across his desk. His desk chair lay completely discarded; he had been working standing up. When he realised who it was, he beamed and pulled a chair that lay under one of the rows of desks to the front of his own.

"Hello, Magic, this is a nice surprise. How are you?" he asked, dragging his discarded seat towards the desk and sitting down, gathering the sheets of paper he had been working with.

"I'm good, thanks," replied Magic.

Lockwood smiled. "You can have a seat."

"Oh, thank you." Magic sat down.

Lockwood sighed. "So, what's going on? Everything OK?"

"Oh—yeah, it's fine, there's just a few things I wanted to talk to you about."

Lockwood's eyes focused. "Absolutely. Go on."

Magic paused for a second before continuing. 'I-I wanted to tell you about something—*different*—that happened yesterday in class."

Lockwood nodded, and waited silently. He laced his fingers and listened, placing his elbows on the desk.

Magic stammered. "Er—well—it may sound silly—"

"Don't worry. Continue."

Where should she start? Chronological order, maybe?

"I was walking home, and this—*figure*—this *being* was—there, on the street—I know it seems normal, but this one was…odd. It looked *inhuman*."

Magic it all in one breath, her subconscious trying to get it out of the way. The expression Lockwood gave her, a confused, curious frown, made Magic cringe deeply inside and regret even coming to his office. Surprisingly, though, it was not the reaction she had expected from him—he didn't seem to be one bit taken aback about what she had told him, or look at her like she was insane.

"Well," Lockwood began, still frowning. "That certainly is quite unusual." A pause. "Did you see their face?"

Magic frowned at the memory. "No, I only caught a glimpse of them."

"That's… *interesting*. Well, thank you for telling me." Lockwood paused again. Magic knew he was deep in thought. "Is there anything else?"

"Er—yeah, one more thing," replied Magic slowly.

"Sure. What is it?" Lockwood smiled now.

"I-I was in Maths, and everything was normal. And then, out of nowhere, my calculator started acting—funny. It began to vibrate, and very quickly got violent. It started shaking so hard that it made so much noise against the table, so I picked it up, and then it froze. But, right after, a bunch of numbers flashed across the screen and disappeared, then flashed, then disappeared, making little beeping noises. A split second later, a—I guess you could say *threatening*—message appeared on it."

Lockwood didn't say anything. His expression was dazed, almost lost.

"Er—sir? That's it."

"No, I know. I'm just thinking about what you said—do you remember what the message read?" he asked her, still frowning thoughtfully.

"Yeah, hold on…" Magic thought for a second, frowning too. "Oh, yeah—*he who goes in, does not come out*—and something about a girl—hold on." Magic scrunched her eyes shut, racking her brains. "It was something about—oh, yeah!" Magic's eyes flung open. "*Past the treacherous sea, she will lie…*"

The frown slid off Lockwood's face.

"Well…that *is* unusual…"

His face went completely blank. His change in expression alarmed Magic. She just sat there and stared, waiting for a reaction.

Then, an expression of horrible comprehension dawned upon his face, those kind eyes of his twinkling madly.

"Magic, where have you put that calculator?" he asked quickly. It was like a switch had been flipped on inside his brain.

"It's in my bag."

"Could I have a look at it, please?"

"Sure…" Magic rummaged through her backpack, digging her hand all the way to the bottom until the top of the backpack reached shoulder-length, and extracted the calculator. She handed it to Lockwood, who immediately took it into his hands, studying it.

"Do you mind if I keep hold of it for now?" he asked her, not looking up. He flipped the device over in his hands, and then met her eyes. "I need to…examine it."

"Yeah—OK," replied Magic, utterly bemused.

Lockwood stowed the calculator in a drawer to his right, and the smile he had worn at the beginning sprung back onto his face.

"Is that all?" he asked her, his tone lighter.

"Uh—yes, that's it. Thank you," she added quickly.

"Not at all. Have a lovely day, and say hello to your parents for me," said Lockwood with a wink.

Magic smiled. "Will do."

He gave her another departing smile as she left the room. She felt stunned, almost numb at the unexpectedness of his reaction.

Magic met Charlie, Chloe, Maria, and Will on the way to Art, where she told them all about Lockwood's response to the calculator and the figure, which, in her opinion, seemed much more unexpected than both of those occurrences.

"You told him about the figure too?" asked Chloe.

"Yeah… I thought, while I was there, you know," replied Magic.

The conversation continued throughout the Art lesson.

"You said he looked disturbed by it? Do you think he knows something we don't?" asked Maria in a low voice, while flicking her paintbrush across her canvas and spraying purple paint everywhere.

"Dunno, he just looked concerned," Magic responded, watching Will flailing his hands furiously, trying to get rid of pieces of newspaper that had stuck to them. Occasionally, the Art teacher, Miss Sherry, a very smiley woman with unusually straight teeth, who wore a tight-fitting pink dress and black boots and sported short, wavy blonde hair, would circle the class in an attempt to see what the students were up to. Maria and Magic's conversation would cease until she was out of earshot once more. Once Will had successfully got rid of the sticky paper, he joined in. Charlie and Chloe stayed silent for a while.

"D'you think…nah, can't be," Charlie spoke after a bit.

"Ah, thank you for that useful input, Charlie," said Maria coolly.

"Well, I thought—I know this sounds silly—I'm probably wrong—it just can't be true—"

"Get on with it!" hissed Maria, shooting anxious glances round the classroom to check if anybody was listening.

"Well—" Charlie began, and Will and Maria leaned in, while Magic listened in, still painting, "—what if he was involved in it somehow…Lockwood."

"Nah, can't be," said Magic immediately, looking up from her work. "He knew my dad—and—well—why would he want to somehow corrupt my calculator into displaying bizarre messages? I mean, he barely knows me, he has no reason to poke at me, anyway."

"But hasn't Slay already proven that last point invalid?" asked Will, a trace of an angry frown flashing across his face.

"I think you've both got a point," said Charlie, wiping the table down with a wet cloth to get rid of Maria's purple paint stains. "But back to what you said, Magic, I think he probably knew what was going on, but not exactly in on it." Charlie walked over to a nearby sink and twisted up his now paint-stained cloth, water flooding out of it and slapping onto the metal bottom. He then placed it upon a drying rack and returned to his seat, wringing his hands.

Despite her friends' reassurances, Magic went from completely shaking off the calculator's strange behaviour as a trivial malfunction to worrying about it constantly in a short space of time. She had never heard of an ordinary piece of stationery that had acted of its own accord; the situation definitely seemed fishy, but she tried not to think about it too much.

After Maths (Miss Glant had finally showed up after a day off sick), the group confided in Tom Lockwood's response.

"Well—I agree with Charlie. There's no reason for Lockwood to want to harm Magic. I think he was just alarmed by the sudden strange story," Tom had said, before walking off with his Year 11 friends.

P.E took place in a huge courtroom towards the back of the school. The P.E teacher, Madame Damsypelt, a skinny woman with dirty blonde hair cut into a pixie cut, was extremely energetic. During breaks in the lesson, or at any time possible, the Charlie, Chloe Maria, Will, and Magic discussed the calculator's eerie message. Magic would've thought that after that incident, there would be other strange occurrences round the school. Nevertheless, the school seemed to be as normal as can be, as if the incident hadn't occurred at all; the word may have not reached the other students yet, if it was going to spread at all.

Once P.E had come to an end, Magic really anticipated entering the History classroom. She wasn't sure how Lockwood would act towards her after she told him what happened. Magic's trepidation increased as she walked solidly towards the end of the third-floor corridor towards History. Taking a deep breath and trying to keep her anxiousness contained, she scraped up all her courage and pushed open the door.

Magic wasn't sure what to expect, but it seemed like she shan't have worried at all; despite the morning's events, Lockwood greeted her and the rest of the class with the same kindness and welcoming smile they had received the previous lesson. After the class had taken their usual seats, Lockwood raised a hand to silence them.

"Great to see you everyone. Ian, put that away please, not in the lesson."

The boy called Ian snarled and stuffed hastily into his bag what looked like a duck-shaped yoyo. Sitting next to him was Michelle, and on the other side was

Phillipa. He then whispered something to Michelle, who giggled uncontrollably, flashed a frightful grin at Magic, which sent a sudden chill up Magic's spine, and then nodded, still grinning. Magic narrowed her eyes at the back of their heads, suspicious.

"Thank you, Ian," continued Lockwood. "Now, as I was saying, we will be carrying on with what we were learning about in the previous lesson—" There was a wave of 'Yes!' across the class. Lockwood smiled. "Yes, exciting—but we must look over the questions from last lesson before carrying on with our tasks."

Throughout the lesson, Magic stole quick glances at the boy called Ian; although she knew that there was no way she was going to work out what he said to her by staring at them, she couldn't help stealing glances every now and then; he had hazel-coloured hair, which was quite long, parted to the side and tucked behind his ears. His evil brown eyes glinted in the light from the torches Lockwood had just lit, his malicious grin frightful. Although he was just a child, supposedly not capable of inflicting damage upon anybody, Magic still couldn't shake of the feeling that what he and Michelle found simply a feeble joke is viewed as outright dangerous in the eyes of others…

"Don't you think they're up to something?" said Charlie anxiously, peering over his shoulder at the place where Ian, Michelle, Phillipa and a bunch of other students lay giggling, Michelle's arms wrapped round her waist, and rolling round with roaring laughter. It was lunch time and the five of them were sitting on their own table in the cafeteria. Tom hadn't returned from his lessons yet.

"I know! You don't miss anything, do you?" Magic asked him.

"Neither do you."

"I saw Ian whisper something to Michelle and she burst out laughing," said Magic, chancing a glance over Charlie's shoulder at what she thought was a sickening scene. "Oh, who cares, probably something stupid. He doesn't seem the bright type to me." She rolled her eyes.

"Oh, no, he isn't," said Maria matter-of-factly, one leg on top of the other and absorbed in a magazine, which she perched upon her knee. She looked up. "In fact, I don't think he knows anything at all. Completely blank every time a teacher asks him something, and yet he walks round the school as if he owns the place," she snarled towards Ian and his now roaring gang.

"They're so *thick*." She threw them a nasty look and returned to her magazine.

"Tell me about it," said a new voice. Tom had just joined them, sitting down, pulling his bag off and setting it down behind him. He had just left his classmates. "To be honest, I think they're just seeking attention."

Outside, Charlie, Chloe, Maria, Will, Tom and Magic sat down at their usual bench spot.

"Look at the idiot, swaggering round like—like he's impressive," hissed Will, who stared at the birch front doors that Ian and his gang had just exited from, still giggling. Will made a retching motion and looked away. Chloe sniggered.

"Don't worry about it, you don't have to look at them—they're just—*stupid*. Ignore them, they want you to react," said Chloe, still grinning. She gaped at a spot over Magic's shoulders, before her grin twitched then faded.

"What's up, Stocklin?" teased a malicious voice.

Magic whipped round defensively in her seat. There stood Ian, evil as ever, arms crossed and grinning triumphantly. He looked to his sides, where Michelle, Phillipa and a few other boys sniggered.

"Go to hell, Byers," Charlie spat immediately.

"Ooh, not very friendly, are we? What did you say, Stocklin?" Ian threw back.

Very quickly, Magic found *herself* fuming. She didn't need this, and it was uncalled for. She already had enough to deal with and didn't need their stupidity added to her overflowing plate.

"You heard him," Magic snarled before she could stop herself. *"Burn in hell."*

It all happened very fast.

Byers lunged at Magic but ended up slamming into Charlie; his fist made contact with Charlie's jaw, and he landed with a loud *thud* on the ground. Maria squealed with fright and threw herself at Charlie's side, where blood was now spilling from his mouth onto the floor; in retaliation, Will grabbed a fist of Byers' clothes and kneed him in the stomach, who doubled back in pain and stumbled. One of Byers' gang members, a large, muscular and stupid-looking boy seized Will by the hairs on his head, elbowed him in the neck and then punched his nose; blood splattered all over the boy's face and he threw Will away in disgust. Magic reacted instinctively; she threw herself onto the ground beside Will, as Maria had done for Charlie. Chloe ran over moments later, having checked on Charlie.

"Are you OK?" Magic whispered shakily.

"Don't worry," replied Will, his voice hoarse as he wiped his face onto his sleeve with his free hand. "At least I look cool." He grinned. Magic smirked back, rolling her eyes and pulling him to his feet. He swayed a little on the spot and steadied himself. His jet-black hair had shot up in all directions, but his glinting grey eyes remained in focus.

"YOU'LL BE SORRY FOR THIS, MORONS!" screeched Byers as he stalked away, still clutching his stomach, up the stairs and out of sight, his gang bringing up the rear. They had gathered an audience as the fight went on, and Magic flushed as most of the people in the playground stared, some horrified, some amused, at the injured.

Magic ran over towards where Maria still sat crouched down next to where Charlie still lay.

"Are *you* OK?" she asked him, now.

Charlie flung an arm across his face, covering his eyes. "It all happened so fast. I swear, once I get my hands on him, I'm gonna—" began Charlie, but Maria interjected.

"No! Charlie, you can't, you'll get into more trouble," cried Maria, trying to stay as calm as she could.

"Well, it'll be worth it," snarled Charlie, as he pulled himself to his feet, blood still dripping from his mouth. Maria ran over to her discarded backpack on the floor, rummaged through it and hastily pulled out two white handkerchiefs. She ran back to Charlie, handing him one, and then jogged over to Will and gave him the other.

"Thanks," said Will and Charlie gratefully, mopping up their faces, Will's voice still hoarse from being hit in the throat.

Magic was trying to process what had just happened. Her eyes flickered from Will to Charlie, still wiping their faces, to Chloe (who was guiding the boys towards the places on their faces with the most blood), to Maria, who looked utterly terrified, and to Tom, who had just stood there throughout the entire ordeal, his jaw hanging open. He didn't say a word, just stared.

"Oi! What's going on over there?"

Miss Ross was moving swiftly towards them, looking flustered and shaken, whisps of hair sticking out in all directions.

"Byers came picking at Charlie for no reason, and he attacked both him and Will," Magic informed her at once. Some may call her a sneak, but that was the least of her concern at that moment.

"I don't know why on *earth* he would do such a thing. If you speak the truth, he must have just made up that cock-and-bull story that you and your friends had turned up looking for a fight; he has just informed me."

There was an instant uproar of outrage.

"Miss Ross, it's not what you think, that stupid—" Will said a rude word, and Maria elbowed him in the side as Miss Ross cried out disapprovingly. "Sorry, miss— he made up the story so we'd get into trouble!" spluttered Will, spitting blood.

"It's true!"

"Yeah!"

"They're lying!"

"It's not what you think—"

"Why would we ever go up to—"

"Very well! Miss Smith and Miss McFee, would you kindly escort Mr Brakk and Mr Stocklin up to the First Aid room? Mr Wright and Miss Kenfield, please come with me, we are going to the headmaster's office, you can inform him of what has just happened."

Miss Ross gestured at Maria and Tom to follow her, who still looked shaken. They glanced back anxiously at Will and Charlie and followed Miss Ross into the building. They looked slightly odd; Tom was a whole head taller than Maria. Curious eyes followed them into the building all across the playground until they were out of sight.

"C'mon," muttered Chloe, "people are staring at us, let's get to the first aid room, those injuries look bad."

Still clutching Maria's handkerchiefs to their mouths, Will and Charlie followed Magic and Chloe up the steps and into the building, a wave of whispers echoing from outside into the building.

Chapter Seven
The Second Sighting

A large woman in white robes and blonde curls stood waiting for them in the First Aid room, holding a tray full of what looked like boxes of plasters and bags of wipes. At the sight of them, she set down her tray on a nearby stool and placed her hands on her hips, her lips pursed.

"Dear, dear, did you girls give these boys a hard time?"

"No, of course not," said Chloe quickly, shaking her head frantically, her tiny, black curls swaying in unison. "They were beaten up by two boys in our year."

"Hey, now! That is simply unacceptable!" cried the woman. "Mr Brakk, please take a seat on that bench, yes, that one, dear—Mr Stocklin, if you would lie down, I need to have a look at your nose—oh, it really is awful…kids having a go at each other these days…"

Will took a seat on a bench towards the left of the door of which they had just entered. Charlie lay down on a manual hospital bed directly opposite the door.

"Would Miss Smith and her friend like to sit down? What's your name, dear?" the woman asked kindly, turning to Magic.

"Oh—er—I'm Magic Mcfee."

"Lovely name you've got there! Well, I'm Mrs Primrose, it's lovely to meet you." She stuck out a fat hand. Once Magic shook it, Mrs Primrose gestured to the bench Will was sitting on, still clutching the handkerchief to his face, and Magic and Chloe took their seats.

"D'you think he'll be OK?" Magic whispered into Will's ear, playing nervously with her hands.

"Oh, he'll be fine," replied Will, his voice slightly muffled as he spoke from behind the handkerchief. "It could be worse."

"I guess…"

It took over thirty minutes for Charlie to be tended to; nevertheless, he finished looking quite ordinary considering their huge fight.

"How are you feeling?" asked Magic quietly as he took a seat next to her. Charlie put a hand to his nose.

"A lot better—blimey, I have to give it to them, they got me good." He turned and smiled at her, his mouth slightly swollen. "Why are we looking so worried?"

"I dunno, unexpected, I guess…"

But Magic in fact was not just shaken from these unexpected events… She had seen Byers and his friends whispering mere minutes before the fight had happened. Could it be possible that they were planning to do more than harm her friends?

Magic's short daydream was interrupted by the finishing of Will's patch-up.

"Better?" she asked him hopefully as he approached them, healed with just a small plaster on the area between his neck and his jaw.

"Yeah, much. Still sings a bit, though," he replied, rubbing his jaw. His voice was much less hoarse now that he had been tended to.

Chloe looked up at the clock above the manual hospital bed and slapped a hand to her forehead, which startled everybody in the room. Even Mrs Primrose turned round in alarm.

"We're late to English!" she cried, her face falling in terror.

"Oh jeez, Slay's gonna kill us—"

"Holy crap!"

"We're so dead—"

The four of them hastily thanked Mrs Primrose and scrambled out of the room, leaving her looking stricken at their sudden departure. They were even more horror-struck when they tumbled into the deserted, silent quartz corridors and suddenly remembered that they had left their backpacks on the field outside. They bolted towards the birchwood doors, where they tripped out of the building and sprinted across the field, the only sound coming from the soft crunches of grass beneath their feet.

Chloe scooped up her backpack from the ground, Magic picking hers up from the bench table and Will and Charlie from the seats. Then, they bolted back into the building, their bags slapping against their backs, the hurried *clitter-clatter* of four pairs of feet against quartz reverberating off the walls.

They climbed the stairs three at a time, their joints aching by the time they reached the top.

They burst open the classroom door and rushed inside, taking their usual seats furthest away Slay's desk, ignoring as much as they could the silence that fell as they entered. Slay turned his head slowly towards them, his expression glittering with a deep hunger in his eyes as he prepared to pounce upon his prey. Magic willed herself not to meet his expression—or even glance at him from the corner of her eye—as she took her seat in the middle of the backbench amongst her friends, staring at her trembling hands on the table. It was like there was a magnetic tug pulling her face downwards, where she wouldn't be able to fault it and even shift her glance a millimetre upwards.

Inevitably, seconds later, the jeering began.

"Well, dear children, look who decided to show up! Why do you feel you are excepted from following the school rules? Surely, you understand simple instructions? *Don't be late to class!* Or would you like me to pantomime?"

Ian Byers and his gang sniggered delightedly. Magic clenched her jaw, not moving. She knew if she so much as moved an inch, or unlocked her teeth, she would scream and yell and unleash all the anger waiting to climb up through her mouth.

But, for Magic, withholding anger was like trying to stop herself vomiting.

"Will and Charlie were injured, in case you haven't noticed, and we were in the first aid room!" she cried out with fury before she could stop herself. The anger was climbing her throat, but was not fully satisfied—it had not been fully released or quenched. Before Slay even spoke, the anger flared white-hot.

"Well, I am sure a nice little trip to the first aid room shouldn't have taken more than a minute?"

Slay's mad eyes were positively roaring with delight now. Magic was blinded with anger and almost lost control—she couldn't prevent her eyes lifting from her hands to Slay's pale, cold face, his frighteningly high-arched eyebrows raised even higher, which made him look petrifying, while his thin lips pointed upwards in a satisfied smile that anyone could easily think looked like an attempt to hide a grimace.

Chloe tugged at Magic's elbow, and Magic didn't need to look at her to know that she was utterly alarmed. She could feel her trembling as Magic was. Chloe hissed in her ear.

"Magic, please, he isn't worth it!"

"But, of course, this school is *gold* you people walk on, is it not?" Slay continued to jeer, all the while Magic sat there, fuming mutely. She was surprised she hadn't caught fire yet.

"How long did it take you to come up with that one?"

The angry being that had been waiting to climb out through Magic's throat burst through and diminished every last bit of control she had left.

A second flashed by, but it felt like an epoch.

The ringing silence was penetrated by Slay's voice, now cold instead of amused.

"Detention. Four o'clock. My office. Don't—"

"I don't know where your office is!" Magic yelled. Her classmates' stares were the least of her concern!

"—be late." Slay finished with an unmistakable air of triumph behind his now icy voice.

Slay didn't speak to Magic once more throughout the lesson, but merely kept throwing her nasty looks, which took all she had left of her to ignore. Nevertheless, she ploughed on through the English lesson without uttering a single word. At least the angry being had tumbled out of her mouth, instead of having to restrain it and shove it back down her gullet every now and then, before it crawled back up to near-surface level. Magic was worried however, that a new being was germinating in the pit of her stomach. This being was called Fear.

"What the hell was that for? The LUNATIC!" Charlie clenched his fists by his sides, his voice shaking with uncontainable anger. "Detention? For being late because we were *beaten up?*"

"No, actually," answered Chloe in a voice barely audible than a whisper. "It's because Magic may have pushed her luck with Slay. In case you haven't noticed, she's the only one whose been put in detention." She set her bag on the wooden bench table for the umpteenth time that day.

"Yeah, well, he started it, if he had just shut up and—and believed us, none of this would've happened! He didn't shout at Byers and his gorilla friend for beating us up, did he, he just shouted at us because we were *late!*" intervened Magic, completely losing it now. "*What—is—his—problem?* Picking fights with *students?* WHO DOES THAT?"

Everybody turned to look at her blankly. She probably looked mad and red in the face, but she didn't care. A full minute of silence passed.

She pulled herself together and asked, with the calmest voice possible, "Where is his office, anyway?"

"Not far from the classroom," said Will, who began pacing. "The room opposite, actually." He stopped in his tracks, staring at the sky. "Why d'you think he's always out to get us?" he asked thoughtfully, still gazing at the sky with a hand on his chin.

"Exactly, don't you see? Magic and Will both see it, Chloe, remember when he almost killed Magic and I? Slammed us into a wall!" cried Charlie in earnest.

Chloe looked at him with a slightly retreating look on her face before responding, "Well, I was only looking out for her. D'you think I want any one of you slammed into a wall again?"

Maria bit her lip but said nothing. She just stared at the grass, her gaze solemn. She usually was the one who piped in, but she remained silent.

"What're you thinking, Maria?" Magic asked her when her anger had subsided a bit more. Magic unclenched her fists she just realised she had balled up, to find deep nail marks engraved into her palms. She scowled irritably at her hands.

"I-I don't know what to say to you, Magic. I'm sorry, I really don't."

At five to four, Magic slumped up to the third floor, dragging her feet up the crimson-carpeted stairs and taking as much time as she dared. When she reached the door opposite the English classroom, she scowled at the silent corridors and then the door, before wrapping three times at the door, not even able to bring herself to hesitate.

"Enter," a voice commanded.

Slay's office wasn't much like any office Magic had ever entered before; at first, she thought she had entered a pitch-black room, but she soon realised that almost all of the furniture present in the room was a deep black colour; the bookshelves, which supported hundreds of cluttered and dust-covered books on either side of the room; the window behind the desk was framed with two red velvet curtains that hung either side of it like hair; a small circular black table was crammed into a corner on the right, supporting a dusty vase filled with blood-red roses; both chair and desk were pitch black; it couldn't have been a harsher colour contrast to the pale man occupying them.

"Sit down, then." Slay leered.

Magic slumped sulkily into yet another black chair facing the desk.

"Do you know what you will be doing for me?" asked Slay, placing his elbows on the desk and lacing his fingers.

"No." Magic answered carelessly.

"You'll be sorting out some old files for me." He gestured to the bookshelf to his left. There was a whole shelf dedicated to cluttered and crammed dusty folders.

"All of them?" asked Magic, sitting up with dread.

"Yes, all of them." Slay's lip curled into that unpleasant smile that Magic learned so quickly to detest. "You will remain—"

"And how long is this going to take?"

"—in this office as long as it takes to complete your task," finished Slay, raising his voice. There was a long pause, where Magic considered arguing before immediately thinking better of it. With an irritated sigh, she started towards the black bookshelves to flick through the first of many folders, and her dreaded detention began.

She remained trapped in the dark office for what felt like hours, getting up from time to time to reach for another dusty folder, wiping her palms across her jeans when she had finished with the previous. From time to time, she would catch a glimpse of the field outside and she would silently long to just jump out the window and escape; she never thought in her life that deserted grounds would look so inviting. Slay kept his head down, not looking up once, and occasionally sparks of fury would splutter within Magic, but she wouldn't let them light fully. She would maintain her self-control for the duration of this detention, which means she would not look at Slay once. She had to say, that was a task that would not prove difficult at all.

After a while, the sky began to tweak from dull white to dim grey. *Three hours or so must have passed by now,* thought Magic.

It was only when Magic's gaze flickered absent-mindedly to the field outside for about the hundredth time when she saw it.

A tall, cloaked figure who appeared to be holding a stick-shaped object that very much resembled a stuff was peering out at her from in between two bushes in the grounds below. Its concealing cloak fluttered eerily behind it in the breeze, the only moving entity amongst the frozen scene below besides the shivering grass.

The being called Fear that had begun to germinate within Magic hours earlier exploded and was immediately renamed Panic. Magic dropped the folder she was carrying in shock and the files within spilled out all over the floor and across part of Slay's workspace, the last of them fluttering to the ground. Panic not just crawled, but sprinted out of her mouth as Magic yelled at the sight.

"What in the name of—" Slay began angrily, but Magic wasn't listening; she dashed towards the velvet-framed window and her eyes scanned the grounds for the figure, but there was no sign of him. Magic growled with mingled fury and panic and hurried back round the desk to pick up the discarded files, pink in the face. Once she straightened herself, her eyes met Slay's cold, dark ones.

"I think that is enough for today. You may leave." His voice was cold and furious; Magic needn't to be told twice. She placed the folder back onto the end of the shelf, leapt towards her backpack, threw it onto her back, and bolted from the room.

Oh, how liberating it felt to finally be able to tear through the school corridors after being trapped in that awful room for so long—she was free.

And then, she tumbled out into the darkening front grounds and that's when it hit her.

She was not sure that anybody had notified her parents that she would be late home.

Oh, God.

Magic tore mindlessly out of the gateless doorway that led to Creavey High.

Though the journey would have taken ten minutes, it took five this time with Magic's speed.

"Where have you been?" cried Mr McFee, when Magic had burst into the house, panting, her hands on her knees.

"David is that her?" cried a shaking voice from the dining room. "Oh, thank goodness! Yes, yes, we've found her, she's here!"

Mrs McFee came running into the hall in her white silk nightdress, her eyes red and puffy. She burst into tears.

"I'm sorry, I'm sorry!" cried Magic desperately. "My English teacher isn't exactly a bright ray of sunshine, so he threw me in detention—"

Magic explained the whole story, from the fight that had occurred in the grounds to Slay putting her in detention, raising her voice over Mrs McFee's continuous wailing. However, she was careful not to mention the part where she had seen the cloaked figure. When she had finished, Mr McFee raised Magic's chin with his hand, so she had to look into his eyes.

"Why didn't you tell us you had a problem at school, honey?"

Magic opened her mouth to speak, but nothing came out; she was speechless. Why *hadn't* she told them? Ah, but she had told somebody about *something*...

"I told Mr Lockwood, everything's sorted. If anything happens, I'll tell him. I'm sorry I worried you."

Mr McFee let go of Magic's chin and his shoulders relaxed. Mrs McFee's sobbing ceased. They seemed to really trust Remy Lockwood; something about him always made them feel reassured.

"It's odd that nobody at school told us, though," said Mr McFee, frowning in thought. "They should have at least told us, right? That *is* odd..."

"Yeah..."

Did anybody in the school even know that Magic had been held hostage in Slay's office that afternoon?

Magic was too overwhelmed to eat, so she climbed up the stairs and entered the safety of her bedroom. She changed into her nightdress and slumped onto her bed.

Ding-dong.

Oh, come on! The doorbell! *When* would she get a break?

She crossed her fingers and hoped silently that it was only a parcel being delivered.

But then, there was a swing of a door and an outbreak of a murmur of happy voices. She bit her tongue and waited for the murmuring to diminish. Surely, it didn't take this long for someone to drop a parcel off?

Magic heard the distant slam of a door and groaned into her pillow when the murmur of voices didn't disappear. So, they had guests now. Great.

To her utter displeasure, the murmuring was growing louder. No! Not up here! They were going to come in here, she knew it.

Inevitably, there was a silent pause before a soft knock on her door.

"Come in," Magic croaked, straightening up and darting over to her desk chair. Magic was utterly dumbfounded at the tall, kind man with brown wavy hair, corduroy trousers and a chocolate-brown travelling cloak standing in her doorway, smiling.

"Hello, Magic. Can I talk to you?" asked Mr Lockwood softly.

"Er—yeah—sure—" Magic stammered, not having enough time to face her confusion, and he closed the door behind him, before striding across the room and standing by her desk.

"Do you mind if I sit down?" he asked her.

What the hell? "No, it's fine," replied Magic, trying to sound as casual as possible while wondering in the back of her mind as to what on earth her History teacher was doing in her house, striding in so casually.

Lockwood pulled the stool by Magic's desk to a place where he could face her and sat down, hands on his knees. There was a pause and then he heaved a great sigh.

"Magic, have you seen that figure again recently?"

The question sent a physical jolt through Magic's body. Did Lockwood think she was mentally disturbed and needed help, or did he believe that she was telling the truth? Magic tried to pull herself back together, trying to figure out how on earth the world worked—he asked her the question minutes after it had happened—

"I don't think you're crazy, Magic." he said in a reassuring voice, as if he had read her mind. "I just need an answer from you."

Magic thought it best to be truthful in this situation. There was no way he didn't already know the answer. "Um... yeah, yeah... I saw it today. How did you know?" she blurted out, before she could stop herself.

"I have my sources. Mr Slay was telling me you reacted quite dramatically at something you had seen out of the window."

Damn it. Did that man have to go babbling about everything? "Right…yes. Yes, I did." Magic replied awkwardly.

Lockwood's gaze shifted; he definitely seemed to be more alert than usual. "I am here to ask one favour of you; if you happen to come across anything unusual again, alert me immediately." There was a silence as Magic nodded numbly, not even half aware of what she was doing.

"Right," said Lockwood, breaking the silence and getting to his feet. "If you ever need anything at all, you know who to ask." He smiled at her and strode out of the room, leaving Magic even more confused than she was before. However, one of her questions had been answered: she wasn't imagining it. The figure had been real. Something was quite suspicious about him and his behaviour. And *was* that a staff he was holding? If it was, how dangerous could this being possibly be?

Magic scrambled back into bed, her thoughts all creating collisions in her mind. Nothing she knew fitted together or made her scream out *'Oh!'* in understanding. She just remained more confused than ever before, wondering what in the world all of this meant.

Trying to clear her brain, Magic got up (why did she even bother getting into bed?), strode across the room, and turned off the bedroom light. She blinked a couple of times and waited for her eyes to get adjusted to the darkness before manoeuvring through it, back to bed.

She pressed her palms into her eyes, elbows on her knees; something wasn't right, but she knew that already. The question was *what*. *What* or *who* was causing all this commotion? She pressed her palms harder into her eyes, white sparks popping out in her closed vision. It was enough with Ian Byers and his cronies looking for trouble all over the school; she didn't need any more commotion.

In that moment, everything seemed unclear. None of the pieces of the puzzle that were Magic's thoughts had fit together. Yet.

But, as she finally turned over in bed, Magic at least knew one thing: this school year was going to be a disaster.

Chapter Eight
Birthday Wishes

September whooshed passed with unexpected speed as October came by, bringing with it ice-cold weather that nipped noses and numbed fingers. All round the school, students were clutching scarfs over their mouths and noses, trying as fast as they could to escape the freezing-cold of the school corridors and taking refuge in the warmth of the candlelight from their classrooms. Charlie, Chloe, Maria, Will, Tom and Magic's homework had already reached an alarming point, and when Tom wasn't spending time with his Year 11 friends, they would while away the hours after school finishing off homework in the vast expanse of the school library, pulling out book after book from the shelves and becoming absorbed in its words. On the evening of the twenty-ninth of October, the group sat cluttered round a dark oak, round table, pieces of parchment, books, quills and empty ink bottles scattered all over the desk, everybody working their hardest. Magic had been so absorbed in her work that she hadn't noticed someone tapping her shoulder.

"Magic!"

She looked up suddenly to see Will clutching a huge pile of books, looking amused about something.

"What's up?"

"We—we have to go… Ross asked us to meet her now in—in her office."

"O-OK then, let's go…" But as Magic stood up, closing her book and tucking it under her arm, she felt a hand grasping her shoulder and pushing her back down into her seat.

"Wha—?" Magic started, confused.

"Not you, just the five of us," Will said quickly, removing his grasp from her shoulder and gesturing silently towards the others. There was the scraping of chairs and the slapping of bags against backs. They smiled down at Magic sadly.

"Sorry, I don't know why she's singled you out," said Will, and to Magic's utter astonishment, Will turned to the others with a huge smirk plastered on his face, which even more incredulously they returned. At this point, Magic was so bemused she just sat there gaping as the five of them got up and left her to her thoughts. *Why me? They've probably been called to talk about schoolwork from last year,* she thought to herself. *Yes, that would be it. There's no other explanation as to why she'd single me out.*

OK but—the hell?

Magic came to realise that ever since the calculator incident she began to feel more curious towards things that were usually considered ordinary. At quarter to seven, she packed up her books, parchment, quills, and empty ink bottles and left the library. Her friends still hadn't returned from Ross's office, but she couldn't wait any longer—she had told her parents she'd be home by seven. Very reluctantly, Magic trudged along the school corridors, the *click-clack* of shoes against quartz, out of the large front doors and into the cold October night. Magic pulled her jacket tighter round herself as she rummaged through her backpack, extracted the empty ink bottles and dumped them in a nearby recycling bin. She trudged along sadly, with a sense of slight irritation, at what she didn't know.

Magic practically strangled herself in the jacket, pulling it as tightly as she could round herself as tiny drops of rain began to splatter against her skin. She scowled as the tighter she pulled, the deeper the straps of her backpack cut searingly into her shoulders. In a haste to arrive home before it began showering, she adjusted her backpack into a more secure, painless position and broke into a run down the dark street, water splashing everywhere as she sloshed through the puddles.

Too quickly for her liking, it began drizzling, the light splattering sounds of water against concrete echoing off the ground. She could barely see anything through the slanted shower of drops.

It seemed like an eternity before Magic finally skidded to a halt in front of her house door. She wrapped frantically at the wood, but nobody answered. Confused and surprised, Magic shuffled through the damp grass of the front lawn to take a peek through the gap in the curtained windows. She lifted an arm above her eyes to shield herself from the rain, eager to get a better view. Through the slight slit in the curtains, she could see the soft light of the living room—so there *was* somebody in the house.

She wrapped at the door one final time, straining her ears over the noise of the rain for any sound from inside. Magic was trying to decide if she'd rather stay out there and get soaked until she was found, or just break in, when the front door clicked, and the door creaked open ever so slowly.

All of a sudden, the lights of the hallway cut to black. Magic took a sharp intake of breath and brushed her fingers against the door, where it creaked ever so gently until it hit the wall of the house. She held out a hand to stop it from hitting her when it rebounded. She blinked a couple times to try and adjust to the darkness.

"Guys?" Magic whispered into the blackness, her throat raw with trepidation. "Mum... Dad?"

Magic began to panic; there was not one sound coming from her house, yet she had seen the light on just moments before. She stepped over the house threshold, the floorboards creaking eerily. She lifted an arm up shakily, her fingers tracing the wall for the light switch. When her fingers ran over a lump in the wall, she pressed down eagerly.

"HAPPY BIRTHDAY, MAGIC!"

The light had barely flickered on before Magic had time to process anything. She doubled back in shock, almost tripping backwards over the threshold and out into the soaking night again. Confetti exploded from all directions and the sound of party whistles filled the house, the sound reverberating in her ears.

Charlie, Chloe, Maria, Will, Tom and Mr and Mrs McFee stood with their arms open wide, grinning broadly, sporting pointed party hats.

"What? I—" Magic spluttered, her mouth unable to keep up with the thoughts in her head. "What are you all *doing* here?"

Charlie barged past a smiling Maria and blew a very large *honk* through his whistle. Maria threw him a disapproving look, rubbing her elbow before Charlie replied.

"Here to celebrate your birthday of course!"

"But how did you—Mum! Dad!"

Mr and Mrs McFee approached, holding a badly wrapped, shapeless brown package. Mrs McFee sported a red, flowy dress embroidered with large, white flowers, giving off more beachy vibes. Mr McFee was in one of his classic suits.

"You organised this?" Magic asked, raising her voice over the lively banter and noises of party whistles. The realisation hit her. "So this was the trip to Miss Ross's office, wasn't it?" she cried, astonished.

"It sure was!" Will appeared before anybody could answer. "Jeez, you're soaked, Magic." For Magic was still dripping with the ice-cold rainwater.

"Er—yeah, it's raining cats and dogs out there," Magic said awkwardly.

"Did we go a bit overboard on the confetti?" Maria asked, grinning as she dusted Magic's shoulder of any remaining sparkles.

"You should probably change, dear, or you'll get sick. Here's your present, I hope you like it. Come down for some cake afterwards."

"Er—yeah—thanks, Mum." Magic stammered, as she trudged up the stairs, the sound of the lively banter gradually getting quieter.

How had they gotten here so fast? It hadn't been very long until Magic had turned in after them. And when had this all been planned? Still, Magic felt her face lift into a smile as she walked towards the bathroom door, swelling up with gratitude.

Magic had never given much thought to what she would wear, considering the fact that she had no idea she'd even have to contemplate another outfit before tomorrow. She felt a rush of nervousness as she confronted her closet, challenging her clothes.

She decided she'd be here until her eighteenth birthday if she contemplated it for too long, so Magic decided to go with jeans and a t-shirt, her general clothing style. She attacked her wet tangles with a brush before heading back downstairs.

Maria was talking to Mr McFee in a corner; she turned and smiled as Magic approached.

"Make room for the girl!" Chloe called as she shuffled to the side to make space for Magic on the sofa. Magic laughed as she sat down. Will came to sit on Magic's other side as conversations resumed all round the room.

"Thanks for coming, guys." Magic smiled. "But when did you all plan this? You must be superhuman!"

"Oh, don't be silly," Tom appeared, taking a seat on the sofa opposite them. "We couldn't miss it. It's not every day you turn fifteen!"

"I know, but when did you—?" Magic began, but Chloe cut across her, raising a hand to silence Magic.

"It's a long story, really... Anyway, we've been meaning to tell you something."

"'Bout what?"

"It's Katie." Will spoke now. Magic turned slightly in her seat so she could face him. His jet-black hair shone in the light from the room.

Magic was taken aback; she hadn't expected that. "What's happened?"

"When we were leaving, we saw her in the corridor, just standing there. But she was shaking, she looked so frightened. I wonder..."

"What?" Magic urged curiously.

"Well...you guys remember when Katie and Slay had that row in the cafeteria?" Chloe, Tom and Magic nodded.

"Maybe she was frightened of *him* today...? What if he'd threatened her!"

"Don't be ridiculous, Will," Chloe butt in. "He's a *teacher*...He's...not allowed to threaten a student. It was probably something small...maybe a talk about missing homework?" She cocked her head to one side, deep in thought.

"Yes, but if it was about something that trivial, she wouldn't have been so defiant. Did you not see how scared she looked? Out of her wits!" replied Will.

"I don't know, guys…I could see both things being a possibility, but it was just something about the situation…" Magic began. "It all just seemed so off…and for it to happen in front of so many people, it just doesn't…" Her voice faded.

She had never given the incident much thought, but looking back Magic realised how suspicious it looked. How livid Slay had looked, apparently desperate for something from Katie's grandfather…or it could've just been something trivial, as Chloe had mentioned. But ever since Magic's calculator had acted up, the world just seemed all the while stranger.

"What do you all look so down about?" Charlie asked, sipping at a cup of juice. His face fell when he was faced with more silence from the group. His voice turned more serious. "What is it?"

"N-nothing," Chloe stammered.

Magic was barely paying attention to Charlie as he trampled over and took a seat in the sofa on the right.

"Hmph." Charlie sipped on his tea.

"What?" Chloe challenged.

"You're acting weird." Charlie said, eyeing Chloe suspiciously.

Chloe rolled her eyes. "So much coming from you," she muttered.

"What's going on?" Charlie gave up on Chloe and turned to Tom. "The mental one won't speak."

Tom placed his elbows on his knees. "Nothing, we were just talking about that day where Katie and Slay had a row in the cafeteria." He rubbed his chin.

Charlie's face fell slightly. "Oh."

"Don't you guys want cake?" Mrs McFee sang before the conversation could continue.

"Sounds good," said Will.

The sextet sat at the table; Mr McFee went off for a while to take a business call, while Mrs McFee made conversation.

"So, what does your mother do, William?" Smiled Mrs McFee, wiping her hands on a towel and pulling off her apron.

"She works in a jewellery shop in the city." There was a clatter of forks and knives as some people began finishing up.

"That's lovely," answered Mrs McFee, taking a seat. "How about your dad?"

Will sipped at some juice and smiled. "He's an actual *jeweller*. They work in the same shop."

"Oh, Magic, come see what I got you!" Maria exclaimed excitedly. "Actually, stay right there, I'll go get it!" she giggled and ran into the hallway. Tom winked at Magic.

Charlie, Chloe, Tom, Will and Magic were sitting in the living room and Maria still hadn't returned.

"Er—Maria, you OK there?" Will called out anxiously.

"No—I mean, yes, I'm fine—stay there!" Maria's hollow, muffled voice issued from the hallway; there was still a note of excitement in her tone.

"Oh, jeez. You guys better not have brought anything else." Magic warned them.

"Ah, well…it's been fun," snickered Charlie. Will laughed.

Magic groaned. "Really, guys? It was unnecessary!"

"Don't sweat, Magic, we had to have got you something whether you threatened to strangle us or not. And it was not expensive, we promise, just a little something," Will reassured her casually. Everybody laughed.

"What're you all laughing at?" Maria asked, appearing in the doorway, her hands behind her back.

"You'd know if you'd been here for the past couple minutes. What've you got there?" asked Charlie curiously.

"Magic's present, which is not of your concern," Maria shot back, though she smirked. She stuck her nose up in the air and marched towards Magic, seating herself by her.

"By the way, Will and I coordinated." she said before handing Magic a small, white paper bag.

Magic's fingers trembled as she reluctantly pulled at the red ribbon at the top. A small box lay in the bottom of the bag.

"Oh, no!" Magic moaned. "I didn't want you spending tons of money, let alone bring presents! Why'd you do this? You said it wouldn't be expensive!" she pursed her lips.

"Well, my parents insisted, though I told them you'd make a fuss," replied Will. "Open it."

Magic fumbled with the box, and it opened with a *pop*. A silver necklace pendant lay snug in black velvet, with a word engraved into the metal: *Magic.*

"Aww, guys…it's beautiful." Magic whispered. She pulled Maria into a side hug. Maria squeaked with delight, her green eyes glittering.

"I'm so glad you liked it! Will's parents made a huge fuss, saying they wanted it to be special, so decided to carve your name into it. Isn't it gorgeous?" Maria asked breathlessly.

"It's perfect." Magic replied. "Thank you, really." She turned to Will, giving him a side hug too.

"Ah, it was nothing." Will smiled, giving her a squeeze.

Mrs McFee appeared in the doorway, wiping her brow against her sleeve. She smiled.

"You all having fun?" she asked kindly.

"Mum, isn't this lovely?" Magic gently lifted the pendant between her thumb and forefinger and held it up to the light. Mrs McFee gasped, and her jaw dropped slightly before she tried to collect herself.

"Darlings—children—that was really unnecessary," Mrs McFee said quickly, pursing her lips. "You really are too kind. Oh my…" She took a glance at it once more. "It's gorgeous. Thank you, dears."

Maria's expression glowed.

When the end of the night dawned, Magic accompanied her friends to the door. She yawned and stretched as Charlie pulled up his hood and Chloe finished zipping up her jacket.

"See you later, Magic. Thanks for having us," Maria thanked her, hugging Magic.

"Yeah, it's been fun," replied Magic, catching Will's glance and smiling at him over Maria's shoulder. "We should do it again," she said, pulling away. "And thanks for the presents!" she added.

"Oh, it was nothing," replied Maria.

"Maybe my place next time?" Will suggested.

"Sure, why not."

"Oh, here're your sweets. Bye, Magic!" Will dumped a large box wrapped in patterned wrapping into Magic's arms, and hurried out the door, biting down a smirk, before she could object. Magic huffed in defeat, and could've sworn she'd caught him snickering.

"See you, Magic!"

Magic waved off her friends until they turned a corner and vanished. She closed the door and found her mother smiling at her in the hallway.

"You need to teach me how to get myself some friends as lovely as those," sang Mrs McFee. Magic yawned.

"Yeah, they're great."

Mrs McFee tapped Magic on the nose. "Off to bed, then."

"Night, Mum."

The stars were white flecks against the inky black night-time sky as Magic tucked into bed, staring out the window. She watched the glistening moon float in the air for a while, her heart light and content. She hadn't had a bad day after all. She smiled at the thought.

She traced the rays of moonlight through her window, onto the wooden bedroom floor, where the rays split into bright white rectangles against the dark oak of the floor panels.

Magic allowed her mind to wander, off into the dark clouds of the dusky sky. Before she knew it, she had drifted off.

Her vision was slightly blurry as she ran, as fast as she could, down the familiar, red-carpeted corridors and torchlit brick walls.

MCFEE!

Magic skidded to a halt wear she was, and whipped round, her palms building sweat.

The terrifying form of Marcus Slay the English teacher towered over her, the unusually high arches of his eyebrows pulling together, his face tugged into a deep grimace, the paleness of him as menacing as ever.

W-what? Magic asked tentatively, shaking from head to foot.

Why don't you listen to your friends, McFee? Appreciate *them more. After all, it could be your last.*

Slay's fingers morphed into long, needle-like bear claws and he began slashing at Magic. Magic ducked out of the way just in time. Slay's cackling rang against her skull. He continued to cackle, but the cackling became stranger, more unusual…high pitched…

Slay's terrifying form changed into the shape of William Brakk, his voice uncharacteristically high.

Heya, Magic! I've got some sweets *for ya…*

Will produced a gargantuan multicoloured box, the size of a large dog, out of nowhere. Magic backed away into the brick wall as Will tore at the wrapping with his teeth, pulling out all kinds of sweets and throwing them at Magic. He broke into a sprint and Magic began running, down the endless abyss that was her school corridor, down the everlasting torchlit eeriness, down, Will's unusual, frightening cackling reverberating off the walls.

Somebody should be able to hear him, come investigate, help out?

Oh, no. The tunnel ended. He had her cornered. Magic turned round slowly and backed into the cold, coarse, hard brick, pressing herself against it. She began to plead with him.

Please, Will. Please!

But the new, apparently psychologically insane, Will showed no mercy. He advanced towards Magic, a hungry look in his eyes, a fire there that she had never seen before...

The scene evaporated.

Magic woke up abruptly, sitting up suddenly, her breathing fast and uneven. A shiver caused by a mix of fear and freezing cold ran down her spine; she realised she was drenched in sweat. Magic wiped her brow with her sleeve and stared out the window. It was still dark outside—she decided she couldn't have been asleep for very long.

After processing the fact that it had only been a dream, she shook her hair and slumped back against her pillows, turning on her side to face the wall and wrapping the covers tightly round her once more.

Chapter Nine
Halloween

Magic took the sweets that her friends had gifted her to school the next day, after deciding that she wouldn't be able to finish them on her own. They were munching at them before their classes started, when Ross came into sight, sporting a bottle-green overcoat today, ringing a large bell. The hollow sound of it reverberated throughout the front field of Creavey High.

Magic checked her wristwatch in confusion; they still had fifteen minutes before they had to retreat inside. She frowned up at Will, who was closest to her, but he too looked confused.

"Isn't there still fifteen minutes left?" she asked into his ear over the ringing of the metal.

"I don't know…"

"Seniors!" Ross called over the chattering crowd. The murmuring died down immediately at her word. "Thank you. I'd like to quickly talk to you about the Halloween dance that's being held. I know that your form teachers have already informed you of this event, and that the Year 10s usually help host the ceremony. However, I also know how difficult it is to be a student of your age, juggling your GCSE work with other activities. So, to take some weight off your shoulders, the Year 9s will be helping host it. Nevertheless, if you still feel that you are up to the task, don't be shy to come and speak to me or another member of staff." The glass of her specs flashed briefly in the early morning sunlight before she spun round on the spot and vanished up the front steps, into the vast building.

"Great." Will grinned as the group were heading out of the building during lunchtime. "That was so kind of her to take the *weight* off our shoulders." His grin broadened.

Maria threw him a disapproving look. "Yes," she snapped. "It is, which means you are going to use it as you should, and not take advantage of it. We're supposed to be studying, Will." she told him in a firm voice.

"We *will*, Maria, chill. It's just not like her to be so nice to us. She doesn't do this to all the Year 10s in this school." Will sounded so pleased with himself.

The sextet took a seat at their usual circular wooden bench in the shade of the birch tree. Charlie was fidgeting uncharacteristically.

Maria lifted her face up from the book she had just began reading. "If you need the bathroom, Charlie, the door's there," she snapped, jutting her chin towards the birch front doors.

"You're in a pleasant mood today," he shot back at her. "I wanted to talk to you all about something."

"What is it?" Tom and Magic enquired.

Charlie's face pulled into an awkward expression. He scratched the back of his head. "Are we going to the dance…as a group of friends?"

Magic flushed red and focused on admiring her feet beneath the table.

"That'd be cool. No need to choose favourites," Chloe said, battling her eyelashes in surprising resemblance to Michelle Kurt. The group laughed.

"OK…cool."

On the evening before the dance, Magic's nerves began to skyrocket; her mother had insisted on buying Magic a surprise dress. Her mother was walking up the stairs right now, humming to herself.

Magic jumped up from her bed and began pacing.

"I can't take the tension anymore! Could you show me the dress?"

"Wait, honey, one *second*," Mrs McFee's cheerful voice issued from the hallway. "Let me just make it presentable." she jeered.

"*Mum!*"

"OK, OK, I'm coming in."

Magic barely noticed her mother when she walked in. She was staring at the clothing in her hands.

A fiery red princess dress emblazoned with white crystals at the neckline lay draped over Mrs McFee's arms, wrapped in a plastic sheet. The hem of the dress was lined with pretty, delicate, intricate lace that gave the dress an elegant touch. Magic thought it was gorgeous.

"Wow…" was all Magic could muster at that moment.

Mrs McFee's face glowed. "Do you like it?"

"Love it!" Magic smiled.

"Careful when trying it on, dear, you don't want to lose any of the diamonds."

Magic carefully slipped into the dress, and made sure everything was right before looking at herself in her full body mirror. When she finally saw herself, she gasped. The frock looked much more gorgeous with her body in it. It accentuated the best parts of herself, and she thought it made her figure look amazing. The intricate red lace at the hem of the dress was the perfect touch to it all, along with the glistening sparkle of the diamonds lining the neckline.

"That's beautiful," whispered Mrs McFee.

"It is. You chose great, Mum. I love it, thanks," replied Magic.

When Magic lay in bed that evening, she felt much less queasy than before; her dress had fit her perfectly and she actually thought she might look great the next day. She loved everything about it; from the lacey tips of the hem to the diamond-encrusted neckline, to the brilliant colour of it. She actually was looking forward to tomorrow's dance…she was also excited to see how her friends would look tomorrow, and how the party would turn out. Magic wondered how the school would be transformed into a disco.

However, despite the positive emotions, she felt slightly nervous; Magic had never been good with taking on the unexpected, especially events involving school. She thought that if she remained with her friends and kept a low profile for the duration of the ceremony, she wouldn't have a high chance of being asked to dance.

The next day's lessons sped by in a flash…until the double English period.

The only reason Magic despised Tuesdays was because the last two periods were both her least favourite subject, mostly thanks to her teacher, Marcus Slay, who absolutely detested her.

So, when the hour arrived, Magic walked into the dull English room against her better judgement and begrudgingly took her usual seat at the back, farthest away from Slay's desk for hope that he would not be able to eavesdrop on her conversations.

When Magic had successfully made it through two hours of Slay's rambling without being picked on, she bade her friends a quick goodbye and rushed home to get ready for the Halloween dance before it began at six o'clock.

She spent a good amount of time contemplating whether she should put on a full layer of makeup and decided against it when she remembered that her lack of skill wouldn't cut it. Instead, she lashed on a light layer of mascara, and some deep burgundy lipstick to match the dress. With the help of her mother's hairdressing skills, she tied her hair into a bottom knot at the lowest part of her head, right on top of her neck. When she was finally done, she admired the finishing look in the mirror; she thought it was pretty decent considering her lack of fashion knowledge.

Instead of walking to school, Mrs McFee drove Magic there. Magic didn't want to risk anybody noticing her walking down the streets alone, fully dressed and maked-over.

The evening was crisp and clear, dusk's first few stars appearing against the beautiful azure of the night, sparkles scattered across the dark horizon.

When Magic bade her mother goodbye, the true nerves began to chatter. Magic walked timidly past the large, twirly 'CREAVEY HIGH' sign above the two brick walls and stopped dead in her tracks.

Magic had not expected her jaw to drop so early into the evening; she had barely been there five seconds when she found that she was already full of shock.

Hundreds upon hundreds of orange fairy lights had been rapped upon the branches of trees, spiralling down the trunks, towards the roots. The orange luminescence of the lights seeped through the trees' leaves, causing them to glow a beautiful orange. A huge, flashing, colourful disco floor had been placed in the centre of the front field, dominating the party. Tables draped in white clothes surrounded the dance floor, topped with tempting foods and drinks. Directly to her left was a huge DJ turntable and mixer, being controlled by a delighted-looking and suited up Mark Irvine, loud and upbeat music playing over the sound of excited chatter. Magic hadn't expected the dance to take place outdoors, but she preferred it out here compared to the way she imagined it to be.

Magic heard a gasp from close behind her. She whipped round in surprise.

Maria Kenfield was standing with her hands over her mouth, her eyes bulging with excitement. She wore a long but simple mint-green dress, complementing the colour of her eyes. Her fiery red hair was subdued in a side plait, which almost reached her waist. She sported a smaller dark green pursue, tucked under her arm, for an extra touch.

"Magic! You look *amazing*!" Maria exclaimed.

Magic smiled. "Thank you, and—" she gestured up and down Maria "—nice." Her grin widened.

Maria flushed pink. "Thanks. Have you seen the others yet? I've just arrived." She scanned the crowd briefly for any sign of Charlie, Chloe, Will or Tom.

"Nope, I just came. Should we go look for them?"

Magic and Maria made their way through the crowd, stopping every few moments to search the throng of excited students for any sign of one of their friends. Maria hastily tapped Magic on the shoulder and pointed to a spot behind the fruit punch, near the school's front steps.

Will was leaning on a pillar near the steps, a cup of punch in one hand, the other in the pocket of the black blazer he sported over a white button-up shirt and black trousers. He was deep in conversation with Chloe, who sat on the stairs, wearing a long, black sequined gown with her dark curls thrown up into a high bun.

Magic and Maria walked swiftly over to them. Chloe beamed.

"Hi, guys! You're looking good," she told them.

"Thanks, Chloe. I like your dress." Magic smiled. Chloe glowed. Magic turned to William. "Will, you're looking good, too," she complemented him, grinning.

Will wiped non-existent tears from his face mockingly. "Oh, Magic, you're making me tear up," he teased. They laughed.

Will's eyes locked on a spot over Magic's shoulder, and his face slowly broke into a smile. "Here they come." Magic saw him sip at his drink before she whipped round.

A grinning Charlie and Tom were advancing towards them, sporting similar outfits to Will, except that Tom's suit was a deep navy.

"Hey, guys." Charlie greeted them.

"Hi, Charlie. Hey, Tom," said Will.

Tom had a strange, distant expression on his face. He seemed to be staring at a spot across the dance floor, almost angrily.

Chloe got up and off the front steps. "Tom?" she asked tentatively. When he didn't answer, she snapped her fingers in front of his face. "Tom!"

Tom jerked and diverted what was left of his attention to Chloe. "Yeah?" his voice still didn't seem fully present.

Chloe snapped her fingers once more. The black sequins on her dress glittered in the light from the dance floor. "What's going on?"

"Him." Tom jutted his chin towards the place he had been staring at seconds ago.

The unpleasant, sickening form of Mr Slay stood across the dance floor, in his same standard striped green and black suit and tie, his hair gelled in a side parting, the high, devilish arches of his eyebrows prominent; his outfit didn't at all acknowledge the change in occasion. The mere sight of him sent irksome chills up Magic's spine.

He seemed as if he was trying to blend into the shadows, when Miss Mills approached him, her greying hair tied into a neat knot, and broke into conversation.

"Blinking jerk," Tom scowled under his breath.

"Tom!" hissed Maria. "We don't need any more reason for Slay to hate us, so would you *please* keep your calm?"

Tom sighed in resignation and pulled his eyes from the scene. "Anybody wanna dance?"

"Uh, definitely not," Magic said quickly. "Sorry, that's not a good idea for me, I can barely walk." She laughed nervously.

"Magic, could you walk with me for a bit? I need to talk to you about something," Will asked.

Magic was taken aback at this unexpected request, but she agreed anyway.

"Yeah, sure…"

"We'll be back soon, guys." Will reassured the others, who wore completely confused expressions.

Will led Magic to the side of the school, where the party was still visible, but the sounds of excited chatter and music were slightly more distant.

"What is it, Will?" Magic asked desperately; she couldn't take the suspense any longer, although it had barely been a minute.

"Calm down, come sit over here." He gestured towards a bottle-green bench a few yards away.

Once they were sat down, Magic asked again, "What's going on?"

Will sighed in the darkness. "Well…you know Slay's always been the dodgy kind, right?"

"Er—right." Where was he going with this?

"Well, I don't think he's up to any good. I mean, I know you knew that, but every time he's round he just gives off this weird vibe…" There was silence for a few moments while Magic pondered this. "Remember how frightened Katie had been when Slay had asked her for a word? I know I might be overthinking it, but that's not a normal reaction from a student towards a teacher that I've ever seen."

"Why'd you decide to only talk to me?" Magic asked with genuine interest.

"Well, I figured you'd be the one who'd take it the best. If I'd opened it up with everyone else, I'd have to deal with their outbursts—Maria and Chloe have already told me to knock it off and not bring up the subject again. They don't think it's that big of a deal."

"What do *you* think is going on, then?" asked Magic.

Will sighed and sipped at his drink. "I wish I could answer you. Thanks for coming with me, by the way, I just feel like I needed to talk to someone about it, it's been irking at me for some stupid reason."

"Anytime, Will." Magic smiled in the darkness. "Hold on…" she'd just had a thought. "Should we tell Lockwood?"

"About Slay, you mean?"

"He actually already warned me about him before. Told me he's somebody I don't want to mess with." Magic paused. "I actually don't think that's normal, Will, no teacher personally warns a student against their own *colleagues*…"

"Hmm," Will began. "I really don't know what to say. If Lockwood told you that, then he must know Slay's no good, which means he might've done something in the past that cost him his reputation. At the same time, Lockwood was your father's best friend, so he may just be looking out for you."

"But don't you remember when I told you how worried he looked when I showed him my malfunctioned calculator? It was like he knew exactly what was going on…" The memory of it sprang a new branch of curiosity in Magic's mind.

"Who said that had anything to do with Slay, though?" Will questioned, frowning into the darkness.

"Who knows?" Magic sighed in frustration.

"What's up?"

"I don't know, I just wish I had answers to the unexplainable…my English teacher despises me the second I arrive at school, my calculator was handing me death threats and I see a creepy bloke who was probably spying on me from a dark alleyway? There's no denying something's up."

"Oh, I forgot about that," said Will, his tone becoming more serious. "Have you had a thought of what could've been up with that guy?"

"I think it's *my* turn to suggest that I could've been overthinking the situation." Magic sighed. "He could've just been some ordinary guy minding his own business—I may just be making a scene for no reason. In my defense, though, I could've sworn he was holding a stick, it almost looked like a staff. And a cape, too!"

"I…" Will's voice faded.

They sat in silence for a bit, listening to the loud chatter and enduring the crazy music of the party, watching people laugh and dance, students and teachers alike.

"Should we go back?" Magic asked tentatively after a while.

"I'm not exactly up for enduring Maria's moaning voice begging for me to tell her what we talked about." He laughed.

"We can stay then. It's been fun, Will."

"Yeah…"

Another pause.

"Speaking of Lockwood," Magic began, "have you seen him today?"

"Uh—no, not now. Why?"

"I thought maybe I could ask him now, I don't want people becoming suspicious when I ask him to stay behind in class."

"'Bout Slay?"

"Mm."

Before either of them could say anything more, there was a crunching of grass as Maria walked towards them, holding her minty dress out of the way of the damp grass. The crunching became increasingly louder until she stopped dead in front of them.

"What're you guys up to?" she demanded.

"We're just chatting about Slay," replied Will defensively.

"Oh." Maria looked surprised. "Still haven't worked out what his deal is?"

"Unfortunately not." Magic sighed.

"Hmph." Maria hesitated. "I don't think we should bother about it too much. Like I said, we don't want to give Slay more reason to hate us."

Will chuckled. "Told you she'd say that," he said to Magic.

Magic thought this over. "She might be right."

Chapter Ten
Examinations

November flurried past in a rush, December welcoming icy winds, and bright white skies. However, the excitement of the Christmas holidays was downplayed because the end of term also meant something else—end of term examinations.

Magic had initially regretted taking History as a GCSE subject, but that had all changed when she had met Remy Lockwood. Something about him made the subject all the while more interesting, and exciting. Her outlook on the subject had completely changed. She felt like she also liked the teacher because he hit close to home—he was quite close to her father, so she knew for sure he was a man of trust.

It was a couple days before their first exam, which would be History. The group sat in the school library, quills scratching against paper in the candlelight. The atmosphere in the vast room was calmer than usual, mainly because students were so endorsed in their work. The evening was one of calm twilight, the twinkling of the stars glistening through the glass of the vertical windows.

Magic looked up from her notes when Charlie appeared round a corner of a bookshelf, tucking a book under his arm.

"Hey, guys, I was wondering…" Charlie began, pulling a seat out from under the table. The loud scraping noise cost him some disapproving glances and hisses from people across the room.

"Sorry, jeez…" he muttered under his breath. He cleared his throat. "Are any of you up to much in the holidays?"

Magic set her quill in her ink pot. "I don't think so. Why?" she asked thoughtfully.

"Well, I'm not doing much, and I wondered if you guys wanted to stay over."

"That could be fun," said Maria, though she didn't look up from her work. "I don't see why not."

"Yeah, I'll check with my parents." said Magic. She suddenly felt excited.

"Cool."

They whiled away the hours in the dim light of the library, eating through page after page of books, parchment, and resources they had been given in classes. Magic felt an urge to make Lockwood proud, so she definitely wanted to do well in his test. She was going to have to work really hard so as to not fail him.

Magic had dedicated most of her study time to revising for History, despite the fact that she knew she'd be tested on other subjects.

Whether she liked it or not, she was going to have to prepare for an English essay. And whether she like it or not, she knew she had to do well. But she'd deal with the pressure of all of that when she passed History.

Six days until her History exam…Magic was bound to make it to the top five people with the highest scores in her class…Five days, she began incorporating Maths and Geography revision…Three days, thank goodness she wouldn't be having an Art exam this term, which meant more priority to her other subjects…Two days, she would ace this exam…One day…

The morning of her first examination at Creavey High was quite the jittery one for Magic. Her nerves skyrocketed as she walked into school in the morning. It didn't help that students were frantically flipping through their notes here and there, desperate to cram in as much last-minute revision as possible. Magic decided to head in early to avoid feeling pressured.

At 8 a.m. sharp, the Year 10s were called to the assembly hall, where they would be sitting their examination (the History room was much too small to be able to fit the entire year group in there at once).

"Good luck," Magic murmured to the others before Ross pushed open the doors, and they headed inside.

The assembly hall, which was usually primarily empty, was filled with row after row of wooden benches and tables. At the end of the hall, a row of chairs, presumably where the teachers would be sitting, stood; the chair on the end, however, was occupied by Lockwood, in his classic corduroy ensemble. At every other seat on the benches, a paper and a quill had been placed.

Magic took a seat where she was instructed, diagonal to Will, and the bench in front of Chloe. She couldn't see where the others sat from where she was.

Lockwood stood up and cleared his throat as Miss Ross rushed towards her seat.

"Alright, Year 10, as you know cheating is not permitted in this school, so for your own benefit, I would recommend that you keep your eyes on your own paper. I don't have much more to say to you—you have one hour. Good luck. You may begin."

A brief moment of shuffle, and quills began scratching paper. Magic was determined to make her teacher proud, so she gave it her all.

"Whew!" Charlie stumbled out of the assembly hall an hour later, wiping his brow against his arm. "How do you think you've done?" They began heading out. "Maria, quit looking like that when everybody knows you're probably going to score the highest."

For Maria had exited the room, biting her nails in anticipation. "What did you guys get for question eight? Oh no, I've screwed it all up!" she cried.

"Woah, relax, Maria, if you're stressed, how d'you think that mouth breather Kurt's feeling now?"

"As if Michelle gives a damn about how well she does," Magic muttered.

"Fair point," replied Charlie.

Maria's shoulders slumped; that seemed to have relaxed her a bit more. "Tom's lucky he wasn't cooped up in there. What were the Year 11s doing?" she asked in a lighter mood.

"I don't know, but I can tell you that he's not missing out," replied Charlie. His expression changed. "Hey, have any of you seen Chloe or Will? I wonder how they've done."

"No, I don't think they've come out yet, I haven't seen them."

They had reached their usual spot of the circular wooden bench under the tree. Magic stretched and slumped onto the wood.

"Tired?" asked Maria.

Magic yawned. "Yeah. At least it's over. I hope I do well, I wanted to make Lockwood proud."

"Same here!" a new voice joined the conversation. Magic turned to see Chloe advancing towards them, followed by Will.

"Why the long face?" asked Charlie when she slumped down next to him in a sulk.

"She thinks the answer she changed at the last minute is probably wrong," answered Will, taking a seat.

"Yes, and that's a perfectly reasonable think to be angry about," Chloe snapped.

"I wasn't badmouthing you!" Will exclaimed.

Chloe's eyes slowly widened, and she sat up straight.

"Cool," said Will.

"Didn't that seem more like an actual *mock* exam to you, rather than those smaller, less-important end of term exams?"

"And?" challenged Will. He rolled his eyes when she wasn't looking.

"They're important!" she moaned, and let her face drop onto her arms.

"So what's the point you're trying to get across?" Will talked to Chloe's large mass of hair.

"Just leave her alone, Will." Charlie sighed. "She'll come round."

Their Maths examination was next; Magic walked out of the exam room feeling pretty confident. They had no more exams or lessons that day, so they spent the time outside.

When Magic arrived home, she had to face the dread of revising for English. She had no idea what the essay question was going to be; she had grown up with a dislike towards the subject, so she had never been truly encouraged to put in the effort. But when Slay came into the mix, that dislike had turned into hate.

Magic scraped together a rough essay plan that she'd try to memorise, and then moved on to Geography.

It was late evening by the time Magic went to bed that night, so expectedly when she awoke the next morning, she was feeling tired and drowsy.

She didn't feel all that confident when she reluctantly trudged through the same large doors and took her seat in the examination room, and certainly didn't feel up to seeing Slay that day. Luckily, he didn't seem to have noticed her when she took her seat.

Magic was glad when she anxiously flicked her eyes to the top of the paper:

How does Dickens use language to present Marley in the novel 'A Christmas Carol'? Use quotations to support your answer. (25 marks)

She had anticipated a question on language. With a sigh of relief, she scribbled away.

"That was the most excruciating thing I've ever had the displeasure to do in all my fifteen years, and believe me, that is saying something." Charlie groaned and lay his head in his hands.

It was noon at Creavey High, and Charlie, Chloe, Maria, Will, and Magic had just left their Geography examination, and once again taken their spot at the round wooden bench; they sat at it so often it was as if it belonged to them. They hadn't seen Tom all day, since he was a year older and didn't attend the same classes. It just so happened that Magic had picked the same GCSE options as her friends…she wondered who she would've became friends with if she hadn't.

"Yeah, same with me, second to only having the displeasure to lay eyes on you five days a week," a malicious voice sneered.

Magic wasn't at all bothered to deal with the sight of Michelle Kurt, so when her doubts were confirmed and was met with her blond head and thick layer of makeup when she turned round, she huffed in frustration.

"Where're your friends, Kurt?" Magic challenged her.

Michelle batted her eyelashes and then squinted at Magic through narrowed eyes. "That's none of your business, *McFee*," she shot back.

"Get lost, Michelle." Charlie's tone was exhausted.

Charlie looked surprised when she turned round, throwing one last devilish look over her shoulder, and left them be. He clearly hadn't expected her to obey.

"Well that was easier than usual." He chuckled. "So, are you guys down to stay over at my place? You can come over Friday night."

"Tomorrow?" asked Magic, sitting up.

"Yeah! Haven't you forgotten that tomorrow's the last day of term?"

"Wow…" Magic had been so endorsed in her schoolwork she'd forgotten to keep track of time. "Yeah, I'll ask Mum and Dad."

"Cool. Will, did you say you're coming?" Charlie turned to Will, placing his elbows up on the table.

"Yeah, I'm coming."

"Maria?"

"Yeah…oh, what? Oh yeah, I asked my parents, they said sure," Maria replied distractedly without looking up from her book.

Charlie diverted his gaze back to Magic. "So, there's just you, then?" He smiled.

Magic was slightly bemused. "Wait—what about Chloe?"

"I might not be able to come, I might be going to Venice with my mum and dad." Chloe sighed. "But if not, then I'm rushing straight over to your house." She grinned.

"Is Tom coming?" Magic asked Charlie.

"No, he can't, he's starting his GCSE prep in the holidays. His examinations are starting in May," Charlie replied sadly.

Will yawned and put his chin on his hands. "Poor bloke."

"Mum, Dad, I wanted to ask you something," Magic proposed at the dinner table that night.

"Go ahead, darling." Mrs McFee put down her fork, with a small *clank* against the porcelain of the plate, and tuned in. Mr McFee stopped chewing.

"You know my friend Charlie Stocklin?" asked Magic anxiously.

"Ohh, that lovely boy with the blond hair?" Mrs McFee remembered, smiling.

"Er—yep, that's the one," replied Magic. "You see, he invited me to sleep over with Will, Maria, and Chloe, if she can come. Could I go?"

Mr McFee continued chewing. "'Course you can. Pack your stuff and you can walk home from school with them if you'd like," he replied, and then smiled. "They're a lovely bunch."

"Yeah, they are. Thanks, Dad." Magic returned his smile and went to rinse her plate in the sink.

She lay in bed that night, excited about the following day—it was just what she needed, a relaxing, fun beginning to her Christmas break. She wouldn't have to be worried about that bone-headed Michelle Kurt and her cronies, including Ian Byers, or her grades or living up to Slay's expectations. It was a good three weeks where she could just relax and have no priorities.

Except homework.

Friday flashed passed faster than she thought it would, and before she knew it Magic was at the front of the school, waiting with Charlie for Maria, Will, and Chloe (Magic was privately delighted that Chloe's trip to Venice wasn't happening). When the three of them appeared, they headed off down the street.

"Are you alright there, Magic?" asked Charlie sceptically, for Magic had to battle the trouble of holding two very heavy bags; one full of her personal essentials and the other with school stuff.

"Yeah, I'm fine," replied Magic. She adjusted her school backpack further up her back, and slung the other over her arm.

"I don't live too far, I walk to school every day, so you won't have to put up with battling your bags any longer." Charlie chuckled.

"Sounds good."

"Hey, Charlie," began Maria, "d'you still live in that same cottage you used to?" Charlie turned to her. "Yup, the very same."

"Ooh, I like that one, it's quite gorgeous," Maria answered excitedly. Her fiery red hair glistened in the daylight. Charlie smiled at her.

The rounded a corner, onto Hargrove Wing. The stone pavement narrowed, so Maria, Will, and Chloe walked in the back, while Charlie and Magic walked in front of them.

"Have you ever been to Charlie's house, Will?" asked Magic. They passed different cars of all makes and colours.

Will's voice came from behind Magic. "No, I—"

There was a hollow *thud* and then an "*Ouch!*"

Magic whipped round suddenly to find Will rubbing his forehead with one hand, the other holding back his dark hair. He stood inches away from a black, rusty lamppost.

Maria was snickering, and Chloe was laughing openly.

"You *idiot*," Maria jeered. "It was right in *front* of you…"

"Shut up, Maria," growled Will, and he began walking again. Maria put a hand to her mouth to stifle her giggling.

"You OK, mate?" Magic asked, though she was trying not to smile.

"Yeah, fine." Will winced.

"Guys, come *on*!" Charlie yelled from the end of the lane; he evidently hadn't noticed what'd gone on and continued walking. "My house is right *here*!" he jabbed his finger at the building he was standing by, though Magic could not see it from where she stood. The four of them broke into a run and sped off down the lane.

In a matter of seconds, Magic skidded to a halt by Charlie and placed her hands on her knees, drawing ragged breaths.

"Home, sweet home," Charlie sang.

The cottage was quite miniature and sweet; not the kind of house you would expect to find on a lane like this one. A dark oak wooden door with a golden knocker introduced the cottage, which resembled a hut on the outside, with cute square windows and white curtains lining the inside.

Charlie pushed open the metre-high brown gate and stepped onto the cobbled pathway leading to the two stone stairs by the door, which was surrounded by grass. It creaked open gently and he held it open for the other four to make their way in.

Peonies and rosebushes lined the edges of the small meadow in the front of the house; Magic could hear a faint streaming sound which sounded like water, somewhere in the distance. She assumed a hose was left running somewhere.

"You…have a nice house, Charlie." Magic turned to Charlie slowly on the spot, closing her mouth just as slowly and grinning.

"You haven't even gone in yet." He grinned back. He jogged up to the front door and then began fiddling with his pockets. There was a faint clinking sound; the sound got louder when he pulled out a set of keys from his right pocket.

"My mother isn't home right now, so we have the house to ourselves."

Chapter Eleven
An Early Christmas

"Where's your dad?" Magic asked him curiously, walking towards him. Chloe shut the gate behind her with another creak and followed Magic.

"He's on a business trip to Warsaw. Wipe your feet, or my mum'll kill me," Charlie warned.

Magic approached the two stairs and waited for Charlie to open the door. He slid the silver key in the lock, turned it, and the door clicked open.

When Charlie stepped into his house, Magic brushed her feet against the 'welcome' mat.

The inside of the Stocklin house was generally what Magic would've expected a cottage to look like; the carpeted floors were a deep brown, while the walls were a deep burgundy, with eccentric golden patterns covering almost every inch of them—the house colours overall were made up of quite muted tones. To the left, the brown-carpeted staircase led supposedly to the upper bedrooms. The door at the end of the corridor was open, and Magic could see half of what appeared to be a small kitchen. There was a glass door in the wall of the kitchen which led to the garden.

"Er—follow me," said Charlie awkwardly.

Charlie advanced over to the first room on the right. He tugged at the golden doorknob and the dark-oak sliding door glided open with a soft rattling sound.

The room inside was as cosy as can be—the same eccentric theme was kept up with the furniture—spongy armchairs and sofas in dark colours were arranged in a semi-circle round the fireplace, where a pile of grey coal lay in the grate. The round wooden coffee table was made of the same dark oak as the sliding door (dark oak seemed to be the preferred wood in the house); a stack of coasters and a candlestick holder stood upon it.

Charlie pulled at the white curtains of the square window that Magic had seen from outside the house. A stream of daylight flooded into the room, and the view of the grass, flower bushes and the road and cars outside took over.

"Nice place," said Magic, looking round the room.

"Thanks." Charlie grinned from the window. He staggered over to the nearest spongy armchair and threw himself at it, crossing his hands behind his head.

"Make yourselves at home, guys." He yawned.

"Cool TV," said Maria, pulling her bag off. Magic hadn't noticed the set in the corner of the room.

"Thanks," replied Charlie. "Oh yeah, you girls can drop your bags off upstairs, last room to the right at the end of the corridor."

"'Kay. Come on Magic, Chloe."

The three girls trudged up the flight of stairs, which curved to the right at the very top. There were four identical white doors, two to the right, perpendicular to each other, and two down on the left.

"He said last on the right…right?" said Magic. She pointed to the furthest door on the right. "That one." She pulled at the doorknob and pushed it open.

The walls on the inside of this room were painted a refreshing lilac. The two beds against the wall on the right were covered in sheets of deeper purple and white, fluffy pillows. An oak wardrobe and cupboard stood directly opposite them on the left. A vertical mirror was propped up on top of the wardrobe, and a large window took over the wall facing the door, framed by puce velvet curtains. The theme of this room simply screamed *purple*. It was simple, yet elegant.

"Sorry—one of you'll have to sleep on the floor, the guest room can only fit two beds," a voice issued from behind them.

"Charlie, I would appreciate if you could announce your presence instead of trying to give us a heart attack," snapped Maria. Charlie leaned against the doorframe, his arms crossed, grinning.

"I don't mind sleeping on the floor," Magic offered. Before the others could object, she persisted, "I insist. Besides, it's only one night, relax."

"Are you sure?" asked Maria in an unconvinced tone.

"Positive. Should we eat something?" Magic changed the subject before Maria could change her mind.

They munched on fruit bars and orange squash while flicking through the telly.

"Where's your mum work, Charlie?" asked Magic after a while, scrunching up her wrapper.

"At Heathrow airport." Charlie yawned, kicking his feet up on to the coffee table.

"Isn't that far from here?"

"Yeah, it is. Well, it depends. Sometimes it takes forty-five minutes for her to get to work, other times it takes over two hours."

"Wow." It was enough of a struggle for Magic to walk to school in the mornings when her parents couldn't drop her off, carrying all her books on her back; her struggle looked like a joke next to what Mrs Stocklin had to face on a daily basis.

"Where're you boys sleeping?" Maria asked, not taking her eyes off the TV.

"The room first to the right," replied Charlie, also staring at the television screen.

"Er—where's the bathroom?" Magic asked Charlie awkwardly.

This time Charlie broke his gaze away from the screen. "Room next to yours." He smiled.

"Right. Thanks."

Magic stepped onto the cool ceramic of the Stocklin's bathroom floor. There was nothing really special about it, other than the row of blue flowery patterns that started halfway up the wall. Besides that, it was your standard bathroom—a sink was the first thing on the left, followed by the toilet and the bath against the back wall. A circular mirror and small acrylic shelf holding a pot full of toothbrushes were fixed directly on top of the sink.

Moments later, Magic turned the golden knob of the sink and stared at her reflection in the mirror; the way her dark hair fell down her shoulders, the way her ocean blue eyes twinkled in the bathroom's light.

Magic remembered that she'd packed her friends' early Christmas gifts in her bag, which is why it had been so heavy. She'd hand them out when she returned.

Once in the hallway, Magic heaved the massive bag onto her back, and put it down again in procrastination. She decided to simply take them all out and bring them into the living room, just in case she accidentally pulled out one of her private personal belongings in front of everybody.

How in the world Magic's bag managed to fit all of the gifts, plus her clothes, was beyond her. It was more of a large duffel bag, but it was still fascinating.

"Oh, Magic, you didn't have to!" squealed Maria once she opened her present, to find a pearl bracelet with a pink, heart shaped crystal charm hanging from it in the bottom of the box.

"And *you* didn't have to buy me that necklace." Magic smirked, folding her arms. Maria pursed her lips, but she didn't argue.

Magic gave Charlie a maroon scarf; Will a new jacket and Chloe a similar bracelet to Maria, just different colours ("They could be like friendship bracelets!" she cried happily), with a purple charm instead of bright pink.

"Magic, you really didn't have to—"

"This wasn't necessary—"

Magic lifted a hand up to silence them with mock authority. They immediately fell quiet, smirks forming on all their faces.

"*First* of all," Magic began, trying to sound firm, though it was evident her tone was masking laughter, "if anybody *dares* spend any money on me for Christmas, when we go back to school, I will steal the paintbrushes from the art room and *shove* them up your—"

"Oh no," Charlie interrupted with mock fear. "Well, I'm terrified. Magic is handing out death threats, guys, we should probably take cover." A small sound of laughter escaped him on the last word.

"Don't *you* challenge me, Stocklin." Magic smirked sarcastically. "Are you saying you are willing to fight me?"

"I will *whack* you with this gracious gift you have presented me with, Magic," said Charlie, going down on one knee and laying the scarf across his arms.

"What the heck, Charlie…" Magic laughed.

"That is barely a threat," Chloe piped in. "I will *strangle* you with this—er—noose." Chloe twirled her bracelet round her finger, spinning it in circles, and broke into silent giggles.

"OK, enough, enough." Magic waved her hands frantically, trying to stifle the number of death threats she was receiving before they could increase. "The point is, the gift you guys bought me for my birthday cost more than all of your presents combined, so I don't want to hear it."

Maria opened her mouth to speak, but then closed it and smirked. She clearly had ways round it, but Magic was too unbothered to deal with it at that moment.

"Whew." Magic wiped her brow against her sleeve and slumped into a chair. "At least I escaped death. You can sit down now, Charlie."

She exchanged grins with him as he too slumped back into his seat.

"So, what do you guys want to—" Charlie began, but he was cut off by the *ding-dong* from the front doorbell.

"Oh—that would be Mum!" he hopped out of his seat and jogged into the hallway.

She had been so distracted that Magic hadn't paid attention to what time it was.

The sky outside was a deep blue hue, but the starry sprinkles still hadn't littered the horizon.

Magic found her breathing speeding up as she heard the front door click open followed by some unintelligible murmuring.

Seconds later, a blond, curvy woman with large ringlets falling down her shoulders appeared in the doorway. She wore a navy-blue blazer with a matching skirt, tights, and high heels; under it she donned a simple white button up shirt, with a flowy red scarf. Her bright, flashy smile reminded Magic instantly of Charlie.

"Hello," said Chloe shyly. Magic flushed.

"Hello there, dears." Mrs Stocklin's voice was sweet and warm. "You having fun?"

"Yes, it's been great," replied Magic timidly.

Mrs Stocklin turned towards Magic and tilted her head to one side.

"You must be Magic! You have a lovely name. Are you enjoying school?" she asked Magic.

"Yeah, it's good—and thank you." Magic flushed deeper.

"That's great to hear. So, you all are doing well?" Mrs Stocklin asked the whole group. They nodded in unison.

"Great—how does dinner in half an hour sound?"

"That's fine, Mum, thanks." Charlie appeared in the doorway and placed a hand on his mother's shoulder. She dropped one last smile and headed off towards the kitchen.

Precisely half an hour later, the five teens were called to the dining room, where they munched on mushroom pasta and steak.

"You're a great cook, Mrs Stocklin," Magic complemented her truthfully.

Mrs Stocklin smiled in delight. "Thank you, love. And you're a great friend. All Charlie does is talk about you," she added, flashing a quick look at her son.

Magic was beyond surprised to hear this. She raised her eyebrows, but quickly lowered them and her head snapped in Charlie's direction, who was blushing deep red, staring into his lap. Embarrassed, Magic too flushed red and stared at her own lap, playing round with her fork. Secretly, she felt warm inside, and was glad that her friends genuinely liked her.

Minutes later, Charlie's mother returned from yet another visit to the kitchen.

"Well, I think you all should hop to bed, it's nearly quarter to eleven," she said.

Quarter to?

Where had the time gone? Magic was enjoying herself so much that the time seemed to have slipped away. Although she was having fun, she admittedly was starting to get slightly drowsy.

"You girls can take as long as you need in the bathroom upstairs, feel free to have a shower, and if you need anything, please don't be afraid to ask me," Mrs Stocklin continued, with yet another smile. She was a very smiley woman. "I assume Charlie has shown you were you'll be sleeping?" She raised an eyebrow at her son.

"Yes, Mrs Stocklin, he showed us. Thank you," replied Maria.

Magic's tiredness was getting the better of her. She decided to turn in. "Goodnight Mrs Stocklin, thank you for everything," she said, standing up and tucking her chair in behind her. "Night, boys," she added quickly, for she wasn't sure if she would see them again that night.

"It's nothing, dear. Have a great night, girls."

Chloe and Maria got up and followed Magic out the sliding door. Magic yawned on the way up the stairs, and she was desperate to change into her pyjamas.

"D'you guys want to go in first?" Magic asked them when she reached the bathroom door.

"No, it's fine, you go ahead," Chloe replied as she came round the corner.

"We'll change by the time you're finished," said Maria, pushing the door to their room open. "Take as long as you need." She smiled before slipping into the room.

Magic brushed her teeth and then headed back downstairs to reach for her duffel bag. She changed, subdued her dark locks into a long plait, repacked her toothbrush, and headed into the hallway, where she found Maria in a pick satin nightdress, to allow her to use the bathroom.

Chloe was in a purple two-piece pyjama set, which matched the purple theme of the room.

"Hey, Magic," Chloe greeted her as Magic shut the door behind her. A mattress lay perpendicular to the two beds, with a folded blanket and pillow set aside at the edge.

"Hey, Chloe."

"I like your pyjamas. They match your eyes," Chloe complemented her, and sat back on the bed nearest to the window.

"Oh, thanks." Magic slumped onto the mattress, moved the pillow to the opposite end of the blanket, which she shook open until it spread out. She lay back, covering herself and then clasping her hands behind her head. The only thing other than the wardrobe and cupboard that wasn't purple in this room was the ceiling, which was a dazzling white.

Magic heard shuffling come from an area above her head; she heard Chloe's bed creak as Chloe was supposedly tucking herself in.

The door then gently clicked open, and Maria walked in, carrying her toothbrush, and shut the door behind her. She tiptoed to her backpack and shoved the toothbrush in the front pocket. She then headed over to the light switch by the door, switched the lights off and strode over to her bed, rolling headfirst onto it and landing in a sprawl. The three of them laughed silently.

"You comfortable down there, Magic?" Maria whispered into the darkness.

"Yeah, don't worry," Magic replied in the same low whisper.

Laughter was issuing from the corridor; it sounded like the boys were heading out of the bathroom. A door slammed shut and the laughter became slightly more muffled, this time coming from the wall to Magic's right. There was a huge thud and then a louder outbreak of laughter. Magic smiled to herself.

"Sounds like the boys are having fun." She smirked into the darkness.

"Sounds like they're attacking each other with pillows," said Chloe.

"Boys," Maria huffed. Magic could imagine her rolling her eyes.

"Today's been fun. Sad it passed so quickly." Magic sighed. A ray of light from the window slid momentarily across the dark ceiling as the sound of a car engine fading in and then out from the street outside interrupted the conversation. Where could people be going at this time?

"Yeah. Thanks for the gifts, Magic," Maria thanked her.

"Yeah, the bracelets were gorgeous..." Chloe added.

"Guys, please don't try and flatter me into letting you spend money on me for Christmas, because it's not going to happen," Magic stated firmly before their flattery could carry on. The girls broke into silent giggles, and Magic joined in.

The laughter in the boys' room had subsided; Magic assumed that they had already fallen asleep, or perhaps they were conversing quietly.

Chloe and Maria were whispering silently above her, but Magic was too tired to tune into the conversation. Her eyelids slowly began to droop; she turned on her side to face the right wall.

It had been a wonderful day, and Magic had gotten just what she needed; a relaxing day well spent goofing round and being silly with her friends. Mrs Stocklin had been wonderful, and she herself had admitted that Charlie talked about Magic a lot; she smiled subconsciously in the darkness.

Although their time had been well spent, and she'd only barely spent a day at the Stocklin house, Magic was still sad to know that she'd be heading back home tomorrow. Oh well, she'd definitely be back.

The last of the girls' whispers filled her ears before Magic's conscious slipped away and she drifted off.

Chapter Twelve
The Diamond of Dominion

The next morning, Magic was the first to wake up. She pulled her toothbrush and hairbrush from her bag and headed straight to the bathroom.

It had been a pretty good sleep—a chill one, with her friends. Not another sound had come from the boys' room after they had stopped pillow fighting.

Magic yanked the hairband out of her hair and began undoing her plait. She yawned silently as she ran her fingers through her locks, and then with her hairbrush. Once she brushed her teeth, she ran the tap and cupped her hands so they'd fill with water, and splashed it onto her face.

She decided to go back and fetch her duffel bag to slip into some decent clothes and met Will in the corridor.

"Hi, Magic," he croaked, rubbing his eyes.

"Morning, Will." She moved aside to let him pass into the bathroom, and headed back to her room to change.

Magic was surprised to find Will in the living room, sitting fully dressed when she headed downstairs.

"Well, you're fast." She grinned, taking a seat by him.

"Yeah, I don't like to spend too much time getting ready in the morning," he replied, grinning back.

There was a sound of cluttering pans and pots from the kitchen.

"Other people are awake?" Magic asked, surprised that she hadn't bumped into anybody in the hallways.

"Yeah, it's not too early," replied Will, and he pulled back his sleeve to check his wristwatch. "It's nine-thirty, nearly. Mrs Stocklin is used to getting up early, since she needs to make the whole drive to Heathrow, so she prepares breakfast before leaving."

"Right," Magic replied. She cringed slightly: it had been obvious.

There was a pitter-patter of footsteps in the hallway as Mrs Stocklin arrived, in her usual smile, at the doorway. She sported the exact same uniform she had arrived in the previous evening.

"Morning, Mrs Stocklin," Magic greeted her.

"Morning, dears," Mrs Stocklin's voice showed no trace of drowsiness, as if she was a superhuman who didn't require sleep to survive. Had Magic even heard Mrs Stocklin head off to her bedroom last night?

"I've made you all breakfast, it's all on the table in the dining room. If any of you need anything, just ask Charlie. Have a lovely day."

"You too, Mrs Stocklin," replied Will and Magic.

"Thank you so much for everything, Mrs Stocklin, you really didn't need to," Magic thanked her timidly.

Mrs Stocklin simply shooed them away. "Oh, nonsense, loves. Alright, I'll see you soon!" Moments later, there was a rustle by the front door as Mrs Stocklin picked up her handbag, and then the swish and slam of the front door.

"So...what d'you want to do now?" Will asked Magic. The words were barely out of his mouth before there was a slam of a door from upstairs and some quite murmuring broke out in the hallways.

"Well, looks like the others are up," said Magic. She stood up. "Guys?" She called out.

"Someone's in the bathroom." said Will.

There was a creaking of stairs and a soft thud, and Charlie appeared in the doorway, his blond hair ruffled, rubbing one eye.

"Well, hello," Will greeted him.

"Hi." Charlie yawned.

Will smirked. "I beat you yesterday."

Charlie grinned. "No, we agreed it was a tie."

"From what I heard of whatever you were doing yesterday, you were trying to kill each other." Magic interjected.

"Heard?" Charlie dropped his hand from his face, confused.

"It sounded like one of you was being thrown against the wall," Magic clarified casually.

"Yes, it did." Maria walked through the door and strode over to the nearest chair. She kicked one leg on top the other. "We'd—well, I know I'd—appreciate it if you didn't make so much noise at midnight when we're trying to catch some Zs."

"Well, we're terribly *sorry*, we didn't realise you were the only one in the house," Charlie replied coldly.

"Guys, it's fine," Magic interrupted quickly before the situation could escalate. "I was too tired to be bothered, I fell asleep really quickly." She relaxed a little bit when they didn't pursue the matter. "You guys hungry? Charlie's mum prepared us breakfast. Where's Chloe?"

"Upstairs, getting dressed," Maria replied. She squinted coldly in Charlie's direction. "She didn't sleep too well last night."

"Well then, maybe she needs to visit a doctor," Charlie snapped back. "And, yes, let's eat."

Magic was glad when they finally sat down and began munching on toast and muffins. Chloe joined them a few minutes in, and as Maria had said, she indeed looked like she hadn't got one wink of sleep the previous night; there were dark circles lining the bottom of her eyes; the whites of her eyes were slightly red. Hey tight black curls where slightly out of place, some springing out in odd directions here and there.

"You look tired, Chloe," Maria said, before sipping on some orange juice.

"Shut up, Maria," Charlie snapped.

"What? Have I said something wrong?" she smirked.

"Guys, don't fight," Magic again tried to bubble down the anger before it rose too high.

"Yeah," Chloe croaked. She paused. "I should head home. I don't feel too well."

"Already?" Charlie looked disappointed, and so was Magic.

"Yeah, so should I," Will spoke, standing up. "I promised my parents I'd help them out during the holidays at the store…it was robbed."

Maria spat out the juice she was drinking, and Charlie chocked on his food. Magic's jaw hung open in disbelief as her fork slid out of her hands.

"*What?*" Magic cried out. "What did they take?"

"Bunch o' jewels. Each and every single one included at least one diamond." Will replied, downcast.

"That's ridiculous! I'm coming with you right now!" Magic exclaimed, getting out of her chair and starting towards the door.

"How could you not tell us this before?" Charlie demanded.

"Well, because I was afraid that this was the way you'd react." Will sighed. He grasped Magic's elbow before she could walk out. "And Magic, please don't bother, it would only make my parents feel worse that I told you and got you all worked up."

Magic stopped in her tracks and sighed. "Fine, but you have to keep us updated. And if you need any help, we're here." She folded her arms in resignation. "Well, I guess I'll see you guys at school. It's been fun. Thanks for having me, Charlie."

Magic went to retrieve her duffel bag from upstairs, and then grabbed her school backpack from the hallway.

"Bye, guys." Magic hugged her friends in turn. "Oh, and get well soon, Chloe. Will, you know if you need anything. OK, see you at school."

December flurried by bizarrely quickly, blending into January, the new year bringing with it some more icy cold weather, rainy afternoons and harshly windy nights. In the last few days of the holidays, Magic felt excited to be returning back to school and seeing her friends.

However, she wasn't very ecstatic about one thing.

Facing Slay again after her detention with him was something that Magic definitely wasn't looking forward to. The thought of him caused white-hot anger to bubble deep inside her; she clenched her fists each time the ghastly image of his face popped into her mind in order to stop herself from lashing out. Slay's loathing towards Magic had definitely not been unrequited.

The night before her first day back, Magic turned in early so that she could make sure all her homework was done, clothes washed and had all her necessary belongings for the following day.

Magic scanned the front field for any sign of Charlie, Chloe, Maria or Will. She knew that Tom would've gone in much earlier. It had barely been a few seconds before she felt a tug at her arm.

"Hello, Will." Magic smiled in relief, beaming. She couldn't stand being alone much longer although it hadn't been long at all. They exchanged a quick hug. "You seen the others?"

"Nope, I've just arrived. We should head to Spencer's room before it's too late. They'll probably be there soon."

They jogged up the front steps, and when the birch door slammed shut behind them, the chatter from outside died down immediately, the sound of the double doors slamming cutting it off immediately. As they headed down the corridor, the *clitter-clatter* of shoes against quartz broke the ringing silence within the walls.

"It's awfully silent for it being the first day back, I can't see anybody." Will scanned the corridor anxiously.

"Miss Spencer should be in her room, though." replied Magic, though she too was slightly suspicious of the lack of activity within the school. "But you're right, it's usually more crowded, and we always have juniors wreaking havoc here."

Will frowned. "Maybe they're on a school trip?" he suggested.

"I don't know...on the first day back? Highly unlikely," Magic replied, sceptical.

"Let's just go to our form room and check if anybody's there. If not, we'll wait outside for them."

"'Kay."

The sound of clattering, echoing footsteps continued. Despite the eerie emptiness of the school, they proceeded along the corridor.

They were about to turn a corner towards the senior corridors, when there was loud breakout of noise.

"It has *nothing* to do with you, I would appreciate if you could simply allow *me* to deal with it!"

They stopped dead in their tracks.

A cold, icy, trickling feeling was slowly tracing Magic's spine. It was too early in the day for Magic's happiness to be crippled by Slay's icy, malicious voice. Nevertheless, she and Will automatically ducked round the bend in the corridor and listened in carefully.

All was silent for a moment. Magic threw a panicked expression at Will, but he gave her a reassuring glance. Had Slay heard them come in, and then come to an abrupt stop? Did he know they were there and listening? It would've been impossible for Slay not to have heard Will and Magic; it was completely silent when they entered the building and the sound of their footsteps had been extremely loud. Magic was starting to worry but took a sigh of relief when Slay didn't seem to react.

"I'm sorry, Marcus, I cannot do that."

Will had to swiftly put a hand to Magic's mouth in order to stifle her gasp. The soothing voice of Remy Lockwood issued from the last room round the bend in the corridor, which was slightly cracked open. Magic couldn't stand it; her curiosity overwhelmed her. She shuffled ever so slightly round the corner, so she could get a clear view of what was happening through the thin slit between the door and the wall.

Slay's stance was livid, like a predator prepared to spring upon its prey. He stood behind a student's desk, both his arms gripping the edge, spread shoulder-width apart.

"Listen to me, Lockwood," Slay spat. The expression on his face was frightening, the high arches of his eyebrows making him look more terrifying than ever. "You stay out of my way, you have no right to accuse me of things you have no proof of." He was still as a sculpted statue.

Magic couldn't see Lockwood through the crack in the door, but she could sense his anger; even through the calmness of his voice, she could filter the anger building up behind it.

"This is not right, Marcus. Let me help you, what you're doing is wrong," Lockwood pleaded. He took a step towards Slay and came into view. He donned his usual corduroy suit, hands in his pockets. Magic could only see the back of his wavy brown hair, though she knew that Lockwood's expression must have told the full story.

"What am I doing that you believe is so wrong?" Slay demanded, raising his already very highly arched eyebrows higher.

Lockwood hesitated. "The diamond does not belong with him, Marcus."

Magic's eyes widened in shock, and her head snapped towards Will, who looked just as astounded as she felt.

Slay's livid expression suddenly morphed into one of fear. Magic was trembling; she had never seen him this way before.

"I don't know what you're talking about," Slay whispered, though Magic could sense the lie.

"Oh, but you very much do," Lockwood responded in his dead calmness.

"I-I would like you to elaborate," Slay stuttered. The fearful look on his face almost caused Magic to pity him, but then remembered how much he had done to make her loath him. She peeled her ears in the deadly silence in hopes of catching every word being said.

Once again, Lockwood hesitated, as if unsure of how much to reveal. "The Diamond of Dominion is destined to remain in its location."

Slay actually doubled back in shock, no longer trying to conceal it. "You know where it is?" he whispered shakily.

"Yes. And I also know how much you have sacrificed in your search for it. Your reputation is worth more than this. Be a good man, and do the right thing, Marcus. Don't let *him* control you like this. He is not worth it, I assure you." He paused. "And I must ask you not to pester young Miss Harrow anymore—she is under enough stress when it comes to her schoolwork. If her grandfather doesn't feel comfortable about revealing the whereabouts of the diamond, I can assist you in finding it…and destroying it before—he—reaches it. You know how dangerous the diamond would be in his possession. You know it would be the right thing to have it destroyed before it lands in his hands. Do the right thing, Marcus. Leave the Harrows be." Lockwood pleaded slowly.

Slay looked utterly petrified. "The diamond was last in possession of Magnus Harrow. The girl is refusing to tell me anything on the matter, let alone finish retelling to me the story she started. The only thing she had dared mention was that Magnus had returned the diamond to its rightful place when he had bought it off the Brakks."

It was Magic's turn to cup a hand over Will's mouth when he inhaled sharply. She stared at him, wide-eyed and petrified at what they were hearing, but didn't dare make a sound.

"And why did he place it where he did once he had bought it?" asked Lockwood, maintaining his calm demeanour.

"Strange things began to happen to him," Slay continued in a hiss. "He was one who believed in legends. He discovered that the Diamond of Dominion was indeed what he had purchased, and knew what he had to do once he received it. The diamond had been lost for decades and couldn't believe he had found it. He decided it would be the right thing to return it to its rightful place, before things escalated. It is a dangerous artefact, Remy. But—*he* is requesting me to retrieve it for him. He greatly values my service. I will always grant my loyalty to him."

There was a long pause.

Lockwood sighed. "This is wrong, Marcus. If you knew it had been bought off the Brakks, why did you do what you did?" Lockwood was again speaking in a code-like manner, as if he knew that Will and Magic were listening. Magic shivered at the possibility.

Slay looked even more petrified, if possible, that Lockwood knew this information. "I-I had to check—to see—to make sure…" His voice faded away.

There was a sudden outburst of chatter in the hallway; students were piling into the building, heading to their classes.

"Oh, jeez," Magic whispered over the chatter.

Slay looked shaken. "I must leave. We'll continue this conversation later."

Will and Magic hastily ducked round the corner and pretended to walk off towards their classroom as Slay burst out the room, fuming, and headed towards the carpeted stairs leading to the upper floors. They didn't see Lockwood leave, but knew he had also fled the room.

"What—I—oh my goodness, Will!" Magic spluttered—her mouth couldn't keep up with the thoughts in her brain, and everything she needed to say. "I—Will! Don't you see?"

Will's breathing sped up. "What're you talking about?"

"It was him! *Slay*! Slay was the one who robbed your parent's store!" The realisation hit her like a smack in the face. "What the bloody heck is going on? They were talking about a *diamond*? *Legends*? Will, this isn't normal!" Magic's head began to throb.

Will attempted to calm Magic down, though he too began exploding. "And Katie! *Katie*! Magic—" His jaw dropped. "Magic, that's it! You remember how Katie and Slay had that incident? That's what Slay had been bugging her about! He wanted to find out more about this diamond—according to him it had last been with Katie's—grandfather, was it? And then go and find it!"

Something wasn't fully adding up in Magic's head. There was still a piece of information that was missing that she couldn't quite put her finger on. "Yes, that all makes sense," she began slowly, "but they kept talking about someone, they never mentioned his name…kept saying 'he', remember?"

Will frowned and straightened up. "Yeah, I remember. Wow, my head hurts…"

"And then there was Lockwood…" Magic lowered her voice so as to not attract the attention of other students. "He was trying to convince him out of something—finding the diamond, or whatever it is? Said it was all wrong…" Magic hesitated. "Hey, Will? Do you think it would be OK to ask Lockwood about the whole thing?"

"I really couldn't tell you, Magic." Will began stroking his chin. "Magic, I think he knew we were listening. Remember how he was speaking? As if he knew somebody else was listening, and didn't want them to know what he and Slay were talking about?"

Magic began nodding slowly. "Yes, he definitely heard us come in, and knew we had stopped to listen, but I'm not sure if he knew it was us." Magic was hot with excitement and nervous energy. She realised she was sweating and wiped her sleeve against her damp brow. "Wow, that was a lot."

"Yeah…" Will agreed. He ran a hand through his dark hair and rubbed his light, grey eyes. "Come one, we'll definitely talk about this later, but we should get to class, or we'll be late."

He was right—the crowd in the corridor had thinned significantly during the duration of their conversation.

Chapter Thirteen
Legends

Will and Magic burst into their form room with seconds to spare. In silence, they took seats in the bend of the horseshoe of desks, trying to ignore their classmate's stares. Luckily, Miss Spencer hadn't yet arrived.

At the front, Maria turned round in her seat to face them.

"Where have you been?" she mouthed.

"We'll explain later," Magic whispered back. She set her bag down beside her desk just as a hurried Miss Spencer walked in. Her blond hair looked windswept, as if she had been running.

During Chemistry, Magic and Will tried to whisper as much of the story as they could to the others. They had gotten to the part where Lockwood had begged Slay to leave Katie alone, when the bell rang, indicating the start of English.

As she walked down the red-carpeted corridors, Magic felt slightly nervous to see how Slay would behave after his terrifying exchange with Lockwood that morning.

When the skinny, frightening figure of Slay appeared, he still looked slightly shaken up, though it was obvious he was trying to compose himself, and behave 'normally'.

"In." He spiked when the class stood motionless outside the English room.

Magic and Will knew they had no chance of recollecting the incident whilst the subject of the story was in hearing range; if Slay caught wind of what they were talking about, they knew that they didn't want to be the reason why his already bad mood took a downfall.

So, the five of them sat torturously at the back of the English room, silently begging the clock's hands to double and triple and quadruple in speed.

After an epoch, when the bell finally rang, indicating their first break of the day, Magic bolted to the door in hopes that she wouldn't be the last one left in the classroom, and that Slay wouldn't have a chance to ask her to remain behind.

"OK, tell us, tell us, *tell us*!" Maria cried desperately, bouncing on the spot as Magic took a seat at their circular wooden bench.

"Right—wait, where were we?" Will racked his brain.

Magic set her bag down and tucked her legs beneath the table. "Lockwood told Slay to not talk to Katie anymore, or something."

"Oh yeah—"

Will, with Magic's help, continued the story from the point they had left off.

They had reached the mention of the diamond being bought off of Will's parents—

"*What?*" Maria sat up straight, slamming the table. Charlie's jaw dropped so low it was in danger of falling off, and Chloe simply sat there, stunned.

"You guys must've heard wrong," Chloe hissed in a delicate whisper.

"I'm pretty sure we didn't," Will confirmed.

"Guys…" Chloe's whisper faded.

"What?" Magic urged impatiently.

"Guys—no way."

"Chloe, can you just—"

"Will, it was Slay who robbed your parent's store! Don't you see? He was—" Chloe began in a tight voice. Even though Magic had already considered this piece of information, the mention of it again sparked another idea in her racing mind.

"—trying to find it to give to that 'him' he kept on talking about! Holey—" Magic finished, and got up and started pacing on the grass, where it crunched softly beneath her feet.

Will looked like somebody had drained his face of colour; he was pale white.

"We don't know that—he can't have—" he spluttered, speechless.

"This *can't* be happening!" Charlie intervened. "You know what, they're both nutters, Lockwood *and* Slay! So you're telling me there's some stupid magical diamond that Slay's after to give to someone, and Lockwood is trying to stop him? Lockwood is smarter than this! How can he honestly believe the rubbish that Slay's coming up with—I mean, we always knew Slay was out of his mind, but now Lockwood too? Come *on*, man, there's no stupid diamond, and the fact that Slay was going after Katie to pursue the stupid fantasy going on in his head—absolute *idiocy*!" He finished in an angrier tone than anticipated.

Magic stopped in her tracks. "We haven't finished the story yet, Charlie," she reminded him calmly. Charlie slumped down onto his arms in silence.

Magic cleared her throat. "Strange things apparently started happening to Magnus Harrow—according to legends, apparently the right thing for him to do would be to return it to its 'rightful place—'" Magic sketched quotation marks in the air with her fingers "—wherever that's supposed to be. And then Slay mentioned somebody wanting the diamond—he looked pretty spooked, didn't he, Will?"

"Oh, yeah," Will replied, nodding, his face still snowy pale. "Frightened out of his wits, which probably means whoever this 'he' person is must be forcing him to get it—threatening him, maybe?"

"Hmm," Maria squinted in thought. "You guys said that all that Magnus was doing was based off of *legends* about the diamond?" she asked.

"Yeah," replied Magic.

"What was the diamond called again?" asked Maria.

"The Diamond of Dominion." Magic looked to Will for confirmation and he nodded.

"If it's a legend," said Maria slowly, "then there must be something about it in the library, don't you think?"

"It's possible," said Magic. "I think we should take a look; we might be able to find something. The last thing I'd want to do is have to ask Lockwood about the whole thing if my curiosity gets the better of me—and I'd hate to admit that we were eavesdropping, as if he doesn't already know…anyway, yeah, I think going to the library might be a good idea. I think I'll head over there after school and pick up a few books."

Magic indeed went for a trip to the library after school; Charlie insisted that Slay had come up with some stupid cock-and-bull story and stormed off. Maria agreed to come and help Magic, but she left a while later with enough convincing from Magic that she looked too tired to walk.

So, Magic decided to start searching on her own. She privately thought it would be easier to search for any information on the Diamond of Dominion on her own, without an over-excited Maria jumping down her throat.

She decided to start looking for any titles relating to the diamond—the library was huge, so Magic knew that she would be there for a long time.

She began pulling books out at random from an aisle labelled *Myths and Legends*. When the first couple books she pulled out were about dragons and vampires, she immediately knew she had to move further down the aisle to possibly find what she was looking for. She strode down the shelves, her fingers tracing the hardness of spine after spine.

Magic stopped in her tracks at an odd-looking, battered book with a bottle green spine whose corners were worn down and eroded.

The writing on the spine had immediately caught her attention.

She frowned and pulled the book off the shelf, slapping it into her arms and striding over to a free table, not taking her eyes off the front cover. In tiny, thin, miniscule golden letters at the very top of the front read:

THE FALLING OF MAGNUS HARROW
AND THE SORCERERS' FIGHT FOR POWER

"He *died?*" Magic cried out in shock. There was no illustration on the hardcover, just those fiery golden words on the front. She flipped the book over and it landed with a *thud* against the table. Nothing. She was faced with an unhelpful block of bottle green nothingness.

No author? Odd. Nevertheless, Magic felt a strange gravitational pull towards the book, as if it were begging her to open and read it. Magic headed over to the librarian and checked it out. She received a few disapproving looks from others, eyeing the book as if it had done them a bad deed. Magic thought she must've looked odd carrying a big clunky book out. She sped up her pace into a brisk walk until she was out the door.

At home, Magic was eager to start devouring the book. She slumped onto her bed, lying on her stomach and crossing her feet in the air. Without a spare of a moment, she flipped open the book and endorsed herself.

Magnus Levine Bartus Harrow—

Harrow. Magic stopped there. She hadn't once paid attention to the fact that Magnus could in fact be in the same Harrow family as…Katie. *Katie.* Hadn't Slay been pestering Katie Harrow?

But of course they were related! It had been so obvious that Magic felt so stupid in the moment. Why else would Slay have been pestering Katie if she had no direct connection to the story?

She sat bolt upright and continued eagerly.

—was known for his special liking and affinity towards strange and mystical objects, hence why he was sometimes given the nickname 'The Spellbounder', because of the way he claimed to feel 'bounded' to the mysterious essence of their magic.

Many millenniums before our time, a young, powerful sorcerer, despite all his already existing strange and impressive abilities, was a greedy and selfish man, and sought to become the greatest sorcerer in the world. He became power-hungry and was desperate to form a creation beyond the reach of any member of mankind. With the help of his abnormal abilities, the young wizard was able to create a diamond that would answer his prayers and grant him all his wishes. He would give it a name that told anyone who heard it the full story of its abnormal abilities: The Diamond of Dominion.

Magic's broken gasp was uneven with excitement and anticipation—she had found the book she was looking for, the book with the answers: she knew it even though she had barely started reading. She continued.

However, the sorcerer was ignorant. He overlooked himself and carelessly threw together a stone, without fully anticipating its strength and power, and how much of a dangerous act he was committing by creating it.

There was, therefore, a fluke in its production as a consequence of his carelessness.

The diamond, it had been said, could only be retrieved and replaced by one person—dead, alive, or not even born yet, the sorcerer didn't know.

In his panic and anger, he went to retract the diamond from where it was kept safe and hidden. Days later, the curse that had befallen him lifted, and he died in the act. He was not the one that the diamond sought.

Centuries later, another selfish sorcerer by the name of Vandalarukk sought out the diamond with the same ignorance and greed as his predecessor. He roamed cities, lands, villages, oceans, but could not locate the Diamond of Dominion. He slaughtered every man, woman and child who crossed his path, disposing of those who did not prove any use in his quest to locate the precious diamond.

It is not yet known whether or not he perished during his travels.

Harrow had read about and, naturally, heard of the evil Vandalarukk, who sought the Diamond of Dominion to seek eternal authority and power. His interest in the abnormal and magical urged him to retrieve the diamond before Vandalarukk could seek it.

However, little did Harrow know that the diamond had been long lost, and its location at the time was strictly secret, unknown.

One day on his search for the diamond, Harrow stumbled upon a married couple on the street, selling stolen trinkets and desirables. He noticed that in the wife's bony arms lay snug a jagged pink rock, which glowed with an eerie luminescence. Harrow knew that that was the diamond he sought, and the wife gladly sold it to him.

Harrow continued on his path, trying to find the place where the ancient sorcerer had once kept the diamond safe, in an attempt to conceal it from Vandalarukk.

With his wit, intelligence and knack for reading clues, Harrow managed to locate the sacred spot where the Diamond of Dominion was destined to lie, protected forever, and he laid it upon its home.

But Magnus Harrow was indeed not the one that the diamond sought out. Once Harrow placed the diamond back, a curse fell upon him, and he later died.

Magic slammed the book shut. She had all the answers she needed.

"OH!" She cried out, standing up straight and dropping the book. "Ouch," she cried, once it landed on her toes. She had just realised something. No, it couldn't be…

Rubbing her foot, Magic picked up the book and threw it onto her bed.

I can assist you in finding it…and destroying it before—he—reaches it…But—he is requesting me to retrieve it for him. He greatly values my service. I will always grant my loyalty to him.

Magic was remembering how Lockwood and Slay had referred to a certain someone as 'him'…could it be possible that Magic had found the 'him' that they had been talking about?

Or was it all 'absolute idiocy' as Charlie had feared?

Magnus Harrow had, according to this book, passed away. Could he have passed away for another, more realistic reason?

He greatly values my service. I will always grant my loyalty to him.

Magic remembered how Slay had been drooling about how loyal he was to Vandalarukk, if that was whom they had been referring to.

The pieces of the puzzle slowly assembled themselves in Magic's head. She began pacing briskly round her room as the sun began drooping down below the clouds. Her brain was whizzing with thoughts, worries, and hunches.

There was something else Magic wanted to address: who was the person that the legend had been talking about?

The diamond, it had been said, could only be retrieved and replaced by one person.

Who was this person? Magic didn't want to open a new window of curiosities, so she tucked that thought to the back of her head to deal with later.

There was another pressing matter irking at Magic: how did Magnus Harrow relate to Katie Harrow, if he did at all? Was he a distant relative, or was he closer than he seemed?

Magic bit her lip. She was sceptical as she thought about asking Katie about the matter. Would Katie take offense, or just brush it off? At that point, Magic decided she barely cared, and that her retrieving the answers she so desperately needed was more important than how others felt about her.

Magic thought she wouldn't be able to sleep through the night, if her interruptive thoughts kept this up.

Chapter Fourteen
Katie's Secret

Magic arose from the crack of dawn the following morning.

As she approached the school front field, she didn't even try looking for her friends; her eyes immediately began scanning the place for Katie Harrow. Magic assumed that she wouldn't find Katie alone, so she'd have to try to find a way to extract her from her clique of friends.

Magic finally spotted Katie with two other girls, chatting in the shade of a tree; her hair was as long and brown as she remembered it, flowing down her back. Magic gathered her courage and marched towards them, trying not to look so desperate. She composed herself when, as she approached, Katie looked away from her conversation.

When Katie realised who was approaching her, her face broke into a smile.

"Hello, Magic," Katie greeted Magic as she stopped by her. "Guys, this is Magic."

Magic didn't have time for small talk—she wanted to cut to the chase.

"Hi, Katie. It's good seeing you. Er—can I talk to you? Alone, if you don't mind?"

Katie looked slightly surprised, but she agreed anyway. Katie's friends threw Magic dirty and disapproving looks.

When Katie and Magic reached one of the short pillars near the front steps, Katie spoke first.

"What's up, Magic?" she asked, leaning against the top of the pillar.

"Look—" Magic took a deep breath "—I-I hope you don't mind me asking…what's the connection between you and Magnus Harrow? If you're related," Magic added awkwardly. She bit her tongue and waited for a response.

Katie's face turned marble white—she began to splutter.

"I—what—? How did you—"

"It's a long story…I'm really sorry to intrude like this, and I know it doesn't seem like something I really need to know, but it is. Could you tell me? Are you even related?"

Katie sighed.

"Well?" Magic urged.

"Magnus was my grandfather."

"I—oh—what?" What had she expected?

"He was my mother's dad, Magic."

Magic's expression changed.

"Hold on…"

Magic trued to restrain the enormity of her reaction as a wave of realisation crashed over her, sending a physical jolt through her body.

The distant voice of Charlie Stocklin filled her ears.

I was walking down the English corridor, and Katie had burst out of Slay's office, looking frightened out of her wits. I asked her what was going on, she just mentioned Slay interrogating her about her grandfather. About something he had, I think.

Oh, how stupid Magic felt, of course he was her grandfather!

Magic was fighting hard to contain herself. She bit down on her lip momentarily to stop herself from yelling out. "Oh, right," she said calmly. "And also—just please, if I'm offending you, tell me—"

"No, go on."

"If you don't mind me asking—how did Magnus pass away?"

Katie's eyes widened and her bottom lip began trembling.

"It was terrible…unexpected," she whispered. "We didn't know."

Magic hesitated; a feeling of mingled pity and regret was building up in her stomach. "I'm so sorry," she said. "But—did it have anything to do with—" Magic hesitated again, looked round to see if anyone was listening, and said in a low voice "—the Diamond of Dominion?"

Magic didn't know what she had expected; a tear escaped Katie's hazel, watery eyes and glistened as it dropped with a *splat* onto her coat. She nodded frantically as her face screwed up into a pout and a new cascade of tears streamed down her cheeks.

Magic felt bad. She pulled Katie into a hug.

"I'm sorry," she whispered.

"N-no, it's n-not that," Katie cried muffled sobs into Magic's shoulder. Katie seemed to hesitate. "It's—it's h-him."

Magic froze. Katie must've realised because she tensed up, too. Magic pulled away from Katie but kept her hands on her shoulders. "Slay?"

"How—"

"I heard him talking. I know about your grandfather. What's Slay been telling you?"

Katie sniffled. "He—he just w-wanted me to tell him where the d-diamond is. Thinks I know where it is just b-because my g-grandfather had it."

"Tell him to back off!" Magic could sense anger threatening to build up inside her, but she swallowed it down.

"I h-have, but he's so *relentless!*" Katie moaned. "I've tried to run away whenever he c-comes, to s-save me from t-talking to him." She wiped her eyes with the hem of her jacket sleeve.

"What is his *deal?*" Magic asked, mostly to herself.

"I don't know…anyway, I should probably get back to my friends…bye, Magic."

Magic removed her hands from Katie's shoulders as she slipped away.

So her question had been answered: they *were* related, which is why Slay had been pestering Katie so much—Slay wanted answers…just like Magic.

"Magic! Where've you *been?*"

Magic was brought back to earth as she was met with an anxious-looking Maria, followed by Charlie, Will, and Chloe.

"I saw you with Katie," said Will.

"Yeah, I was asking her about something," Magic replied slowly.

"What?" Charlie demanded.

Magic slapped a hand to her head. "Oh, right!" The others looked alarmed.

"Magic, are you—?"

"Of course, I haven't told you guys what I found out yet! I was at the library yesterday, remember?"

Charlie's face sunk into a grumpy grimace. "Magic, I bet you anything that stuff's a load of—"

"No, it isn't—"

"I forgot you went yesterday! What did you find out?" Maria exclaimed, her eyes widening as she began bouncing on the balls of her feet.

"Well…you see, it's a lot…oh, hold on, I have the book, here—"

Magic slipped her bag off and extracted the large, clunky bottle-green book from amidst her other belongings.

Maria's face morphed into confusion. "No author?"

"I know, it's odd." agreed Magic.

"Well, let's read it!" Chloe spoke for the first time, trudging over to get a closer look. "Wow, this *is* long…" she muttered, running her fingers over the stacked pages.

"We can't read this all now," said Will sadly.

"You don't need to! I literally just read the first page, and there's everything you need to know!" Magic encouraged them. She slapped the book into Will's arms. "Take a look!"

Will raised an eyebrow as he flicked open the scruffy hardcover. Chloe, Maria and even Charlie leaned in eagerly.

For the next few moments, Magic watched as four pairs of eyes, grey, brown, green, and blue, moved side to side rapidly, their facial expressions brightening up even more as the eyes moved down the page.

When Charlie finished first, he crossed his arms. "I still don't know if it's legit…"

"I mean, I don't blame you," Magic replied. "I found this book among others about the Loch Ness monster and the lost city of Atlantis."

"But they wouldn't just make up some random story about this," Chloe finished reading and joined the conversation. "Magnus Harrow was a real guy."

"How do you know that?" Charlie challenged her.

"He is, Charlie," Magic interjected. "That's the whole reason I was just with Katie. I was asking her about him. He's her grandfather. The grandfather you had been referring to, to be exact."

There was a thud as the book slid out of Will's hands and landed open-sided on the concrete of the stairs.

"Of course! His name is *Harrow*! How did I not see this before?" Maria cupped a hand to her face, and then hastily began fiddling with the ends of her flaming red hair.

"You couldn't have, there's probably a million Harrows on this earth," Charlie said dully, rolling his eyes.

All throughout her lessons that day Magic was extremely distracted; so distracted, in fact, that had it not been for Maria, Magic would've spilled too much sulphuric acid into their flasks during Chemistry.

"Magic!" Maria grabbed and heaved at Magic's elbow. Magic was shaken out of her numb state, having been unconsciously working at the practical, completely unfocused due to her mind being submerged deep in her thoughts.

"Where do you think that diamond could be?" Magic asked distractedly to no one in particular, as Maria slipped the acid beaker out of Magic's hands and out of her subconscious reach.

"Magic," Charlie hissed, picking up a strip of magnesium with a pair of tweezers. "Not here."

"But think about it," Magic continued as if Charlie hadn't said anything, her expression distant. "A diamond that everyone's looking for—well, almost everyone who knows about it, of course—it must be hidden so well...it could be anywhere on earth." Magic cocked her head to one side thoughtfully. "What if we could get to it first? Before Vandalarukk could lay his hands on it," Magic added in an undertone.

She hadn't intended for Charlie to hear her, so she jumped in shock when Charlie made a low growling sound in the back of his throat, clenching his fists at his sides. Magic's attention was immediately diverted from her thoughts to Charlie as she was forced to pull herself out of the large abyss that was her thoughts, her head arriving back in the Chemistry lab.

Magic noticed the loud, booming Mr Clark heading in their direction. She quickly picked up a pair of tweezers in an attempt to look like she knew what she was doing. As Mr Clark approached, she heaved a sigh of relief; at least Charlie's inevitable wrath that had been about to crash down on her could be delayed.

"Now, let's see..." Clark's cheerful voice radiated across the room over the light chatter of the class. He beamed. "Ah! Very well done, Magic, very well done! You've added the perfect amount of acid. Make sure to be careful while adding in the magnesium, you don't want to harm yourself...well, I'll let you carry on investigating exothermic reactions." He nodded happily and strutted off to the next group.

Maria pursed her lips as Magic grinned at her.

"It's not funny, Magic, we've got to stay focused," Maria cautioned, placing her hands on her hips.

"I was asking a question, that's all," Magic replied. "I don't know why Charlie's getting all worked up," she muttered.

Chloe and Will were a pair, almost finished with their practical. Maria liked them very much, but she was a fierce competitor. She glanced briefly at them from over her shoulder, and then whipped back round anxiously.

"Come on, Magic! *We haven't even added the magnesium yet!*"

"Relax, Maria," said Magic, trying not to smile at Chloe and Will's pantomime of imitations of Maria, which she could see over Maria's shoulder. She lifted her eyes from them to Maria's face. "Clark just told us we're doing well."

"He said *you're* doing well. He didn't even look at us." Charlie growled. Magic was startled slightly at his voice; she had forgotten he was there.

Will rested an elbow on the lab tabletop, slumping his face into his hand. "I smell jealousy," he teased.

"Shut up, William."

"Oh, jeez, you know he's angry when he uses my full name."

The rest of January blurred rapidly into February; the announcing of the new month, however, did not bring with it a change of weather. The icy frostiness of the air nipped at the tips of fingers and reddened the end of noses.

The teens' workload had piled up dangerously high, resulting in their days mostly spent in the peace of the vast library. It felt like they spent more time there than their actual classrooms.

One night in late February, Magic had slumped onto her bedroom desk during the early evening, fed up with her mountain of homework. She slammed her exercise book and pushed it towards the window; she decided to take on the rest of the mountain later.

She sighed, stretched and got up, making her way to her small, rustic bedside table (over the course of the past few months, additional furniture had been added to her room), where *The Falling of Magnus Harrow* lay, cover down. She yawned, picking up the eroded, bottle green manuscript and laying back against her bed headboard, flicking on her bedside lamp.

Magic became more and more obsessive over the legends of the Diamond of Dominion as the weeks passed by. She had been unable to gather much more information from the library as the authorless book seemed to be the only one with details on the matter. Nevertheless, this book wasn't going to bore Magic any time soon—she would read and reread extracts on a regular basis, focusing particularly on the ones on Magnus Harrow. However, she had not yet found any additional information worth remembering.

She sometimes thought it foolish that she was focusing so much on a supposed made-up fairy tale—however, had the exchange between Lockwood and Slay not taken place, and a legend possibly confirmed real, she wouldn't have even bothered.

Magic skipped over extracts on Magnus' early life, trying to extract more information on the sorcerers, or the diamond's possible whereabouts.

There was a knock on the door and Mrs McFee poked her blonde head into the room, holding a green mug in one hand, her other on the doorhandle.

"You doing OK?" Lauren asked her daughter.

"Yup. Just reading."

"You mind if I come in?"

"Sure."

Mrs McFee entered the bedroom and gently shut the door with a *snap*. She tiptoed over to Magic's bedside table and set down the steaming mug of hot chocolate.

"Thanks, Mum," said Magic, as Mrs McFee took a seat on the edge of the bed. She gave her a smile and a wink.

"Tell me about your book," said Mrs Mcfee, jutting her chin towards the bottle-green hardcover in Magic's hands.

"Oh—" What should she say? "Just some old fairy tales," she invented wildly.

Her mother chuckled. "Schoolwork serving you well?" she asked, looking at the mountainous load of text an d exercise books piled up on Magic's desk.

"Haha, yeah. Eventually, I'll get through it though."

"Of course, you will." Mrs McFee smiled. There was a couple moments' pause. "We didn't name you Magic by accident." She gave Magic a pat on the leg before leaving the room.

The words momentarily rung in Magic's ears, having more impact on her than was probably intended.

We didn't name you Magic by accident. The words felt empowering, encouraging. Magic felt like she could take on the world.

There was a small pool of guilt building up inside her as she remembered a thought she had had a few days ago.

What if she could get to the diamond before Vandalarukk could find it?

She shuddered slightly. It was something Magic would do…but was it worth it? Risk it all for something that might all just be make believe? She might end up like Magnus and everybody else who tried to retrieve the diamond—perished. She surely was not the person the legend spoke of, the one and only person who could touch the diamond and remain unharmed.

Still, her pool of guilt bubbled higher as her desire to retrieve the diamond grew stronger. Not the desire to use it, but get it before Vandalarukk, or anybody else untrustworthy, could lay their hands on it.

We didn't name you Magic by accident.

The words throbbed against her skull.

Chapter Fifteen
The Third Sighting

Magic would've rather taken on her pile of homework from the night before once again than sit through ten minutes of—especially one from Slay—an English lesson.

So, when the bell rang indicating the end of the final break of the day and the start of period five, Magic reluctantly trudged across the field and up the carpeted stairs, sulking silently behind her friends.

"Do I even need to ask you what the matter is?" Chloe sighed as they approached the beginning of the dim corridor, where the rest of class was gathered, murmuring silently.

"Nope." Magic pouted.

They had just come to an abrupt stop when the door flung open, and the students jumped in shock.

Two seconds in and Magic's blood had already begun to boil at the sight of Marcus Slay's malicious, evil, twisted smile in the doorway. She gritted her teeth together, the scraping sound stinging at her ears, and stalked through the door with her fists clenched. She unintentionally brushed against Slay's arm, which twitched at her touch.

Magic picked up the pace and slumped at the back of the class, as far as possible from Slay's desk (as usual).

Charlie, Chloe, Maria, and Will filed in beside her, depositing their bags beneath the bench tables. Magic was pressed into the dark wall, and, leaning against it, she decided she didn't care. Even though it meant that she wasn't going to attract much attention, and Slay probably wouldn't notice her, the snarl still didn't leave her face.

How was she going to endure this? She may have been overreacting, but then Magic remembered the amount of injustice Slay treated her with—slamming her and Charlie into a brick wall and calling her out for things she had no control over, just to get under her skin. Her snarl deepened at the thoughts.

Though when Magic remembered the day when Slay looked terrified out of his guts because Lockwood seemed to know more information than anticipated on the Diamond of Dominion, she wasn't sure whether to feel pitiful or satisfied.

This was going well. Slay was rambling away at the chalkboard, though Magic wasn't filtering any of it. She didn't even know what the lesson was on. It didn't matter, though. Slay had forgotten to pick on her today. Well, it seemed like he had.

Good. So far, so good, Magic thought. *If I can keep this up for another one and a half hours, I'll be good.*

One hour left. Magic's throat had gone raw from lack of speech. She noticed Maria giving her anxious looks from the corner of her eye.

Magic hadn't shifted weight at all during the lesson, so her head felt glued to the wall, her elbow digging into the smooth wood of the table.

She tried to keep the anger bubbled down, low, where it couldn't erupt. Though at this point, Magic still hadn't grasped why she was getting worked up. It seemed that even Slay's mere presence could drive her internally mad.

Forty-five minutes—this was going swell, Magic thought, *minus the nearly uncontainable anger. She* could sit through another forty-five minutes. That was nothing for her. Easy.

Magic diverted her gaze out the window, brushing the grass and the trees below, saluting the sky above.

There was a bird sitting on top of the round wooden bench that Magic and her friends usually sat at, shaded by the shadow of the birch tree. Nice. It pecked at the wood, supposedly trying to catch a bug.

A small robin flew down, cautiously approaching the bench. He was a black and orange spot amongst the dazzling green of the grass.

Should he proceed? Would the much larger raven chase him to death? He seemed to be having a mental battle…just like the one Magic had been having. Huh. Magic wouldn't have ever thought that out of everything she could relate to in her life that it would be…a bird.

Magic felt a sharp, eye-watering nudge in her ribs.

"Magic!" Maria cried in a hoarse whisper.

"What?" Magic whispered back irritably. Maria had broken her peace, causing Magic to remember where she was.

Locked up in a room with a terrifying beast for a teacher. Magic wouldn't be surprised if Slay grew horns and a mane at that moment.

"I would like a volunteer to step up and help me with this scenario."

Magic growled internally at Slay's awful, malicious voice. It aggravated her even more than usual, as throughout the whole lesson she had managed to block it out.

"We can't keep going over the basics! We should be writing GCSE-level essays and yet here I am trying to teach you how to punctuate sentences! Ridiculous," Slay spat. "Now, who would like to volunteer?"

Not one pupil raised their hand, or even shifted weight. It didn't even sound like anybody was breathing.

Slay's black eyes scanned the room. It was like a wave passed over the students, cutting their breathing.

Although she had been praying that it wouldn't happen, Magic had slightly been expecting it. So when Slay's eyes rested on her face, she didn't even react.

"McFee—" Slay smiled that awful, twisted smile "—would you like to come and help me insert the appropriate parenthesis in the correct place?"

Even though he asked the question, it sounded like more of a demand. Some of the kids turned to look at Magic sadly, others didn't even move. Magic's growl faded for a split second, but then it was replaced with a worried frown. She felt her face adjust to make it look more defensive. As she lifted her head off the wall, she felt the blood in her face flow frantically, as if even it was trying to escape. She swore internally.

Magic was reminded greatly of *Jurassic Park* as the atmosphere in the room tensed up when she slowly walked down the aisle between the desks; it was so silent you could hear a pin drop.

The floorboards creaked slightly as she approached the chalkboard. *Tyrannosaurus rexes can sense smell,* thought Magic. *Not gonna help me much dwelling on it. He's already seen me.*

Slay leaned smugly against the window frame. He stuck out his hand, a piece of white chalk pinched between his thumb and forefinger. Magic took it, standing as far as she could from him as possible, and tried not to touch his hand again. She tried not to make a face of disgust as she turned to the chalkboard.

Magic wasn't worried because she didn't know the answer, but rather because only time would tell what Slay had in store for her. She knew that she wouldn't just be able to sit back down and then call it a day. Slay would want a piece of her before she left, the perfect opportunity to humiliate her. The Tyrannosaurus Rex was hungry.

Magic raised her hand over the board, planning to draw in a bracket. It seemed like everybody else in the room had forgotten how to breathe. Or maybe they had just lost their lungs. Normally, the air in the room shouldn't become this unbreathable when a teacher asks for a child to help at the front of the class. A child probably wouldn't think twice, it should be completely ordinary. With Slay, however, it was a different story—you just never knew what to expect when it came to him.

Magic drew in the first bracket, the smooth sound of the chalk against the board the only one in the room.

Magic moved to draw in the second bracket, when something out the window distracted her out of the corner of her eye.

She thought it was that black raven again, but once she checked back, she realised the black object was far from it.

Her blood ran cold.

Lurking behind the birch tree was a dark, shadowy, masked figure, which appeared to be carrying a long, heavy staff. Magic tried to seep her gaze through the mask, but the hood of the cloak the figure sported was too big for her to make out anything from underneath it.

It felt like somebody had compressed her lungs—condensed them into a small pulp that made them impossible to breathe through. Was it stalking her? Magic began to tremble on the spot—the thought of the rest of the class staring at her had flown from her mind—this was the most important thing right now. She had to find out who it was.

Magic reached out a hand towards the window almost reflexively—she hadn't taken her eyes of the figure since she had spotted it. Its dark cloak fluttered in the breeze, as eerie as an abandoned scarecrow.

Magic took a step towards the window—she had tunnel vision. Magic had been robbed of all senses—the figure was all she could see.

Magic was pulled back to earth when she felt something slippery beneath her foot. All the background sounds of fidgeting kids and birds' distant chirping filled Magic's ears once more.

She pulled her gaze from the scene outside and looked to her feet.

Magic hadn't realised she had dropped the piece of chalk—the rest of the world had been blurred, and she had gone numb—until she saw the two halves of it strewn against the floor, white dust scattered everywhere, covering the floor.

Magic slowly lifted her foot off the ground, and dusted her trainer. She quickly glanced back out the window, but the figure was nowhere to be seen. A wave of quiet snickering travelled the room, and a pool of regret was filling up inside Magic. She was devastated that she had lost him once again.

"Would you like to take us with you on your little fantasy, McFee? I'm sure we'll find it as entertaining as you make it seem."

Magic had completely forgotten that Slay was in the room, so she was completely relieved when she realised his tone was laughing rather than livid. She'd take his sneer over his anger any day of the week. Silent giggles erupted round the class.

Confusion was added to Magic's pool of regret and frustration—why wasn't Slay yelling at her for dropping the chalk? It had made a huge mess!

"I just dropped the chalk, sir," Magic replied, only half there. "That's all." She tried to save herself. "I could clean it up, if you want."

"No. This cues your dismissal." Slay's voice was dead, cold—though Magic could detect the fury behind it.

There was an immediate loud sound of haste shuffling as the class shoved their books into their bags and heaved them onto their backs, making a run for the door.

Magic made to go and get hers from the back of the classroom and then get the heck out of there, but she ran into Charlie halfway down the aisle.

"I've got it, let's get out of here," Charlie mumbled over the noise. Magic's backpack dangled from his left arm. Magic turned round quickly and sprinted out the door.

Magic put one hand on her knee, and the other on her chest to control her panting. None of them had spoken one word until they reached the field outside.

"What—happened—Magic?" Charlie breathed, throwing his and Magic's bags onto the round bench.

"H-hold—on," Magic's chest was rising and falling rapidly, the sharp intakes of breath scratching at her throat—but not just because she had been running so fast.

Maria, Will and Chloe burst out of the front doors and jogged over to them, pushing past students who threw them dirty looks in turn, their bags slapping against their backs.

"What the hell—?" Chloe began, but Magic had regained her breath.

"It was him." Magic straightened up and gave her a dead stare.

Will caught on immediately. "That—that same figure? Magic, it's been a while since you've seen him, are you sure—"

"Positive," Magic cut him off firmly. She knew what she had seen.

"*What* is his deal?" moaned Maria. "Are you absolutely sure?"

"*Yes*," Magic emphasised through gritted teeth.

There was a few minutes' pause, silence between them except for sharp breathing. The students had slowly filed out of the field as the group had been conversing.

Maria muttered quietly after a while. "This is odd…"

"I'm surprised Slay let you off, though," Charlie said with a frown.

"Yeah—" Magic nodded lightly "—if it had been any other day he would've had me stay the whole evening to clean it up."

"Any other day?" Maria piped in, the parenthesis obvious in her tone.

"An ordinary one…if that exists anymore," Magic added in an undertone.

At home, Magic tried not to think about the incident during dinner; she didn't want to worry her parents, and she wasn't exactly the best at hiding things.

So, naturally, when Magic tried not to think about it, she thought about it even more. A frown formed on her face as she chewed her boiled potatoes.

Mr McFee's exhausted face mirrored hers. "Is anything up, dear?"

Magic's frown faded. *Goddamn reverse psychology*, she thought. She studied her father's face—it was the face of an overworked, middle-aged father. His much more prominent eye bags were slightly purple, his eyes wearily watery. The chocolate brown locks of his hair stuck out in all directions, as if he had been electrocuted.

He was probably more tired than he looked, and Magic didn't want to add to that.

"Nope…just something at school." Magic tried to muster a smile.

"Oh, that's nice, dear." David McFee's head didn't seem to be at the table at that moment. Magic didn't bother—she knew what it was like to be mentally distracted.

The sun didn't dip down below the horizon until round seven that night; the days were getting longer now that the end of February was nearing. Magic didn't know how she felt about that. She could barely cope with the lengths of the days as it was.

As Magic slumped into bed, she couldn't resist; she had to think about the day's incident.

Who was that man? Why did he keep on showing up wherever she was? Was it a coincidence? Everything happens for a reason. Was he after *her*, or something else? *Somebody* else?

She remembered the book she had read on Magnus Harrow and the sorcerers. She tried to imagine what Vandalarukk would look like—he was a very powerful sorcerer, after all—according to the legend. She still wasn't sure if the book could be trusted as there was no author's name on the cover.

A sorcerer would be tall, towering, and fierce. They would have a fearless face and a mind you could never shift. An untwitchable sneer.

They would wear a long, intimidating cloak that blew in the wind, accentuating their bravery.

Their stand would be firm and stubborn. Determined and unmoving.

They would have jewels of all colours, shapes, and sizes. Silks and satins of all expenses. Maybe even a wizards' hat, for heaven's sake.

But most importantly: *every sorcerer bears his magical wooden staff.*

It looked as if Magic had figured out who that cloaked figure was.

Chapter Sixteen
A Strange Disappearance

"*Vandalarukk?*"

"Magic, how is that possible?"

"You could've just been seeing things!"

"It doesn't make sense."

"A *sorcerer stalking* you?"

"Guys, hear me out, OK!"

There had been outbursts from Chloe, Maria, Will, and Charlie at Magic's possible realisation. The noise had costed them a few anxious and dirty looks from across the field.

"Keep it down, guys, please!" Magic pleaded.

"You're crazy, Magic." Charlie proposed.

"Thank you, Charlie," Magic thanked him coolly.

"Rich coming from you, Charlie. And what if she's right?" Chloe interjected.

Charlie squinted at Chloe through narrowed eyes for a moment, and then threw his hands in the air with outrage. He was already tall enough, and now with the added height he towered over them.

"I'm sorry, I need a moment! This is just—" He sighed and strode over to their round birch bench, slumping onto the wood with a *thud*, elbows on the table and running his hands through his hair in frustration.

"Charlie, why are you so determined not to believe me?" Magic asked tentatively.

There was silence for a few moments, except for the twittering of birds in the distance, and the low chatter of students echoing throughout the field.

"It just doesn't make sense," he replied in a calm tone. "Where is the logic behind this?"

Magic thought for just a split second, and then her face twisted into a frown. "You see, I haven't got to that yet—but Lockwood is a very smart guy, and he wouldn't just put his trust in a story if her didn't absolutely think it was real and backed up by *evidence*," Magic added quickly at the crease between his eyebrows. "He's a historian, for God's sake, he's all about the evidence."

Charlie took this in for a few minutes. The girls and Will stared at him in silence, waiting with bated breath.

"OK," he finally said. "I'll believe you and Lockwood if I see it for myself."

"Are you calling Magic a liar?" Will fired at him.

"What—? Of course not!" Charlie looked shocked as to how Will could accuse him of such a thing. "It's just that…I'm also all about the evidence." He grinned.

The other four couldn't help but return it.

It had been a while since Charlie, Chloe, Maria, Will, and Magic had caught up with Tom because of his gradually increasing workload. Magic could imagine how hard it would be for a Year 11 student to keep up with everything, considering how much she was already struggling to stay on top of things in Year 10.

So, they were quite surprised to bump into him in the junior corridor on the way to their form room. He looked pretty much the same, carrying his usual chocolaty brown handbag, matching his hair and eyes, other than the dark purple circles pressed into the skin under his eyes.

"Tom, you look tired," Chloe said as they stopped in front of him. "Let's stand here, before we get run over." She gestured to the side of the corridor. Students were indeed filing in rapidly, the sound of their footsteps and continuous chatter ricocheting off the walls.

"Yeah. I need to get this essay in." He gestured to the exercise book in his hands. "How're you guys doing?"

"You should worry about yourself, Tom, we're fine. Get some sleep."

They bade him goodbye and watched him turn a corner before speaking again.

"Poor lad," said Charlie. He grimaced. "Year 11 looks like fun."

"Yes, it does. Now come on, before we're late," Maria urged.

During lunchtime, Magic couldn't quite focus on her friends' conversation. Four tables across the room, she was trying to examine each of the girls' faces, but she couldn't see clearly because they were huddled so closely together, far away from everybody else sharing their table. They looked frightened and overly observant, constantly looking over their shoulders as if expecting a monster to walk in that instant. With a small pang of realisation, Magic recognised them as Katie Harrow's clique of friends, the ones Katie had been conversing with on the day Magic had went to ask her about Magnus. Magic scanned the group for Katie, but she was nowhere to be found; the seat she usually took up was vacant.

"Hey, where's Katie?" Magic asked no one in particular, her eyes not leaving the girls' faces.

"She's probably ill or something. Why?" Maria asked, placing her bottle of water on the table and staring over Charlie's shoulder at the scene.

"Look at her friends," Magic whispered. "Don't they seem out of place? They're usually quite bubbly, and now they seem…off."

Chloe stared anxiously at Magic's face. "You're oddly watchful today," she deduced.

"Well, yeah…nothing's normal anymore. Everything just seems so odd to me now." Magic paused and thought for a second. "It's kind of exhausting."

Will looked over his shoulder at them. "It's probably nothing…but why do they look so scared?"

Maria looked stricken. "Will!" One of the girls caught his eye and he whipped back round.

"What?" he snarled.

"Don't stare at them!"

"Says you!"

"Guys, cut it out," Magic demanded in a monotone. She was too used to their feuding that she didn't bother getting worked up.

"If Katie's just ill, why do they look terrified out of their wits?" Will questioned.

"We don't know that she's ill," Maria replied swiftly.

"And we don't know that anything's wrong with her at all," snapped Charlie.

"Then why wouldn't she be in school if she's completely fine? I know her parents, they came over, remember? They don't seem like ones who'll just take her out of school for a biking trip…" Magic responded.

"At least we have History all afternoon." Chloe tried to lighten the mood, pulling her gaze from Katie's frightened friends. "Lockwood's a good lad. What're we doing again?"

"I don't know, we're supposed to be starting a new topic today," Maria replied.

Lockwood was a man who didn't think there was such a thing as arriving early to a class, so when the five of them turned up to the shabbily fitted black door with the bronze eagle knocker ten minutes before the lesson was due to begin and found it slammed shut, they hesitated.

"D'you think he's in there?" Charlie whispered anxiously.

But Magic had heard something. "Shh!"

She thought she would have a heart attack. She was caught up in this *again?*

"Listen, guys! There's someone in there!"

Indeed, there was a pair of muffled voices issuing from behind the door. One sounded dismissive, while the other furious. Magic pressed an ear to the door, begging herself not to make a sound and expose them. She beckoned to the others to come and listen, and they did the same.

"How could you let this happen?" Lockwood demanded. It sounded as if he was fighting explosive anger. Magic imagined a fire blazing in the heart of his eyes.

"What did you want me to do? *I cannot control him!*" Slay's voice responded in a dead but pleading tone. Magic's eyes widened at the others, who looked just as she felt.

Slay muttered something inaudible, and Lockwood laughed coldly. The sound was uncharacteristic; it sent chills down her spine.

"Of course we can't involve law enforcement any further, Marcus." Lockwood's cold sneer issued in response. Magic had never heard him this way before. "What do you expect them to be able to do in this situation? Her parents already rung them late into the evening after the girl did not return." There was a long pause. Magic couldn't feel her face.

Finally, Lockwood spoke again, this time his tone more collected. "I told you before not to let this happen. Did you really think you could stay out of this and pretend it didn't? Do you really think the police will be able to track her down and rescue her? This is insanity!" Despite his tone starting collected, it gradually filled with the same fury. He spoke in a whisper. Magic had to really strain to catch every word he uttered. "She'll die, Marcus. He'll kill her. And you don't care." Another pause.

Magic hadn't realised that her breathing was adjusting to match Lockwood's mood; her chest was rising and falling rapidly, her ear numb from being pressed deeply into the wood. She looked at her friends. The colour had completely disappeared from their faces.

"They'll never find her, not unless they know how to get there," Lockwood finally spoke. "It's dangerous, but somebody has to—"

The school hallways were filled with a loud, ear-splitting ringing sound, signalling the end of lunch. As their classmates immediately appeared from round the corner, Magic quickly pulled her ear from the wood just in time for Slay to slip out of the room, his face hard and white, his eyes dead. He tried to avoid everybody's glance, darting quickly from the scene.

A dishevelled Lockwood then appeared in the dark doorway, his wavy brown hair slightly ruffled, and donned his usual corduroy ensemble. Despite having just been furious with Slay, his eyes remained focus and friendly. Magic had an uncomfortable feeling that Lockwood knew they hadn't just arrived seconds ago.

"Hello, everyone," he greeted the class in his usual smooth, friendly tone. "Come on in."

Magic went in first, anxiously making her way to her usual spot at the front. She tried to act normal as her friends took their seats on either side of her. Magic thought it was slightly obvious that they looked unusually shaken and hoped that Lockwood wouldn't pick up on it.

During the course of the lesson, Magic tried to remain focused, but she wasn't as up for the lesson as she had been before they had eavesdropped, maybe because she knew now that Lockwood was trying to hide something.

She stared at the clock. Had it only been five minutes? She figured she was going to be here for a while if time had decided it would pass by that slowly.

Again, Magic found her mind drifting off, out of the classroom, completely out of the school.

So, she was stuck once *again*. Who was this 'she' now? In *danger*? What the *hell* was going on? Everything seemed so shady and suspicious. Magic remembered how frustrating it had been when she was trying to figure out who that 'he' Lockwood and Slay had been referring to was, and how everything had clicked when she realised it was Vandalarukk. If only the bell hadn't rung, maybe Magic would've found out who this 'she' was, instead of having to discover herself.

But this time, Magic didn't have a head start—they had not mentioned much on this girl during their conversation, so Magic was having to walk into this completely blindly, not knowing where to start or who to ask.

She remembered Lockwood mentioning parents…so this girl must be young, then? Magic reckoned that if she didn't know who Vandalarukk was prior to hearing about him, then this girl wasn't likely to be anyone she knew.

One and a half hours left of the lesson…Magic was feeling hot, tired and irritable…One hour left…Why was she even getting worked up about the whole situation, anyway? Half an hour left…It technically wasn't any of her business, so she shouldn't really be worrying about it…Fifteen minutes…But how could someone not be intrigued when a *sorcerer* was possibly involved? Ten minutes…Although, didn't Magic technically *have* something to do with it? She had seen the same sorcerer the day before, after all…

Magic sprung up in shock as the bell rang and the noisy shuffling sound of scraping benches and backpacks being heaved filled the classroom. Just as Magic was about to leave, she could've sworn that Lockwood gave her a fleeting smile before she disappeared from the room.

"We're going about this whole thing the completely wrong way."

Charlie, Chloe, Maria, Will, and Magic had stumbled out of school, shoving past students who didn't have a care in the world, chatting away completely unbeknownst to all the chaos that was happening behind closed doors.

Once the five of them had left the building, they had thrown themselves at their round wooden bench and their brains had immediately sprang into action.

Charlie had just spoken, and he was rubbing his forehead, his face scrunched.

"What do you mean?" Magic responded, her own head throbbing.

"Why does this even matter to *us*? What has it got to do with any of us?" Charlie raised his head from his hands. He seemed to hesitate. "I mean—for all we know, it could be dangerous. Do you really want to get caught up in it all?"

"Says you!" Magic exclaimed in reply. Before she could carry on, Chloe cut her off.

"Oh—so all of a sudden what we've been saying all along makes complete sense and it's not 'a load of rubbish'?" She folded her arms, her lips pursed.

Charlie flushed. "Well, I guess I needed to see it again to make sure I wasn't imagining things," he replied defensively.

"Did you guys catch him dropping the 'she' again?" Will spoke up. "I mean, why do they have to keep using goddamn pronouns?"

"Guys, he knew we were listening," Magic muttered through clenched teeth. "I'm telling you he knew we were listening."

"How?" asked Maria.

"When I left…I don't know, he just kept looking at me as if he knew I knew something I shouldn't. It wasn't mean or anything, it just seemed like he knew. And the fact that they keep referring to people using pronouns. Funny how we always show up at the wrong time, don't you think? How we keep getting caught up in things like this I'll never know…"

"Right?" Maria grinned in response.

They laughed it off, and Magic ignored the edgy feeling in her stomach.

Maria had stalked off to ask Lockwood a question about their homework assignment, so the group left without her.

When Magic stepped over the threshold to her house, she heard the small murmur of a television screen coming from the living room. It sounded like her parents had arrived home early.

"Hello, love," Mr McFee greeted her distractedly, not taking his eyes off the flat screen. He lay across the sofa, his head rested on the arm, legs crossed. "How was school? Getting along with the teachers?"

"What—oh yeah," she replied. "Where's Mum?"

Mr McFee yawned. "In the kitchen, as usual." His mouth twitched upwards slightly.

"Yes, indeed." Lauren McFee appeared in the doorway, donning her orange flowery apron, a large, round silver tray piled with sandwiches in one hand, a platter of juices in the other. As she strode over and placed the two trays on the coffee table, she asked, "How was school, dear?"

"Good."

Mr McFee smiled in delight and immediately hopped up to grab a sandwich. Magic hadn't realised how hungry she had been, so was glad when she munched on her own.

When Magic's father seemed relieved of hunger, he spoke up as Mrs McFee squashed herself in next to Magic.

"Your uncle's flying in from America next week," David McFee announced casually, and he smiled at his wife. "Your brother's always full of surprises."

Magic perked up. "Uncle—Mickey?" Magic hadn't seen her uncle in a while—he'd always be busy with work and tied up in his schedule. She was very fond of him, however, and excitement began building up inside her, though she was too tired to show it.

Magic snapped her head towards her mother, who was glowing. "How long's he staying?"

"Told you she'd get excited," Mr McFee mumbled round a mouthful of sandwich.

"Two or three days, he's barely carved them out. You know how busy your uncle is."

Mickey McFee was a hedge fund manager on Wall Street, New York. When Magic's grandparents had separated long before she was born, Mickey had gone to live with his father in Los Angeles, while Lauren had remained in England. When Mickey had finished his education, he moved to New York because of the 'better career opportunities'. He was a very charismatic and caring man, which is why Magic was very fond of him.

Magic gulped down her sandwich in happy silence as she listened in on her parents' conversation. They were so endorsed that they didn't notice her slide out of the room until she was climbing the stairs.

"Goodnight, dear!" they called from below.

Chapter Seventeen
Intruder

Magic jumped on the balls of her feet as the front doorbell rang. She bolted to the door before anybody else could, a grin breaking across her face.

She had barely opened her mouth before her head was pulled between two arms and she was lifted off her feet, a strong, attractive perfume filling her nostrils.

"Hello," a charming voice spoke into her ear. "Didn't think you'd be this excited now that you're older."

"Of course I'm excited!"

The older brother of Lauren McFee was a spitting of her—the same dazzling blue eyes glimmered down at Magic as he set her back down. His beautiful grin broke across his face at Magic's smile. His chestnut brown hair was parted to the side and swept back neatly, looking very professional. He sported his usual black suit that he wore to work.

Magic adored this man very much because he was her number one supporter—through thick and thin, even though he wasn't always physically there, she knew there was always a passionate fire burning for her deep in his heart.

"You're starting to look the exact mirror reflection of him, Magic." David McFee appeared, and he clapped his brother-in-law on the back. "Look at you, almost twinning, eh?"

"She just needs a briefcase and suit, and we'll be identical." Mickey chuckled, patting David's back. "Oh, and a fine Californian accent," he added with a wink. Magic laughed, and he gave her a squeeze.

"Go upstairs and get ready," he whispered in her ear. Magic frowned at him questioningly. He straightened up and smiled. "Let's go on a little trip. I haven't seen you in a while." He winked at her once more.

Magic knew her uncle. She nodded at him suspiciously, but smiled nevertheless. "'Kay."

Ten minutes later, Magic clambered down the stairs in a pair of jeans and a jumper. Mickey was waiting in the corridor, his hands clasped in front of him. He had abandoned the blazer of his suit, wearing only his long-sleeve white button-up with his black trousers. He was quietly humming to himself.

"Ready to go?" he asked as she stepped onto the landing.

Magic leaned out of the car window, the cool midday wind slapping her hair back behind her. The houses standing side by side were a colourful blur in Magic's vision; her eyes welled with cool tears as the force of the wind pulled her mouth into an awkward smile. The rumbling sound of the cars was low and smooth, and oddly, soothing.

Mickey chuckled as Magic pulled her head back into the car and rolled the window up. She smoothed her hair out and looked over at her uncle, who was humming cheerfully to Radiohead's *Talk Show Host*.

"You like Radiohead?" she asked surprisedly.

"'Course I do…you sound shocked, you don't like them?"

"No, I think they're great. One of my favourites, actually."

Mickey grinned. "That's my girl. You've got taste." He gently tapped against the steering wheel to the beat of the song.

Magic allowed her ears to tune out and absorb the music. She sang the words along with the song in her head.

Gloating behind the curtains for the buzz…
The buzz…
The buzz…

Magic got a little carried away singing along mentally…and hadn't realised she'd started singing aloud.

"*With a gun and a bag of cigarettes, and nothing…*"

"Nice voice, kid." Mickey lowered the volume so he could hear her voice. "Carry on." He smirked. Magic rolled her eyes, but sang, nevertheless.

Mickey and Magic strode round the gorgeous flowerbeds, passing by excited and quite chatty visitors. The golden orb suspended in the sky that was the sun shone thick rays that glazed the green grass and brightened the flower petals, but didn't warm the chilly atmosphere, however. Children were gathered round the glistening, smooth surface of the lake, happily throwing bread to a small flock of ducks near the lake's shore.

They strode down the murky yellow pathway, enjoying the relaxing warmth of the sun's rays seeping through their skin.

"So, how's the high school life been serving you, kiddo? You doing good?" Mickey asked Magic.

143

Magic gently brushed her fingers over the crispy leaves of nearby bushes as they ambled past them.

"Yeah...to some extent." Magic forced a laugh. Whoops—she forgot how good Mickey was at reading people.

"OK, tell me," he demanded immediately. "Who is it that's bothering you?" Mickey raised an eyebrow as he slid his hands into his pockets.

Magic sighed. "Really, it's fine—"

"Magic, I insist."

She sighed again.

"There's this—"

"Kid?"

"Well, there is, but they're not as annoying as my English teacher."

"Name?"

"Slay. Marcus Slay I think it was."

"*Slay.* That's ironic."

"I know."

"What'd he do?"

Magic huffed. "He just has something against me. It's like he's trying to find excuses to pick on me."

"Ah, I see..." Mickey pondered this as he stepped aside to allow room for a lady to push her pram along the pathway. "D'you notice any particular pattern with the way he behaves?" he asked as he moved back onto the pathway.

Magic thought this over before answering immediately. "I don't think so. It seems to me he tries to be malicious at every chance he gets."

They entered a quieter part of the park, surrounded by trees that slightly drowned out the sound of the excited chatter, along with the happy rays of the sun. The atmosphere became much more tranquil, almost like they were in a completely different place.

The pathway became neater, and less dusty, and a fence with black, chipping paint cut off the pathway from the rest of the forest at the sides.

When they were deep enough where they wouldn't be overheard, Mickey leaned against the fence. Magic stood opposite him.

"What *is* his deal?" Magic murmured, mostly to herself.

"I'm sorry, honey." Mickey sighed, but then his expression became serious. "Magic, people like that usually are trying to get you off track. Stay in your own lane, and don't allow obstacles to cause traffic on the road you're driving on."

"But he's a bump *in* the road. I can't swerve him—well, I can, but I don't want to have to change paths to avoid him. I should be able to go my own way."

The gentle sound of twittering birds allowed Magic to dodge a space for a deep, meaningful silence to occur. She didn't want to have time to think on the matter.

"But why should a small bump in the road matter? It only lasts for seconds and then the road is smooth again," said Mickey, a small crease appearing at his forehead.

Magic tilted her head to the side as she pondered this. "I guess you're right."

Mickey chuckled.

"But whether he's in my way or not, he's just a bit—off..." Magic's voice trailed away.

"Hmm. In what sense?"

Magic huffed. "In alphabetical order, or order of importance?"

Mickey chuckled again, and Magic smiled a little.

"Whichever," replied Mickey.

"OK," began Magic. "Well, first of all, he looks like a serial killer. Second of all, he has weird, suspicious conversations with teachers about un—"

"Wait a minute," Mickey interrupted quickly. "You've been eavesdropping?"

"Don't act like you didn't do it," Magic contradicted him.

"No, I'm not penalising you." Mickey chuckled. "You know I used to do it all the time. Just don't get yourself into trouble, kid."

Magic raised an eyebrow at him.

"Sorry. Carry on."

Magic thought for a second and then carried on. "Oh yeah, and he always looks at me and my friends like the devil...oh! *And* he's recently been torturing Katie into giving him some information about—"

Magic cut herself off. How much should she reveal to her uncle? She did trust him, after all, but how much of what she knew would be safe to spread?

She decided she'd only tell him if he questioned it.

"—about something. She always looks frightened every time he's in the room, so she always scatters before he gets the chance to call on her."

"Oh, my," said Mickey, shaking his head, and then pausing. "That's not normal at all."

"I know. Katie hasn't been in for a few days."

"Oh. Let's hope she's OK, then."

"Yes."

Mickey thought for a moment. "Do you get on with your other teachers fine?"

145

"Yeah, they're all great, except for *him*."

"It's alright, hun, relax. Don't stress too much about it."

Mickey lifted Magic's chin up with his finger so she had to meet his eyes.

"It'll all be alright. I promise." he said quietly. His blue eyes were burning so fiercely it was hard not to believe him.

Magic plastered a smile on her face. "Sure."

"That's my girl." Mickey smiled, and he hugged his niece.

When the sun began to shine a dim yellow rather than piercing white, indicating that sunset was close by, they headed home.

As she stepped over the threshold of her house, Magic was surprised to find all the lights off.

She flipped them on with a *click*. Magic had assumed her parents would be here when she returned. She frowned in confusion.

"Where're my parents?" Magic turned and asked Mickey. The car keys in his hand clattered and clinked against the table near the door as he set them down, and began taking off his jacket.

"I'm sure they'll be here soon. Probably took the chance to go out…I don't know, though, let's see," replied Mickey, adjusting the cuffs on one of his sleeves.

"It's awfully quiet. I'm used to the television being on all the time," whispered Magic. She couldn't explain why a slight sense of fear randomly began to build up in her. She shook herself out and ignored the feeling.

"Don't worry, I'll call them. Go and change, I'll be down here. We'll probably order food or something." He winked at her. Magic smiled, but still felt uneasy.

As she climbed the stairs, she heard the faint murmuring of Mickey on the phone. Her parents had apparently left to look at new furniture to replace some in the living room, from what she could hear.

Magic didn't descend immediately once changed. She stared out the window, not entirely sure why she felt so blank, almost exhausted. It was a strange feeling, and she was unsure how to deal with it. The sky outside was a deep purple now, but the white flecks that were stars still hadn't appeared yet. She had the strange desire to grab a can of white paint and spray it across the sky, just so she could admire the twinkle of the stars.

Her eyes flicked towards the book on the Diamond of Dominion, where it lay open face-down on her desk.

She was about to go and reach for it to take with her downstairs, before she heard it.

There was a faint clacking sound against her window. The sound would come irregularly, every couple of seconds. It sounded as if rocks were being thrown against it.

Another *clack*. Though this one was more like a *clunk*. It was much deeper, meaning the objects being thrown at her window were much larger than before.

Magic backed away immediately, startled at the random occurrence of this strange sound. She moved way back, as far away from the window as she could, her back flat against the wall opposite.

Suddenly, the window began to quiver in place. Magic's eyes widened with confusion and then paralysing fear as the window slowly began to move upward. She took a sharp intake of breath as a black gloved hand reached under the window's pane and heaved it upward.

Whenever Magic watched crime films, this would be the moment where she would blame the characters for not running away. But, now, when she was faced with the situation in reality, she finally understood why those characters had just stood there, paralysed.

The window slid open with a *whoosh*. Another gloved hand reached over the windowsill, heaving its owner's body upwards.

Magic flinched as a person clambered into her room, pulling one leg over the windowsill, and then the other, before they stumbled onto the ground.

Magic stood there, splayed like a starfish across her bedroom wall, utterly petrified with shock, her expression horror-struck.

The figure in her room was dressed completely in black—she assumed it was a man, from the way he was built. He wore all black—shoes, trousers, and a zip-up jacket.

Magic began questioning why she was still standing there instead of running out of the room and calling for help as the man stood up. There was a woollen cloth covering his face, almost like a mask, and she could barely make out his features.

Her heart was drumming frantically against her chest, as if it knew that there was something very wrong about the situation. Magic felt her organs plummet down through the bedroom floor. She had to remind herself to keep breathing as the figure finally stood up…and pulled off his mask.

Magic felt like her face had fallen off.

"*Lockwood?*"

Her face contorted in horror and shock in ways she never knew it could. Part of her was relieved that it wasn't somebody dangerous, but part of her was in a state of near stupor.

Lockwood mustered a smile, as if he hadn't just broken into Magic's room in a way that made him seem like his intentions were far from innocent. His eyes were tired, and his hair slightly ruffled, but his gaze was focused.

"Hello, Magic. I see I gave you quite a scare there," he said casually, holding the black mask at his side.

"I—but—what—why—just—" Magic spluttered, bewildered beyond description.

She took a deep breath to give herself time to process the situation and then released her grip on the wall.

First, she had to address the terrifying entrance.

"We have a door, you know," she said, finally able to form a sentence, in a tone as calm as she could make it.

Lockwood looked slightly embarrassed. "Yes, well, I didn't know if the door was locked, and I didn't want to force at it just in case—"

Magic's head snapped round as her door clicked open, and Mickey stood in the doorway. He was just going off the phone with someone.

"Hey, kid, I heard a noise from here, so I just wanted to make sure—"

And then, he saw Lockwood.

Magic held her breath. She knew the situation looked incredibly odd out of context, and she couldn't even explain it herself.

Mickey's gaze completely faltered, to be replaced with one of utter blow, exactly like Magic felt. The phone slipped out of his hands and landed with a thud on the ground.

"What in seven shades of *hell* are you doing here?"

Magic thought it impossible to feel any more shocked and confused, so what happened next left her at exploding point.

Mickey's face broke into an open-mouthed smile, and he extended his arms out before walking over towards Lockwood, who grinned and clapped him on the back. Lockwood patted him gently in return.

Magic watched, sure that the muscles in her face were completely strained to tearing point at how shocked her expression was.

The two men laughed as they greeted each other like brothers.

Magic couldn't stand it anymore.

"OK, OK, OK, *hold* up," she interrupted them, holding her hands up, not a care whether she seemed overthrowing or not. "*How* in the *name* of *all* of *hell* do you know him?" she addressed her uncle, whose smile slipped slightly.

"We were friends at school! Hold on—" His smile completely dropped off his face now. "How do *you* know him?" he fired.

"He's my History teacher!" Magic paused, allowing for Mickey's face to morph into realisation and for her thoughts to regroup. "OH…oh, oh, oh…yeah! Dad *told* me he was friends with you—" she turned to Lockwood now, who was smiling "—but he never mentioned *you* being friends with him too!" She turned back to Mickey. Her eyes just flickered between her uncle and teacher.

"I have so many questions," Magic whispered to herself.

"Ask away," said Lockwood, his expression clearing. He suddenly looked worried.

"What're you doing here?" Magic tried to keep her voice collected.

"Ah, OK. You might want to sit down, Magic. You too, Mickey," said Lockwood. His expression looked sceptical.

"This is crazy," Magic whispered to herself as she slumped into her desk chair. Mickey lightly took a seat on Magic's bed. Lockwood gently shut the door and leaned against it, before unzipping his oversized black jacket and removing it, revealing a long-sleeved button up shirt.

"Suited up, I see," Mickey teased.

"Mickey, shush for a second," Magic snapped. She didn't even care that she was being rude and, apparently, nor did Mickey. "OK, Lockwood, explain."

Lockwood sighed, and looked almost unsure. "Magic, you don't need much of an introduction, as you seem to have figured out most of the situation yourself."

"Elaborate." Magic's breathing picked up. She just wanted to make sure they were referring to the same thing before she began to speak freely.

"You overheard Mr Slay and I talking about the Diamond of Dominion? Don't look so guilty, Magic, it's alright." Lockwood chuckled. "I knew you were there as soon as you arrived. I only stood in your way to make sure Slay would not notice you there."

"Oh." Magic bit her lip. "Right."

"I also notice that you found the book?" Lockwood asked, jutting his head towards the thick book on Magic's desk.

"Uh—yeah," Magic stammered. "What was it doing in the library?"

"Ah, I must've misplaced it…but no worries, the truth would come out soon enough."

"So what's going on?" Magic urged impatiently.

"I think it best that I get to the point. You see—" he hesitated for a few seconds. "Katie Harrow has been snatched by him."

Magic's heart leaped. "*What?* Snatched by who, exactly?"

Mr Lockwood swallowed, and looked to the ceiling, crossing his arms. "Vandalarukk."

Every cell in Magic's body ignited in flames of anger, fear, and utter terror. A tunnel grew in her vision, and the world round her blackened for a second. Her lungs contracted and restricted her breathing, and her mind plummeted through a dark abyss.

How could this have happened? Why? When? Magic had so many questions that they collided in her head. She suddenly couldn't breathe, and the sound of her own brain buzzing pulled her back out of the tunnel.

"How?" Magic asked in a strained whisper. "Why?"

"Shouldn't that be obvious? Her grandfather was the last known person to possess it, and it hasn't been seen since. He's coercing her into spilling information."

"That's awful," is all Magic could bring herself to say. She brought a trembling hand to her face, and then dropped it, unsure of what to do.

"Where's he keeping her?" she asked after a few minutes, finding her voice. Her throat was raw, almost charred. She didn't want to even think about what Katie must be going through now—she swallowed that creeping feeling of despair down, and listened in.

"That's what we need to find out," Lockwood replied.

Magic just remembered her uncle was in the room. He hadn't said a word through all of this, just listened in, horror-struck.

Of course he'd be confused, thought Magic. He had no idea what they were talking about, and it all seemed like a made-up fairy tale, or complete nonsense, from an outside perspective. There was no way to connect the dots.

"But do we know she's alive?" Mickey asked, speaking for the first time. "You know what he's capable of, Remy."

"Wait, what?" Magic was suddenly confused—Mickey had just joined the conversation, when *he* was the one who was supposed to be confused. "You know about all of this?" She turned to her uncle.

"Yes, Remy's been filling me in weekly," he informed her.

"This—is—crazy!" Magic uttered for the umpteenth time that day.

"But that doesn't explain why you're here." Mickey frowned, turning to Lockwood.

"Isn't that obvious? We've got to rescue her!" cried Magic.

Lockwood chuckled. "Your niece is way ahead of you, Mick. Yes, we've got to save her."

"But how? Where's he keeping her?" asked Magic anxiously. She had one more thought. "And why me?"

"That will unravel in due course. However, I'll answer your first two questions.

"The first—we'll have to go to Pyrithia—"

"To *where*?" exclaimed Magic.

"Magic, listen, and then ask questions," Mickey urged. "We don't have much time."

Magic nodded and then 'zipped' up her mouth, locked it and threw the key away.

"It's the name of the kingdom Vandalarukk's hidden himself in," Lockwood answered her question.

"Ah."

"How're we getting to Pyrithia's kingdom, though? I've heard it's extremely hard to track," enquired Mickey. Although confused, Magic tried to absorb as much sense from this part of the conversation as possible.

"It *is* very difficult to track, but I think I've managed to nail it down," replied Lockwood, nodding. "It's taken months, though. The most difficult part of this whole operation is transportation."

"Ah, of course," Mickey agreed.

"What do you mean? It can't be that far away," interjected Magic.

"Ah, but you see Magic, I'm not necessarily referring to the distance we have to travel, but rather the *way* we'll be travelling."

"Right…and how are we planning to travel?" Magic asked, slightly bemused.

"That part is—a little interesting."

"But extremely cool." Mickey grinned. "Not like anything you've ever seen."

Lockwood grinned, then rolled his eyes. "You act like you know how it feels."

"Know how *what* feels?" Magic asked impatiently. She was frustrated at their lack of explanation, and wished they'd explain without her having to press them to.

"Teleportation."

Chapter Eighteen
Portal

Magic found the word didn't sink in immediately.

"I'm sorry?"

"Teleportation, Magic," Lockwood repeated.

Her jaw dropped.

"You're bluffing."

Lockwood smiled. "No, I'm not."

"This is insane."

"I know."

"There's just no way."

"Yes. There is."

"Tele—but *how?*"

"It's…complicated."

"I'd be surprised if it wasn't," murmured Magic.

There was a short pause.

"So how does it work?" Magic asked curiously.

"Well, you see, it would be easier for him to *show* you rather than spend so long explaining it to you," said Mickey slowly, getting up and heading towards the door. "Did you bring it?"

"'Course I did," replied Lockwood, following him.

Magic didn't even complain about her confusion; she just got up and followed them downstairs.

Mickey led them out onto the dark, grassy front porch. Magic came to an abrupt stop, expecting him to do the same, but when he continued round towards the back of the house, she frowned and followed him, the damp grass crunching beneath their feet.

"Alright, then," said Lockwood once they had walked all the way round to the back wall of the house, "no one should see us here."

He was right; it seemed unlikely that anyone was going to see the strange, unknown ordeal that was about to take place. The streets of Krington seemed as deserted as ever, a peaceful silence coating all the homes like blankets, and the evening was darker than usual. Even while knowing all this, Magic still felt nervous. When had the day come to an end? It seemed like just a few minutes ago she and her uncle were having a chat in the park…time flies like a bullet when you're nervous.

"Magic, I'll have to ask you not to scream," Lockwood cautioned hesitantly as he reached into his pocket.

"Oh, God," Magic whispered. "Is it that bad?"

"It's just not something you see every day…the kind of stuff you read about in story books," Mickey answered her.

Magic could feel her heart drumming frantically again, as if trying to escape her body. Her breathing quickened as Lockwood pulled out an oddly shaped, bulky sack from what she could see in the darkness. She thought she could see the shape of a rectangle pressed against the material. It looked like a box.

Magic watched as Lockwood and Mickey exchanged a fleeting look, before Mickey nodded, and Lockwood unravelled the sack, which dropped with a soft crackle onto the grass.

What it was, Magic didn't know. It looked like an ordinary rectangular-shaped box from her point of view, but she knew that its story wasn't so simple.

Lockwood knelt down and placed the object onto the ground, and that's when Magic allowed herself to gasp.

The object had barely made contact with the grass, before it split in two, duplicating itself, one half flying up in mid-air with a small *whoosh*ing sound, and placing itself on top of the other half with a deep *thud* that shook the ground. That block then split itself just like the previous had, duplicating, and flew up with the same *whoosh*, landing on top of the second block with a ground-shaking *thud*. Slowly and steadily, a tower was building itself.

After this repeated eight times, the blocks began building themselves horizontally for a few moments, and then downwards until it hit the ground with one final, rumbling *slam*.

The mysterious object had just built a rectangular archway all on its own, about two feet taller than Magic was. Magic's mind was frozen in astonishment; she could barely comprehend what was going on anymore. Her mouth had dried up from being open through the entire ordeal, and she didn't even realise.

Out of the corner of her eye, Magic could see Mickey and Lockwood turn their gaze towards her to catch her reaction, their curious eyes gleaming in the moonlight. She didn't take her eyes off the archway.

"What," Magic whispered shakily over her uneven breathing, "was that?"

Nobody answered her. Still not taking her eyes off the archway, Magic watched out of the tiniest corner of her eye. Lockwood dove back into his pocket and pulled a much smaller object which he held between his thumb and index finger. Magic finally turned to see what he was going to do. Lockwood took a hesitant step towards the archway, and threw the tiny object at it.

Magic yelled out in shock as the archway burst into bright purple flames that flickered with a loud, thundering sound.

Lockwood backed away slightly, and Magic mirrored him automatically. Her eyes widened as she stared at the blazing fire that engulfed the archway.

"OK, listen up," Lockwood called loudly over the roaring flames. "We're going to have to go through it."

"*WHAT?*" Magic yelled out in terror.

"Yes, you'll have to trust me, Magic, just trust me!"

"Alright, alright!"

"There's one thing I have to mention first—once each of us passes through, we might not end up all in the same place," Lockwood cautioned.

Magic didn't know her heart would be able to plummet more than it already had. Her blood ran cold, then turned to ice. Was she dreaming, or stuck in a nightmare? She had completely lost her grasp on reality.

"How do I find you guys if this happens?" Magic asked, panicking now.

Mickey walked right up to Magic and put both his hands on her shoulders. "It'll be alright, OK?" he assured her.

She shook her head stubbornly. "Why don't we just all go in together?" Magic asked Lockwood over Mickey's shoulder. Mickey turned round and waited for his response.

"I've never tried it with multiple people at once, it's too risky, God only knows how the portal will react," Lockwood called over the bellowing flames. "We have to go in one at a time, I'll go in first—"

The flames spit violently, and Lockwood's gaze flickered towards them anxiously. He spoke faster.

"We've got to hurry," he continued, yelling now. "It doesn't hurt, I promise, just walk straight in. I'll go first so you can see how to do it." Lockwood sighed. "Alright, I'll see you both soon. Mickey, let her go in after me."

And without any hesitation, Lockwood walked straight into the purple flames. Magic gasp and then squinted, expecting to see a horrible sight. However, Lockwood did not melt to death.

To her surprise, he continued walking after the flames engulfed him, but did not reappear on the other side—Magic could see straight through the transparent flames, and the area behind the portal was as deserted as ever.

"He's alright, don't worry," Mickey told Magic soothingly. "I promise you he's fine."

Magic gulped, swallowing back her panic. Her throat felt charred again.

"It's my turn now," she uttered, terrified.

"Yes, it is. Don't worry, alright? Magic." He grasped her shoulders tightly. "Don't worry. You won't feel anything. I promise. I'll be right there after you. Now go," he urged her. He bent down and kissed her on the forehead.

Magic nodded and approached the spitting flames. Surprisingly, there didn't seem to be any heat emanating from them; Magic expected herself to become drenched in sweat within seconds of stepping near the fire, but not one bead of sweat trickled down her forehead.

She held her breath, and, to avoid procrastination, ran headlong into the flames.

Had she not known the flames were there, Magic would have thought she had just run into a slightly colder room.

She stared down at her feet as the purple flames licked at her, but she couldn't feel anything. Not one ounce of pain or burning. She smiled in relief.

"Keep going!" she heard Mickey call from behind her, his voice distant.

She squinted as she slowly traipsed forwards, her subconscious expecting to walk straight through the archway and back out into the dark Krington evening and the damp night-time grass.

But she didn't.

Magic continued to walk, the crispy noise of grass beneath her feet vanishing. A wave of cold rushed over her, and then vanished as quickly as it came.

Magic took a sharp intake of breath as the cool feeling of the flames licking at her lifted as she walked out of them. The temperature was suddenly normal, similar to the one she had been experiencing seconds before in Krington.

The ground beneath her feet felt oddly bumpy.

She certainly had not just walked through the archway and back out onto the grassy ground of her backyard.

Magic was standing in the grandest forest she had ever lay her eyes on, surrounded by the most greenery she had ever seen in her life. The squint fell off her face, along with her jaw. Some of the trees must've been at least over a hundred feet tall, some of their barks thin and perfectly round, others more shapeless, jagged, and wide, moss creeping up their sides. Smaller saplings were scattered in between

155

these majestic trees, along with even smaller dazzling green bushes with delicate, thin leaves. The ground was scattered with murky brown twigs and discarded leaves, which is why it felt so odd to walk on at first.

The thing that shocked Magic the most about this scene was that the bright light of the sun pierced through the trees, falling in slanted rectangles across the forest floor.

Where was she? Hadn't it just been night time when she left Krington, or even England? She definitely was nowhere near home at the moment.

Although utterly confused, she couldn't deny that wherever she had landed, it was a beautiful place.

She caught the gentle sound of streaming and splashing water that her ears had not absorbed at first. It felt like an enchanted forest, one she would normally visit in her fantasies. Was she fantasising now? Dreaming? There was no way that this was real.

But it all *felt* real. It never felt this real in her dreams. Not like this.

Magic was so amazed that she almost forgot what she was supposed to be doing here. She needed to find Lockwood and Mickey. Fast.

Should she just call out?

It was oddly quiet. Where was the sound of the roaring flames?

She turned round a hundred and eighty degrees, expecting to see the portal she had just come through.

But there was nothing. Just the vast expanse of the forest, continuing out into the distance as if it hadn't just been disturbed by unusual purple fire. She stared out as far as she could, but all her eyes could make out was the green mistiness of the atmosphere, far, far away.

Magic pivoted round, the twigs crackling lightly beneath her feet, and took a deep breath. The sound of the distant water helped sooth her.

"OK," she told herself. She didn't have time to wonder where the portal had disappeared. She would assume it had evaporated.

"Mickey!" Magic called out over the sound of the splashing water. "MICKEY! LOCKWOOD!"

No response.

Magic began trampling through the bushes and murky underbrush, calling out eagerly. "LOCKWOOD! MICKEY! LOCKWOOD!"

She topped suddenly. The trees were thinning, and the atmosphere became brighter. She was reaching the edge of the forest.

Magic continued stumbling through the underbrush, until she walked right out of it.

Her breath was knocked out of her at the sight that followed.

The sun's dazzling rays fell over the most beautiful scenery she had ever seen. It completely blew all the fantasy worlds she'd seen in her dreams, fantasies, and movies out of the water.

She was standing up on a high cliff covered in brilliant green grass and flecks of yellow and white that were daisies—a cool breeze blew lightly at her hair, which billowed gracefully behind her shoulders, and whipped the grass gently.

The splashing sound of the water grew significantly louder. Magic walked carefully towards the edge of the cliff, as close as she could without falling off, and her insides churned as she looked down a four-hundred-foot drop, water rippling off the part of the cliff to her left, and falling gracefully, almost in slow motion, before splashing down into the crystal blue pool of water below, the bright white caps dissolving into a series of tiny bubbles. The bank surrounding it was glazed in lush greenery and more beautiful daisies, the rest of the forest surrounding it.

Magic looked up at the tops of all the trees below; she was so high up that she was level with some of the grand leaves at the top, which gleamed in the sunlight. She stared into the distance to try and see where the forest ended, but just couldn't find it. The green went on and on and on.

The scene was slightly thrilling and did well to relax Magic a little. Now that she had made it out of that mysterious portal safely, she needed to find the others…and didn't anticipate that to be easy at all.

"MICKEY!" she began to call out. "LOCKWOOD!" she called in the opposite direction, belting at the top of her lungs.

They can't have gone too far, she thought. But if they had, how was she supposed to find them? The forest was insanely massive! They could be anywhere.

Magic's relaxed mood was short lived, and she immediately began to panic again.

"MICK—" she cut off.

"Magic!"

A voice called out her name, but it was extremely distant, and barely audible.

"MICKEY!" Magic called; she recognised her uncle's voice at once. "KEEP MAKING NOISE, MICKEY!"

"There's no need Magic, I can see you, I'm over here!"

Magic paused. "What—?"

She turned round frantically, trying to locate her uncle, but he was nowhere to be found. His voice had been less distant and muffled the last time he had spoken. Had he landed in the forest, just like Magic had?

A sudden rustling from the trees had Magic whipping round in fright. *Now* there was a tiny bead of sweat trickling down her forehead.

Her shoulders released the tension they were holding when her uncle stumbled out of the thick trees, looking slightly battered but otherwise perfectly fine. He grinned broadly as he extended his arms out and Magic ran into them.

"You alright?" he asked, dusting her off. "God, you did amazing."

"What—? I didn't do anything," replied Magic quickly.

"Yes, you did. I thought you were terrified, look at you!" he laughed. "Fit as a fickle."

"Right."

He stared out across the horizon, placing his hands on his hips. "Have you seen any sign of Lockwood yet?" he sighed. He squinted slightly in the sunlight as he scanned the scenery. He noticed the waterfall and he immediately looked shocked.

"What?" Magic asked suddenly. "What is it?"

"We've found it," Mickey murmured, mostly to himself. "We—found it."

"Found what?" Magic urged.

"Pyrithia! This is the kingdom!"

"*Where?*"

"We're standing *on* it, Magic, it's inside the waterfall." He smiled open-mouthed, as if he had just won the lottery. "Oh, Remy'll be over the moon…"

Magic was sure she had left her heart in the forest. "I-*inside* it?" she whispered. "*Yes!*"

"What's even in there?" she asked. She stared down at the splashing and fizzing water below, and realised it didn't look so innocent and wonderful anymore.

"You'll see in a while, it can be quite magnificent… but first, we have to find Remy!" he sprang into action.

"OK, OK," said Magic, "do we just—call out to him?"

"Uh—right. Let's start with that, I don't want to have to split up just yet, until we absolutely need to, this forest is huge…"

They began calling out into the distance, from all angles on the cliff. Magic was slightly concerned; this approach would only work if Lockwood was anywhere close by. They weren't sure how far their calls would carry into the forest.

They were calling out and looking for him for almost fifteen minutes. Magic slumped down on her knees, and then squinted as she tried to see past all the trees in her peripheral vision, searching for any signs of rustling or disturbance. Nothing…yet.

Magic sighed just as Mickey called out once more. "Where could he be?"

"I don't know kid…" He looked slightly drained, but then his expression sprung back into life. "But that looks an awful lot like him."

Down on the bank below, Magic could just see a burst of tiny purple flames spring to life, and then a man with brown hair stumbled out of them. As Magic had assumed, as soon as he stepped out of them, the flames shrunk until they disappeared.

Lockwood looked confused for a few moments while staring out at the waterfall, but then he looked utterly delighted.

"Hey, guys! I'M DOWN H—!"

"WE KNOW!" called Mickey. "We're coming down!" He began rolling up his sleeves.

"Huh?" Magic frowned. "How're we coming down? The only way to—" Magic stopped, and so did Mickey. "No, Mickey, I can't jump!" she whispered, her eyes widening.

"Yes, you can! Look," he said. "Remember that time in the swimming pool? The birthday party you had when you were little?"

Magic dug through her exhausted brain and pulled out the memory. "Yes." She nodded.

"Do you remember how frightened you were to jump in? And you realised how easy it would've been if you had jumped in straight away? How relieved you were when you had done it, and found it so fun that you wanted to do it again? This is like that, now."

That made her feel significantly better, and her reassurance also seemed to relieve Mickey.

"OK."

Magic mirrored her uncle, rolling up her sleeves until they squeezed at the top of her arms. She looked at him briefly, his hair flickering in the wind.

"Alright, you ready?" he asked. Magic wanted to get this over with.

"I think so," she breathed.

"Alright, on the count of three. Count with me, Magic. One…"

"Two," Magic squealed.

"…three."

Magic felt the cool rush of wind flow through her clothing as she ran and leapt off the four-hundred-foot-cliff. Her hair was pulled upwards by the wind, along with her arms, and her eyes filled with cool tears, her eardrums full of the sound of splashing and rushing water. The whole forest was a green blur in her warped vision.

Magic had never swum in water with her eyes open before, so when she collided with the white water caps of the pool seconds later, she rammed her eyes shut instinctively as her body made contact with the cool surface and then fell three feet into the icy cold water. She began kicking blindly in an attempt to eventually break through the surface, but her body was starting to go numb with the cold, despite the fact that the sun was shining bright that day.

With a sudden sense of accomplishment, she briefly broke free through the surface, spitting and coughing, before another water cap crashed into her head, pulling her back under.

She kicked frantically down below, unsure of where she was going. She was starting to run out of energy, and feared that she eventually wouldn't be able to save herself.

She kicked and kicked at the waters. Her feet brushed against something—the ground! She must have been swimming towards the edge of the bank. She continued thrashing in that direction, until she was in shallow enough water that she could press both her feet into the ground, achieving crouch position, before pushing herself up and out of the water.

She shuddered in the cool breeze, as she shoved her sticky hair out of her eyes and blinked away the water clinging to her eyelashes. She stepped gently out of the water and onto the muddy riverbank; she was soaked from head to toe, and shivered lightly, but it didn't bother her at all. She had just jumped off a four-hundred-foot waterfall, for God's sake.

"Nice job, Magic. You've done a much better job than him." Lockwood chuckled as Magic stepped towards him. "Look, he's still swimming over here."

Magic laughed with relief at the sight of her uncle swimming over in a perfect breaststroke, before clambering onto the bank, ringing out his hair, and rubbing his eyes. He smiled broadly at Magic.

"Well done, kiddo!" he enthused. "Good job."

"Thanks." She grinned back. "So, what now?" Magic turned to Lockwood.

"Well, now that we're safely back together in one piece, I have to open the entrance to the kingdom," Lockwood replied slowly.

Magic sniffled expectantly. She was suddenly filled with a new sense of bravery. "And how are you going to do that? Mickey said it's in the waterfall, right?"

"Indeed it is," said Lockwood. "Just watch. Oh, and don't scream."

"Why would I? I've seen the worst of things."

"You think?"

Magic shivered a shiver that had nothing to do with her being cold. "What do you mean?"

"Just watch," Mickey whispered from behind her, putting his hands on her shoulders. Magic nodded distractedly.

Lockwood approached the edge of the bank, stepped into a small lunge, and stomped three times, so hardly that Magic could feel the ground vibrating.

Chapter Nineteen
Pyrithia's Hidden Kingdom

Not only did Magic's jaw drop in awe, but she felt as if her entire organ system was collapsing. Mickey's grip on her shoulders tightened.

The ribbon of the waterfall seemed immediately disturbed; the way it was flowing began to twist oddly outwards towards the sides—it was like the flow of water was splitting in two, opening like curtains, the two streams of water now flowing away from each other, and behind it, there should have been some jagged rocks...but there was nothing of the sort.

The waterfall had concealed a large spiral that twirled from top to bottom. It looked very random and out of place, as if it wasn't supposed to be there.

"Wow," was all Magic could muster.

"Woah, we're climbing all that?" Mickey sighed. "Oh well, we should better get going then. We've gotta get a little more wet, kid."

"Are we swimming across again?" Magic groaned. Her hair was sticking a little less to her back now, and her baby hairs were close to drying. She was still drenched, and was unsure as to whether she'd be able to carry the heavy weight of her clothes as she dragged herself through the water. "And *climbing*? What's at the top? How are we supposed to climb that?" Magic privately thought it would be fun, but she wasn't entirely sure what it was.

"They're stairs," Lockwood informed her.

"Ohh, I couldn't tell."

Lockwood led the way, trampling round the bank, the rushing water and crashing ice caps, until he reached the wall of the waterfall, followed by Magic, and finally Mickey trailing behind them. The large curtain of water was inches away from them. Magic was being squirted with miniscule drops of water every time water struck the pool.

"Alright, we've got to walk through," Lockwood told them. There was no introduction to this; Lockwood simply stepped through the strip of flowing water, across the corner of the clear pond, and vanished behind it.

"It's safe, come on!" Lockwood's voice echoed over the loud rushing of water.

Magic hopped across the pond, through the strip of water, closing her eyes momentarily, and landed on cool, flat rock. She landed in a crouch and then straightened herself. The water had smoothed her hair back over her face; more hair had plastered to her back once more, and so did her clothes. She was dripping tiny drops of water that left dark spatters on the brown floor. There wasn't much to say about this part of the place; there was simply a tall, towering spiral staircase spiralling upwards and upwards, the same colour as the floor. The effect of the water streaming across the open face of the area was quite calming. It was a tranquil place.

Lockwood's fringe of brown hair plastered to his forehead and tickled at his eyebrows; he flattened it across the top of his head just as Mickey stepped through the waterfall, his white clothes grey and dripping.

"We should start heading up here," Lockwood said, whipping his head back towards the staircase. "It's a long climb, but it'll give us time to prepare…anticipate what's up there."

Magic shivered with a mix of cold but also flourishing anxiety—she had not given this much thought; she had been too busy being mesmerised over the fact that this whole fantasy was really happening, even though she had gotten over the fact that she wasn't dreaming.

They began clambering up the stairs of cool rock. They had a long way to go, ergo had plenty of time to work out what they were going to do when they were up there.

Magic had zoned out of the conversation for the first few minutes, too busy wondering what the great height they were about to climb would look like from the very top.

"…she shouldn't be too far in, although if he's trapped her for questioning, I doubt she won't be. I think he thinks that she's the one who's able to retrieve the diamond, hopefully he hasn't forced her to do it yet," Lockwood was saying. "The consequences of that are…well you already know, extremely severe."

Although Magic hadn't been listening for the first half, she understood what they were talking about and an overwhelming sense of dread threatened to engulf her—if Katie had already been forced to try and retrieve the diamond, then there was no way that they would find her in good shape…

"Guys," Magic interrupted. The other two stopped abruptly. "Do you *know* where the diamond is?" Things began clicking in her brain. "Hold on…"

"Let's keep moving, then you can tell us what you're thinking." Lockwood smiled, and they carried on up the spiral.

If many had tried to retrieve the Diamond of Dominion in the past, and failed miserably, that means that it couldn't have travelled very far if people were killed on the spot almost every time…there was only one person who would be able to retrieve it without harm, after all, according to the legend.

"Where was the diamond kept? In the kingdom?" Magic asked, her feet starting to ache.

"Yes, according to legend," Lockwood answered with a strained voice from above; he had sped up to the flight above, climbing on top of the heads of Magic and Mickey.

"So could it have gone far?" Magic asked loudly, her voice echoing.

"We don't think it has, it should be here, in the kingdom," replied Lockwood.

Mickey hadn't said anything throughout the conversation. He was gasping for breath every few flights, clutching a stitch in his side; Magic guessed that the occupation of a hedge fund manager in New York never got very physical.

The sound of the rushing water began to quieten after a while. How long they had been climbing for, Magic didn't know. All she knew was that she could no longer feel her legs and felt like she was no longer controlling their movement. They felt so numb it was like they were holding their own, pulling along the rest of Magic's body wherever they desired. The movement of dragging one foot after the other became automatic and almost instinctive after a long while.

"Argh, at last!" Mickey cried.

Magic had been sleeping on her feet for the past God knew how long. So, when she reached the top, a wave of shock snapped her out of her slumber.

They were standing in an extremely high-ceilinged cave, almost as high as the ceiling of a church, and just as wide. There was two feet of space ahead of her, before the floor cut off and a large lake with an unseeable end started off. A wooden boat was tied to a short stake of wood, and Lockwood stood there, untying it.

Magic huffed, her chest rising and falling rapidly. The sudden pause in the motion of her feet made them feel like they were melting. She had never exerted so much energy in one day, and doubted it would end here.

While regrouping herself Magic suddenly realised something.

"How's—this—possible?" Magic huffed in between breaths.

"How's what possible?" Lockwood asked her, not taking his eyes off the tangle of rope in his hands.

"How can the ceiling be so high if we've reached the very top? There was so little space when we were looking in from the outside! The top of the staircase ended so close to the top of the waterfall, and yet—"

"This is no ordinary place, Magic," Lockwood reminded her, raising his eyebrows. "Haven't you already gathered that?"

"Yes, but—"

"Magic, look over there," Mickey cut across her.

At the end of the colossal lake was a small colourful glow. Magic wasn't sure what it was, but thought it would become apparent once they crossed the waters.

"Alright, Mickey, step in." Lockwood beckoned to him. The boat creaked as Mickey took a seat at the front. Magic carefully stepped in after him and sat in the middle row, and finally, Lockwood stepped in the back. Magic realised something else.

"Don't we need oars?" she asked, frowning.

"Oh, no, we won't be needing them," Lockwood answered from behind her. Magic looked at him over her shoulder, confused. He winked at her, before turning round and pushing against the ground behind them, which sent the boat shooting through the lake, the water rippling gently at the sides. Magic stared at the discarded rope and wooden stake almost longingly, before forcing herself to turn round and face the colorful glow at the other end. She had to keep focused on their mission. It was the most important thing right now.

The waters sloshed gently as the boat glided through the clear waters, nothing else apparent that was disturbing it. The glowing light at the end of the tunnel grew very slowly larger, but nothing she could see from the glow seemed to stand out or give Magic any idea as to what was to come.

"What're we rowing towards, exactly?" asked Magic. As the question left her lips, she remembered that they didn't *need* to row it, according to Lockwood. Magic suddenly realised that the boat hadn't slowed down one bit—it was going at the exact same speed as it had when Lockwood had set them off in the beginning.

"Where Katie's supposed to be…" replied Mickey, turning round to face her. "If we rescue her fast enough, though, we *could* find a way to try and transport the diamond to a safe place without hurting anybody, though that would be very risky…let's focus on saving your friend for now."

"No, I don't think we should go anywhere near the diamond as a means to transport it," Lockwood interjected. Mickey gave him a questioning look over Magic's shoulder. Magic turned round to face Lockwood. He had a serious look on his face. "The only reason I think we should even go *near* that thing is if we have any intention to destroy it, before it destroys us." Lockwood seemed to hesitate. "We aren't in school anymore, Mickey. This is all so serious."

Magic assessed her uncle's reaction; the first word that came to her mind when she saw his expression was 'flashbacks'. She shook herself, frowning at her randomness.

The boat continued to tear gently through the water, the rippling sounds soothing in that moment.

They were more than two thirds of the way through. Magic stared at her rippled reflection in the bumpy waters; she looked almost bald because of how wet her hair…still was? Not even her baby hairs had dried almost an hour after she had walked through the strip of water—they stuck to her just as stubbornly as they had when she had first made contact with the waters, but then again, as Lockwood had said, this was no ordinary place.

The boat jerked to a stop as it bumped into the smooth, grey floor, and the source of the glow finally became apparent.

At the end of the boat ride, they were met with a grand, semi-circular room, as wide as the lake, the floor of smooth, grey stone. There were four dark passageways, spaced evenly apart, with flaming torches fixed into the walls on either side. Although these wouldn't have been able to provide much light, the place glowed very oddly and much brighter than the torches could ever have made it.

Mickey stepped out of the boat, and then helped Magic out. Lockwood hopped out after them, and the boat was left discarded at the edge again.

Magic couldn't help but notice that the passageway on the far right was barred with a portcullis that looked almost impossible to break through; the bars were made of thick, dense metal. The rest of the passageways were doorless.

"That's where the diamond is," Magic uttered through gritted teeth, her fists clenched at her sides. The truth popped into her mind effortlessly; she was getting good at this.

"That's right," whispered Lockwood. Magic looked over at him; he had a very alert, almost panicked, look in his eyes, almost as if he was ready to spring if something pounced out of nowhere. Magic thought he looked just like how she felt. Mickey was in the same mode; he was in fighter stance, ready to strike at any blow coming his way.

"Keep on the lookout," Mickey warned them both. "Anything could happen."

"Where could she be?" asked Magic, her adrenaline beginning to spark. Her head throbbed and heart spluttered at the thought that anything, from anywhere, could pounce out at them at any time. It was a mythical, magical world, after all.

"I reckon she's down one of the passages," replied Lockwood, his voice tight. "Alright, everybody stay close together, and do not wonder off without notice."

Mickey and Magic nodded, and followed him as he advanced towards the first passageway on the left—Magic stared at the back of his head, wondering...

This was a very different man from the one who had picked fun at her and her friends during their History lessons, and told her to watch out for her attitude towards Slay. Now, he seemed more defensive, alert, worried, and serious, and instead of directing her *away* from danger, she was being directed towards it...the mere fact that he was her teacher completely flew out of her mind.

They were one foot from entering the passage, when it happened.

WHAM!

Magic got the shock of her life as she felt a strange force, like an invisible hand, pull her backwards so rapidly that the rest of the world was blurry for a moment. She was pulled all the way back to the very edge of the floor in mid-air, to a point where she was in danger of falling into the water. She hung there, suspended, her arms splayed, unable to move her limbs, the invisible force trapping her in its strong grip. Mickey and Lockwood were on either side of her, hung in that same unbreakable suspension, but she couldn't turn her head to make sure they were OK.

A red cushioned throne lined with gold metal fell to the ground with a loud SLAM out of thin air, and Magic realised with heart-stopping dread exactly who, or *what*, sat upon it.

A cloaked figure with a large, wide hood concealing its identity sat, slouched, on the throne, and in its hand, as tall as the throne itself...was a wooden staff.

Magic felt her lungs contract and her blood freeze, her chest tightening even more under the invisible force holding her hostage. She was horror-struck, to the point where she thought her entire body would crumble, and her heart once again was throbbing so hard that she thought it likely it would just burst through her chest. The breath was knocked out of her as the realisation dug into her like a thousand knives stabbing her all over her body—she felt cold. More than cold, actually. She was paralyzed.

This was the unexplainable cloaked figure she had been seeing between alleyways and round school.

It was no longer a figment of her imagination. This was real.

Her head screamed as she tried to control her breathing, her eyes drifting over the rest of the scene.

On either side of the throne, two other hooded figures sat motionless, kneeling down towards the throne as if it was an idol of worship. Their identity was also concealed, and the fear of more unknown crept up Magic's spine. She assumed that the person on the throne was their master, and they were kneeling out of respect.

The figure on the right was much smaller, built almost like a child, but she was definitely older than Magic was; Magic knew it was a girl not only because of the way she was built, but also because a foot of dead straight, reddish-brown hair protruded from under the hood, stopping right above her waist. There was not a single crease in it. She kneeled there, towards her master, her head down, and her hood as wide as his.

Magic couldn't gather much about the identity of the man that kneeled opposite her; nothing hung out of his hood or cloak. He was very mysterious.

Magic's gaze slowly diverted to the elephant in the room, the glowing, horrifying thing in the corner of her eye that she refused to look at, but couldn't help herself, her resistance already limited.

In the top left of the room, nearly hitting the ceiling, Katie Harrow lay suspended in a glowing orb that levitated way above their heads, splayed the same way as Magic was, her head pushed back so she was forced to look at the ceiling. Her hair swam round in the air as if she was in water.

Katie suddenly started thrashing and screaming but could not break free of the powerful orb that held her in place.

The figure on the throne made a petrifying growl of fury before slamming the end of the wooden staff he was carrying into the ground, which shook the whole cave vigorously, the thud echoing thunderously against the walls.

As soon as the staff had made contact with the ground, electric bolts, almost like lightning, struck within the orb, striking the thrashing Katie directly at her chest. She screamed a final blood-curdling scream before she fell silent.

The cells in Magic's skin shivered in place. She didn't have to be a whiz kid to know that this being was extremely dangerous. Very dangerous. And she came to realise in the back of her mind exactly who he was. She shuddered with fear, still held in place like a starfish.

Vandalarukk stood up dramatically, before slamming the end of the staff into the ground, the cave shaking once again.

As the staff collided with the ground, Magic felt the invisible binds holding her above the ground release her, and she tumbled to the ground, her knees buckling under the impact of the drop. Her face collided with the cool stone, and she felt a cut form at her temple, followed by a drop of hot liquid trickling down the side of her face.

She heard two more thuds echo on either side of her as Mickey and Lockwood each fell to the ground with a grunt.

Magic wiped away the blood with her sleeve, but it kept on coming. In the end, she left it as it was and checked her left—Lockwood was still on the ground. He threw her a serious and worried look before she turned to her right, where she found Mickey with a blank expression, not taking his eyes off the sorcerer. He had a small cut at his chin, but Magic could feel that her injury was worse. She felt at her forehead; her hair was sticky as the blood clumped to it, though it was still wet.

Magic tried to make her expression as menacing as possible as her stare penetrated Vandalarukk's hood, but all she could see was his pointed, grey chin. She hid her shiver well this time—she was getting good at this. She would not give him the satisfaction of getting to her.

"*You*," a snarl tore from under his hood. "*You* have been causing me great issues." Vandalarukk's voice could only be described as a growl. It ripped through his teeth like knives. His head tilted ever so slightly towards Lockwood. Magic's menacing expression slipped from her face for just a moment as she witnessed her History teacher snarl for the very first time ever. As soon as she digested his actions, the menacing look on her face reappeared. She would have to get used to his two personalities.

Vandalarukk cackled a blood-curdling laugh as he slammed his staff into the ground once more, and Magic's heart spluttered as Lockwood yelled in pain.

"You are the only *insignificant* thing standing between me, and the Diamond of Dominion, other than this *silly* little girl." Vandalarukk spat on the floor.

Another slam of the staff against the stone floor, and another serious of lightning bolts struck Katie.

"STOP THAT!" Magic yelled over Katie's screams before she could stop herself. Vandalarukk turned to face Magic (she could tell he was shocked at her response, even though his expression remained concealed by his hood) at the same time the hooded girl looked up, throwing back her hood.

As soon as Magic saw the young woman's face, it immediately hit her that she was not much older than Magic—in fact, she looked like she was round the age of eighteen, maybe nineteen. Her skin was a deep, clear russet-brown colour, complementing her dark locks well. Her expression was furious.

"You *dare* speak to the great sorcerer like that," she hissed.

"Enough, Aurora, do not acknowledge the girl," Vandalarukk interjected. "I will dispose of her in the right means."

"Yes, master," Aurora spoke to him like a puppy, her voice quite high-pitched and eager.

Magic gulped but managed to maintain her menacing expression as Aurora gave her a piercing glare. Magic simply stared back into her deep brown eyes, trying to scare her, though she knew it wouldn't do much.

Throughout this whole ordeal, the other mysterious, cloaked figure had not uttered a single thing or moved a slight inch.

"And you?" Vandalarukk whispered softly, turning to the figure to his right that was the only person in the room other than him whose identity had not yet been revealed. The figure trembled at Vandalarukk's feet, quivering in fear.

Another thundering SLAM indicated Vandalarukk's staff harassing the ground again, and the figure's hood slipped off.

Chapter Twenty
Slay Unmasked

Magic's menacing expression completely fell apart, to be replaced with one of utter shock and horror; she had completely abandoned the idea of looking menacing as her eyes widened with shock, and her jaw dropped to the floor. She felt the colour leave her face.

It was Slay.

"*You!*"

Marcus Slay's teeth chattered in a mix of fury and fear. His gaze was stabbing—his hair was still slick and pointy, but he had a subtle, battered look about him. He looked so pale he was almost translucent. Magic wondered if he was bound by that invisible force.

Although doused in fear, anger, and confusion, Magic was desperate for some questions to be answered. She wasn't sure how to come about that though. Should she just ask?

"Why have you been tailing me for so long?" Magic demanded, staring right at what she could see from Vandalarukk. In that moment, she felt very brave. She tried to make her voice sound as cold as possible.

"I was not tailing *you*, young Magic," Vandalarukk replied in that booming growl. "I was after this pathetic, silly girl you call a friend!"

He slammed the staff and the electric bolts struck Katie once more.

Magic could see the pain in Katie's face, the agony in her eyes. Magic suddenly had a thought. Her eyes flickered from the screaming Katie Harrow to the wooden staff in Vandalarukk's grey, clawed hand, and back again.

There was a hand-sized slot at the top of it, supposedly where the diamond was supposed to go. The power that staff possessed was already quite damaging, and Magic could only imagine, with a shudder, how dangerous it would become if Vandalarukk managed to retrieve the Diamond of Dominion.

However, if Magic somehow managed to destroy that staff, even if Vandalarukk managed to get a hold of the diamond, he would not be able to use it—so she wouldn't have to worry about transporting the diamond to a safer space—and it would probably kill him in the process, anyway.

Magic played along.

"And why were you tailing *her*?" Magic asked in a whisper, even though she knew what the answer would be. A plan was beginning to formulate in her head. She didn't think it very smart, but it was worth a try.

"It was vital that I extract all the information I need from her. Her stupid grandfather thought it smart to go get it himself, without a single thought of the consequences of his powerlessness. Such ignorance ended in his death." Vandalarukk ranted, his growl becoming harsher in his frustration. Magic wondered what his expression looked like, but she thought it better not to know. There was not a single hint of pity in his voice as Katie's face contorted in pain at the mention of her grandfather.

"That doesn't give you the right to attack a child," Lockwood whispered. He threw Magic a look full of understanding, and it seemed he had caught on to what she was planning to do. She had begun crawling forward without realising it.

Vandalarukk cackled maliciously, the booming sound ricocheting off the stone walls.

"Nothing stops Vandalarukk from reaching his true potential. I have no use for you anymore."

Vandalarukk paused, before lifting his head up slightly so that the bottom half of his grey face was exposed. His chin was so pointy Magic thought it could slice paper. His thin, ash-coloured lips stretched into a broad grin, revealing a set of dazzling, perfect white teeth. When he spoke next, his tone was excited.

"Rora, dispose of them."

Everything happened so fast that Magic reacted without processing anything.

Aurora leapt up, her black robes falling at her sides, and zoomed over, levitating an inch off the ground, in a blur towards them. She flicked her hand towards the side—

Magic was thrown across the room and slammed into the stone. As she slipped down the wall, she felt the searing throbbing of her head against her skull—the cut in her temple deepened and blood gushed out all over her head, clinging to her hair strands. Her body fell limp against the ground just as she heard a faraway voice yell, "MAGIC!" At the same time, a booming cackle echoed within the room, followed by more slams. The floor vibrated softly beneath Magic's body, and although her conscious was beginning to slip away, she knew something had blown up. Were the others OK?

Her vision clouded as she blinked back blood that trickled down her forehead and into her eyes. She was trembling, unable to speak or yell out. She assumed Aurora thought her dead.

Magic's eyelids began to droop but she knew she couldn't let herself slip away, not like this, not when they were so close to winning. They had made it this far. She would fight till the end.

Magic forced the heavy weight of her eyelids open. From the ground, through her warped vision, she could see Mickey trying to force Aurora's telekinetic abilities off of himself, but to no apparent avail, and the vague scene of Lockwood attempting to retrieve the staff form Vandalarukk in a deadly brawl.

This was Magic's chance. Everybody was distracted and thought her too weak to move. She needed to get up and help Lockwood…but one more injury, and she was sure she would be knocked completely unconscious, if not killed from loss of blood.

But she would fight till the end.

Magic adjusted herself into a sitting position. Her head spun and white sparks exploded in her vision. She felt sick, but the sounds of the multiple fights going on were overwhelming, and she knew she had to get there before something terrible happened to Lockwood or Mickey.

With all the strength she had left in her, Magic stood up, her legs trembling but her mind determined, and she advanced, as fast as her body would take her, towards Lockwood.

Aurora turned away from torturing Mickey and noticed Magic running back into the fight. With a snarl, she raised both her hands and, as if wiping a window, swiped them towards the wall once more. As Magic was launched into the air, Aurora smirked triumphantly and turned back round, resuming her fight with a horrified Lockwood.

This time, however, her aim was hindered; Magic flew towards the passageway closed off with the portcullis, and she realised in mid-air that this was the end. She was going to slam into the gate, and her body would shut off for good.

Magic scrunched up her face, the slam would come any second now—

The impact would kill her—

There was no way out—

A wave of shock and confusion engulfed Magic as she tried to understand why she was still able to consciously think.

Her face felt cold. She was lying on a smooth surface. The stone? She didn't understand. She was supposed to be dead.

173

Magic lifted her face from the floor...*was* she dead? The atmosphere was suddenly darker. The sounds of the battle were so distant and low that they were barely audible.

She was not dead *yet*. She was *dying*. Her conscious mind was just wearing away the last strings that were tied to reality...soon every sound and feeling would dissolve...

But nothing changed.

Magic was still able to hear the sounds just as clearly as she was able to a few seconds ago.

The atmosphere was darker, because she was laying in the middle of the passageway corridor.

Wait—

What?

The passageway corridor?

Magic's vision swam into focus. There, a few feet away from her, was the thick, metal portcullis, still closed as firmly as it had been before. Everything was the same.

Except that she was on the other side of it.

"What in hell—"

Magic got up, the feeling of the pain in her head completely flying out of her mind, and walked towards the portcullis until she was an inch away from it.

Had it opened to allow her to land safely, and then shut immediately after? Magic couldn't recall hearing any noise indicating any movement from it...though her mind was very clouded with the thoughts of her own death as she had flown through the air, so it may have just been that she hadn't paid attention well enough to hear it.

Magic reached out to push against the portcullis, testing its strength, when the unexplainable happened.

Her hand went straight through the bars, as if they were mere shadows.

She pulled her hand back quickly, and wanted to scream out until her lungs exploded, but she knew that if she did, Aurora would turn round and then *really* finish her off.

Magic was mesmerised...so she had flown straight through the gate, and landed in the cool, dark passageway...which she was sure led to the Diamond of Dominion.

The diamond.

If Magic wasn't going to destroy the staff, she was going to protect the diamond.

Without hesitation, she rolled up her sleeves and turn on her heal, and forced herself to march down the narrow, dim corridor.

Magic lifted a trembling hand to her head—it felt as sticky as drying honey. Stopping the most dangerous sorcerer on earth from becoming the most dangerous sorcerer in the universe was now her number one priority. It didn't even bother her that she would probably be killed within minutes of brushing her fingers against the gem. She had no time to wonder about strange phenomena now…she would wonder about the portcullis later…if there was a later. Magic forced herself to believe that if she was able to pass through it, then probably anybody could.

The further she walked down the corridor, the quieter and more distant the yelling, thudding, and cackling became.

As she walked down the dim passageway, she brushed her fingertips against the cool stone walls—it was so narrow in there that she could stretch out both arms and touch each wall comfortably with the tips of her fingers as she walked.

Magic was confused and slightly surprised when she found she didn't feel panicked or scared anymore. She simply felt nervous—nervous to finally see the diamond in person, so she'd finally be able to understand how powerful it truly was, even with the knowledge that it would most likely kill her…

After walking for a while, with a few odd curves in the pathway here and there, the sounds from the battle had completely disappeared. At the end of the passageway, however, there was an odd glow; not like the glow Magic had seen at the end of the lake while in the boat, but a different sort of glow—as she squinted to get a closer look, she could make out colours of purple, pink and green spilling out into the dark passageway.

Magic picked up the pace into a brisk jog—her heart began thumping so shockingly quickly that she could've sworn she heard the sound of her heartbeats echoing off the walls.

She was metres away from the doorless room, before she skidded to a halt in the glowing lights.

Chapter Twenty-One
Crystals

Magic stood there, motionless, and allowed the crashing beauty and mysteriousness of the room in front of her to consume her. She didn't think she had seen anything more beautiful in her life.

Purple, green, and pink crystals of different lengths, widths, and shapes stuck out of the walls and ceiling, pointing inwards, with the most blinding glow in existence that Magic could've been walking towards a colourful sun. They were extremely sharp and pointy, and covered every inch of the room except the floor that not one bit of the ceiling or floor was visible between them.

These crystals had a strange twinkle coming from them—the twinkling was making an odd sound, like the soft clinking of metal objects together. She felt exactly like she was walking into the crystallised side of an enlarged version of a half of a geode rock. It was hypnotising.

The thing within this room that Magic was sure wouldn't be found in a rock full of crystals, however, was a tall, silver support stand. It was so thin that it almost disappeared behind the twinkling light of the sharp crystals.

Magic's shocked expression slipped of her face, to be replaced with a frown of curiosity. She took a step into the room, then paused suddenly, expecting something to come out and attack her. But when nothing did, she advanced towards the stand.

As she got closer to the shining, silver support stand, the thing it was holding became more apparent. At just the mere glance of its fiery gleam, Magic's eyes filled with shocked, triumphant tears.

There, at the tip of the support stand, was a small, short cup.

And within it, a jagged, shapeless, hand-sized rock with the most beautiful, fiery gleam, with hints of crimson, orange and yellow that she had ever seen. It reminded her of a flaming piece of lava.

She was a foot away from the Diamond of Dominion. Should she just take it, and risk her life? Inevitably, the power of it would kill her, but something didn't seem right.

It had all been too easy. She had been able to walk straight through iron bars, down a passageway and into the sacred room where the most prized and sought-after object in the universe was being kept, and not get injured in the making? Surely an object so important and so dangerous would be kept in a better protected place…even the most powerful sorcerers had been killed trying to receive it, for God's sake! Yet here Magic stood, a normal, ordinary 15-year-old girl, inches away from it, completely unscathed and as healthy as a horse…

A bombardment of thoughts, realisations, worries, emotions, and ideas struck her like knives at her body. In that moment, she couldn't breathe. A tight feeling pulled at her chest, suffocating her organs and restricting her thinking. She had lost all sense of logic or reasoning as her organs sunk to the core of the earth, but she found that the cold feelings of dread she had been bottling up the entire day evaporated. The tears in her eyes shivered as a victorious smile broke across her face.

She was the most powerful being in the universe.

Without a single millisecond of hesitation, Magic reached out and clasped her fingers round the gem, and pulled it out of its support stand. She waited for a second to allow something to happen round her, but, as she had expected, nothing did.

However, as soon as her fingertips had brushed against it, she felt a warm, almost electric current flow through her veins, that suddenly empowered her. It simply glimmered in her hand, as if happy it had finally been taken out of its place without having to destroy someone.

The Diamond of Dominion felt warm in Magic's hand and fit right into her palm: it was meant for her to carry.

So, she had retrieved the diamond successfully without obtaining any new bruises, but what now?

Magic looked round her, unsure of what to do next. She definitely was not going to keep the diamond—what use did she have for it? She just had to get rid of it, or find a way to destroy it, or destroy the staff…or both. She was the only one that could without getting hurt.

And then she remembered the battle she had left a few minutes ago, and suddenly felt panicked. Were Mickey and Lockwood alright?

"*You!*"

A high-pitched voice screeched from behind Magic that shocked the life out of her. Magic whipped round, clutching the diamond firmly in her hand.

Aurora stood in the doorway to the crystal room, levitating a foot off the floor—no wonder Magic hadn't heard her arrive. Her dark hair, parted perfectly in the middle, hung dead straight down the front of her long, black robes. Her clear, copper skin gleamed in the colourful light of the twinkling crystals.

But Magic was not afraid. Aurora's telekinetic powers were no match for her.

Magic snarled at her. "What're you doing here? I wouldn't come in here if I were you," she hissed coldly. "You'd get yourself *hurt*." Not that Magic cared about her safety.

Aurora cackled coldly. "*Hurt?* Is that a threat, little one? Please! You are no match for Aurora Rirks' greatest powers! I'll finish you in *seconds*," she spat.

Magic's lips curled. "Are you sure about that?" And she stepped away from the support stand, revealing the empty cup at the top.

Aurora's face fell—she looked beyond horrified. She was afraid.

"Alright, if you say so," said Magic, a satisfied tone growing through each word she said. She held out the diamond towards Aurora.

Aurora immediately dropped to the ground, and backed away, petrified, her hands out in front of her. Her anxious eyes flickered rapidly from the empty cup at the top of the support stand to the fiery, glowing diamond in Magic's hand.

"How did you get that?" Aurora whispered, before locking her eyes on the diamond that sat peacefully in Magic's palm.

"What? You're scared of *this?*" Magic demanded, and shoved the diamond closer to Aurora's face; she flinched, and Magic forced a laugh. "I thought I was no match for you? Hmm..." Magic murmured in mock thought. "Oh, dear, I don't think your overlord will be very happy with you, will he?"

Aurora looked like somebody had slapped her. She was visibly trembling at this point.

"Oh, but I almost forgot, he has *nothing* against your powers! I don't think he'll be very happy when he hears you've said that, don't you think?" Magic continued. The warm, courageous feeling the diamond gave her coursed through her veins.

"I—don't twist my words—" Aurora spluttered, the colour slowly leaving her face.

Magic advanced slowly towards Aurora, the full power of the diamond pulsating through her—it didn't just feel warm, now. It felt hot. Burning.

Magic began breathing heavily—they were in the passageway now. Aurora leapt up into the air in fright, and levitated briskly towards the portcullis entrance.

Magic made it to the end of the passageway all too quickly, to find Aurora ramming the portcullis shut hastily behind her. It shuddered to the ground and the whole cave shook.

The diamond's current flowing through her was electric. She was unstoppable.

Everybody in the room froze where they were, staring in shock as Magic effortlessly walked through the portcullis as if it wasn't even there.

A small hum buzzed in Magic's head. A series of green electric bolts erupted on the tip of Magic's skin—every cell in her body vibrated. The green glow from the lighting crackling at her body reflected off the faces of Mickey, who was in crawling position on the ground, Lockwood, who stood up straight with a tear in his shirt, and Aurora, who just kept backing away in mid-air.

The entire kingdom glowed green.

Magic couldn't bring herself to be shocked or worried or anxious or even afraid at what was happening to her. This was a fantasy world, a world of magic, a world full of make-believe. Nothing could surprise her now.

Vandalarukk was levitating right below where Katie was suspended. He had his arms extended, carrying the staff in his right hand, and he looked like he was ready to pounce.

Magic's eyes lingered on the staff—there, at the top of the wood, was the slot where the diamond was supposed to go.

The green, electric glow that emanated from Magic was so blinding that she couldn't see anybody's faces—the emerald light spilled out all over the room.

Her gaze was set on the wooden staff. Although she couldn't see his expression, Magic knew that Vandalarukk was petrified. But she knew what she was going to do.

She would use the staff and the diamond to destroy the staff and the diamond.

The movement felt instinctive, almost natural—Magic extended her free hand up towards Vandalarukk. It was like the power of the diamond that was channelling through had completely taken over her.

As soon as Magic had lifted a finger, the wooden staff immediately began forcing itself out of Vandalarukk's thin, grey hand. It thrashed and thrashed in his hands, trying to break free of his grip. Terrified, Vandalarukk whipped his free hand round and clasped it round the wood of the staff with all his might—it shook vigorously before snapping free of his grip.

As soon as the staff had left Vandalarukk's fingers, the sorcerer crumpled to the ground in a bundle of black robes, his thin mouth open in a scream of rage, his sharp, white teeth bared.

Magic could not hear him over the fizzing sound of the electric bolts emanating from her body. The staff flew straight into her hand—she grasped it firmly and slowly raised the Diamond of Dominion to the slot at the top.

Magic's hand shivered as she fixed the diamond into the staff, and it clicked in triumphantly.

She could not hear anything but the deafening screeching of her green lightning or see anything behind its blinding green glow. With all her might, she grasped the staff between her two hands, trembling, as she lifted it up, over her head, and in one swift, clean motion, swung it down towards the ground.

Magic let out an ear-splitting scream as a strong, cold feeling tugged at her heart. She caught the room filling with blaring, furious white light before ramming her eyes shut with pain. She could feel nothing, hear nothing else but her screaming, her wailing—

She wasn't the only one screaming—

She could her a new booming, piercing, infuriated growl burst through her ears—

She was sure her head was about to split open—

She couldn't hold on any longer—

WHAM.

Magic crumpled to the ground.

Every ounce of her body was in pain. All she could hear was the odd drumming of her heart.

Strange. She thought she was dying. How disquieting.

Slowly, very slowly, the sounds of the chaos round her snuck back through her ears. The feeling returned to her fingertips, her arms, her legs. She could feel her limbs again. The empowering warmth had disappeared, to be replaced with an empty coldness.

Magic located her eyes and managed to lift them open just a few millimetres. How she still had strength to move even her eyelids, she didn't know.

The first thing she noticed was her hand, laying palm up just a bit away from her. She tried flexing her fingers; they moved willingly.

She looked over her hand, and, there, a few feet away from her, the staff lay strewn across the floor, the tops of it burned and blackened. And there, a few inches away from it, the two halves of the diamond lay shattered; Magic could just about see the jagged bumps where the two pieces fit together. Its colour had turned from fiery red and orange to a glossy, jet-black. It no longer glowed, and looked like all the life had been sucked out of it. The part of the ground Magic had struck looked impacted, too—there was a black shadow dented into the floor, where the diamond had collided, and then shattered.

As Magic's gaze darted past the disintegrated objects, she noticed that the orb Katie had been held in had vanished. Katie had dropped to the ground, trembling, and Lockwood was at her side in an instant.

"No, I'm fine, I'm fine, sir!" she insisted. Her voice seemed so far away and so distant that it was in danger of dissolving. Katie scanned the room anxiously and her eyes landed on Magic's body strewn across the floor.

"NO! Magic, oh, Magic!" she wailed.

"She'll be fine, Katie," Magic heard Lockwood reassuring her. *Was* she going to be fine? Magic wasn't entirely sure herself.

"Magic?" a voice whispered softly by her ear. Something smoothed hair out of her face. It was a warm touch—a hand.

"Mickey?" croaked Magic in a husky voice. Her throat felt charred again, but this time it was much more painful.

"Are you OK, honey? Where does it hurt?" Mickey crooned to her like a baby.

"I'm—fine," Magic breathed. Just when she thought she was getting better, she felt her consciousness slipping away.

When had her eyelids began to droop? The image of Lockwood bending over Katie, the throne, the passageways, the lake, all slipped out of sight…

And she fell into an abyss of darkness.

Chapter Twenty-Two
The Truth

And then—pain.

Magic McFee jerked in her slumber. She jerked again.

"Is she alright?" Remy Lockwood asked anxiously as Mickey McFee scrambled to Magic's side.

Lockwood knelt against the wall of Magic's bedroom, his arms crossed, while Mickey knelt at Magic's bedside.

Mickey frowned, concerned. "I don't know. She should be."

"She'll be alright."

And then Magic opened her eyes.

Her eyes stung, and then watered as she rammed them shut again.

And then it hit her.

It was morning.

It was morning, as in she had just woken up.

As in she had just left the world of a very strange dream.

As in nothing that had just happened in that waterfall seemed real now that she had left it.

But that was impossible. The dream had been too real to be just a dream.

The world was too blurry to look at at that moment. She was tired of looking at things that didn't make entire sense, or didn't tell a full story as soon as you laid eyes on them—messing with the unknown had proven quite dangerous for her, practically life-threatening.

All of a sudden, the pain in her body crashed over her like a tsunami. The sensation felt exactly like the heavy feeling she had felt when she was trying to swim out of the waterfall, but the water just kept crashing into her.

The portal, the purple fire, the wonderland, the waterfall, the staircase, the lake, the passageways, Vandalarukk, Aurora, Slay, Katie, the staff, the portcullis, the crystals, the diamond, the electric lightning, the pain, the pain, and the pain.

And then, the unpleasant feeling washed through Magic again. She tried frowning, but a searing pain leapt through her forehead—it felt almost caked. A bandage? Somebody had wrapped up her wounds.

No normal dream, or any dream at all, could injure her or cause her as great pain as she felt right now. Meaning that the events of a just couple of hours ago were no dream.

She winced as a pain in the right side of her hip announced itself, but she felt much too weak to readjust herself. Her bed felt warm and comfy—it was her safe space, and she would not do anything to disrupt it.

Her legs felt like empty hoses, and her arms had casually turned into spaghetti strands. Her head throbbed angrily, and she let out a low grunt.

"Magic? Magic!" Mickey whispered to her softly. "Are you OK?"

Magic forced herself to open her eyes, and blink back the stinging feeling that poked at them. The world came into focus. Mickey leaned over her, his expression anxious but controlled, and then her eyes travelled to the other side of the room, where she noticed Lockwood hunched against the wall.

Mickey smoothed some hair out of Magic's face. "How're you feeling?" he asked her calmly. "I patched up your injuries for you."

"Yeah…thanks. I'm OK," Magic croaked. Her voice was hush and rough, and her throat felt like it had been evaporated on the sun. She tried swallowing, but it only made it hurt more. "I'm better."

"That's good."

The pain in her throat triggered the unanswered questions of the night to instantaneously creep back into Magic's mind in such focus that the suddenness of it scared her. She suddenly felt a rush of strength, along with a million questions. So many things hadn't made the slightest bit of sense, and she almost crumpled over the overwhelming feeling of it all.

"Oh!" she cried out, scrambling as she sat up in bed. Her injuries burned like lava, but she ignored them.

"Jeez, kid, relax!" Mickey cried out. "You'll hurt yourself again!"

"Where did Slay go?" she blurted suddenly. "I never saw where he went? What happened to Katie? The diamond? *Oh!* Did you see me? I *glowed!* Mickey, I—"

Mickey pushed down on Magic's shoulders, pressing her into the bed stand.

"Deep breaths, kid," Mickey coached her. "We'll explain everything in a second, once you remember how to breathe again…and, yes, I saw you glow, your eyes looked terrifying."

"Yes, I—wait, what?"

Her *eyes* had glowed? That was probably why they were in such pain—

"My eyes—glowed?" Magic whispered hoarsely. "*What?*"

Mickey suddenly frowned in confusion. "You didn't know? They were bright. Green. Glowed like the sun. Looked like you were about to turn into an Avenger or something…don't look so worried, you looked great," Mickey added quickly.

Magic rolled her eyes as best she could without them stinging. "You think I'm worried about what I looked like, whilst ignoring the fact that that *is not normal?*"

Mickey chuckled. "You've been awake for five seconds and have already transfigured into a fireball." Lockwood smirked slightly at this. "Just relax."

A sudden thought popped into Magic's head, the worry sinking to the pit of her stomach. "Do Mum and Dad know about any of this?"

Mickey turned round nervously and exchanged looks with Lockwood. Magic eyed them suspiciously.

"What did you tell them?" Magic asked firmly to neither of them in particular.

Mickey cleared his throat. "Well," he began, "I told them that when I took you out yesterday, you tripped and fell on your head, so I brought you straight home and patched you up…they arrived only minutes after we got here. Had we been a tad late, we'd have had a lot more explaining to do."

"So…" Magic processed this thought. "They don't know—anything?" she asked slowly.

"We thought it best to keep it covered up," Lockwood interjected.

"I can see why," replied Magic. She tried to lighten the mood. "Mickey, you'd better watch out, they might not let you take me out again," she said with a grin.

They laughed. A pain squeezed at Magic's chest, but she ignored it again.

"Wait, Lockwood, how're you here? Aren't you supposed to be in school?" asked Magic. She couldn't bring herself to reflect her shock as she remembered that she, and Lockwood, were supposed to be in school. She had exhausted herself beyond imagination and was completely drained of energy.

"Slay is missing too. I've told them I'm not feeling well," Lockwood replied casually, shrugging his shoulders.

Magic laughed. "You can't do that! And speaking of Slay, did he just evaporate? I never saw him once I came back out of that passageway." Another question, along with a million others, popped into her mind at that moment, but she bit them back for now.

"He fled as soon as he saw that you had been able to walk through that gate, or passageway or whatever," Mickey responded. He scrunched up his face, disgusted. "He immediately knew it was you."

"That could take the diamond?" Magic asked. Another question formed in her mind. If she could ask them all at the same time, she would.

"About that, Magic," Lockwood intervened. "I have to commend you on your bravery. It was a big risk to go and handle an object of such danger without knowing what the outcome would be on your part. But, I am assuming you did this responsibly, you seemed to have figured it out faster than I did." Lockwood smiled.

"That it was me all along…yeah, that was unexpected, but I reckoned that if, as an ordinary girl I could walk through solid material, and a witch, with, like, actual *powers* or whatever she was, had to lift it to get through, I definitely had something about me, so I took the risk…but it paid off, I think…speaking of which, who was that girl, and what happened to the diamond?" Magic had to blurt out two questions in order to reduce the collisions happening in her mind. She vaguely remembered seeing the diamond destroyed across the ground, but she felt the desperate need to ask about it anyway.

Lockwood sighed deeply. "Well, to answer your first question, Aurora Rirks is a young, orphaned girl of Pakistani heritage, who was abandoned by her parents because of her supernatural abilities, as you very well know of."

Magic nodded and shuddered at the memory of Aurora throwing them across the room using the power of her mind.

"She fled her country, in search of acceptance, and kept herself safe using her powers. Eventually, she stumbled across Pyrithia, and began working with Vandalarukk, who took advantage of her abilities.

"Now, to answer your second question: you may not have noticed, but both the diamond and the staff are damaged beyond repair."

Magic pondered this for a moment. She couldn't help but feel slightly sympathetic, almost pitiful towards the girl who had almost murdered her—Magic knew all too well what it was like to feel thirsty for acceptance. She sighed.

"And what about Vandalarukk? What happened to him?" Magic dispensed her questions like a vending machine, but neither Mickey nor Lockwood seemed annoyed by it at all.

"Well, we didn't really stick round to inspect the collapsed robes on the floor after you passed out and Katie was released." Mickey sighed. "Anyway, our job was done, so we had no reason to stick round."

"Hmph. That's—"

Magic was cut off when, suddenly, there was a series of drumming against the door, along with some excited voices. Magic's eyes snapped towards the bedroom door, bemused.

"Who?"

"They're already here?" Mickey sighed again. "Alright, let them in."

185

"This'll be good." Lockwood grinned. "You can come in, guys," Lockwood spoke to the door, his voice raised.

The words had barely left his lips before the door burst open, and in stumbled Maria, followed by Charlie and Chloe, followed by William, and, even more unexpectedly, Thomas.

Magic's face broke into a delighted beam as Maria barged past Charlie, her blazing red hair up in a messy bun, and hurled herself at Magic's bedside, throwing her arms round her neck.

"Magic, MAGIC! Oh, *Magic!*" Maria screamed into Magic's shoulder. She pulled away. "How are you? What happened?"

Maria's entourage of eager questions triggered the rest of her friends to go off with curiosity. Suddenly, everybody was at her bedside, except Tom, who stood in the doorway, scratching his head in confusion.

"Did you see him?"

"Did you see his *face?*"

"The diamond?"

"Did it hurt?"

"Who else was there?"

"Where was it?"

"Where did you go?"

"What else did you find?"

"Was everything true?"

"How did you get hurt?"

"Jeez, Magic, those cuts are huge!"

"Is he dead?"

"Did you kill him?"

"What did you find?"

Magic simply beamed at them, unsure where to start or what to begin with or what to mention first. Though she was too exhausted to start retelling all the events of that night, she wanted to tell them as soon as she could—she sympathised with them a little too much. She knew exactly what it was like to have so many questions you want answered at the same time that you're at bursting point. Oh, how she knew.

"Guys, guys, relax, calm down, she's only just recovering, don't bombard her just yet, you'll find out everything in due course." Lockwood chuckled. He was too used to eager children. "You've got great friends, Magic. Never let go of them." He winked at Magic, just as everybody bent over to hug her at the same time.

"Sorry." Maria flushed deeply. Everybody else looked just as eager as before as they pulled away, their eyes blazing with curiosity.

"What in hell was all of that about? What happened to you, Magic?" Tom asked slowly, very evidently in a state of complete bewilderment.

The reason for Tom's confusion immediately clicked in Magic's brain—Tom had been absent from them for most of the year due to the importance of his exam preparation and the nature of his tight schedule. He had missed out on all their discoveries, theories and realisations. Magic clapped a head to her forehead at the thought of how much he had to catch up on.

"Oh, jeez, you've missed out on a lot..." Magic told him apologetically.

"I can see that." Tom walked into the room and shut the door behind him.

"She'll explain everything to you guys in just a moment," Lockwood told them. He hastily lifted up his sleeve to look at his wristwatch, and then addressed them with a tad more haste. "I've really got places to be, but I've got just a couple things to say first."

Everybody immediately tuned in, their curiosity redirected at Lockwood. Even Mickey looked intrigued.

Lockwood cleared his throat. "Firstly, Magic, I owe you an apology."

Magic was taken aback at this. She had not expected that.

"It was wrong of me to ask so much of you so quickly, and—"

"No, no, no," Magic cut across him, shaking her head. Her friends looked at her with odd expressions. "Lockwood, you only asked if I would accompany you, and I wasn't going to say no. It was my choice to go through that passageway and pick up that diamond, which led to my injuries. You have no part in that. You have no part in any of the rash, sometimes not very thought through decisions that I make."

There was silence for a few moments, and Magic could tell, by the frown on his face, that Lockwood was thinking this through. After a while, a smile broke across his face.

"That's very—*humble*—of you." Lockwood smiled after a while. He seemed to hesitate. "Magic, you really *are* Magic."

Magic hadn't expected him to say that, so she threw him a smile of appreciation. She knew that those last five words would forever ring in her ears in times of despair, to remind her who she was. After all, her parents didn't name her Magic by accident, and was happy that people started to recognise that.

Lockwood began pulling on his coat, when he suddenly seemed to remember something. "Oh, and one more thing before I go," he said quickly, reaching into his pocket.

He rummaged round for a while, before extracting the battered, strange calculator that Magic had given him at the beginning of the year. She took a sharp intake of breath, suddenly remembering the whole story behind the strange piece of stationary.

"You still have that!" Magic exclaimed.

"Yes, I do, and I looked into it, as well," Lockwood told her, as he handed her the calculator.

Magic touched the screen where the eerie message had appeared months before. It looked just as ordinary as it had before it had displayed the message. Had she not known the story behind it, she wouldn't have known there had been anything wrong with it.

"What did you find out?" Magic asked him quickly. "Who's responsible?"

"Well, it isn't very hard to guess—turns out Vandalarukk had bewitched it, thinking it belonged to Slay. Had you waited a little longer, I'm guessing you may have seen some threatening messages directed at Slay, supposedly as a warning to him to hurry up with—"

A muffled ring at the doorbell cut Lockwood off. Everybody turned expectantly towards Magic's bedroom door. There was a swing and a snap as the front door opened and then closed, and then a thunder of the stairs as somebody hastily climbed them.

There was a soft, desperate knock at the door.

"Come in," Magic called anxiously.

The door slowly creaked open, and there, in the doorway, stood a downcast, worry-stricken Katie Harrow. Her hair looked as if she had held a balloon to it, her flyaways sticking up in all directions, and there were dark shades under her eyes.

Katie cried "Magic!" at the exact moment Magic cried "Katie!"

"Hello, Katie," Magic greeted her awkwardly.

Katie stepped into the room just as awkwardly. She bit her lip as her gaze fell upon everybody else in the room. Her brown eyes were troubled.

"Hi, everyone," she said.

Magic was starting to cringe inside at the awkwardness of the situation. It was very evident that she was holding back a lot of thought.

She strode over to Magic's bedside and knelt down beside her.

"Magic…"

"How are you, Katie?" Magic asked her, trying to diffuse the tension.

Katie burst into sobs.

"Magic, oh, Magic, I'm so sorry!" Katie wailed hysterically. She wrapped her arms round Magic and cried into her shoulder. "It's all my fault! I—"

Katie's muffled sobs broke off when Magic put a hand on each of Katie's arms and pulled her away, so that she could look at her.

"Don't be stupid," Magic said to her very seriously. "It had to be done. I—I—" Magic hesitated as Katie sniffled, her red eyes puffy with tears. "I am the girl the legend speaks of. Either way, I *had* to be the one to end it all, so suck it up, because I'm fine, and whether you liked it or not, it had to be done," Magic told her firmly.

"So—so you're not mad at me?" Katie asked her hopefully, her voice trembling.

"Katie, how could I be? You haven't done anything!" Magic exclaimed incredulously.

"I-I just wanted to make sure," Katie sniffled. "Magic, I really appreciate you coming to save me. That was really brave of you." said Katie in a small voice.

Magic smiled. "That's what friends do for each other, right?"

Katie gave her a watery smile.

Magic sighed, trying to remember where the conversation had been at before Katie had arrived. "So, what were you saying about the calculator, Lockwood?"

Lockwood snapped out of the daydream he was having. "Oh, yes—I was just saying that if you'd let the message display itself for a little bit longer, you'd probably have seen a death threat directed towards Slay, or something like that. It's just a guess; I don't have much to go off of."

"I'm sorry, a calculator handing out death threats?" Tom interjected, evidently unable to stand his confusion any longer. "Somebody's got a lot of explaining to do. Magic, how on earth did you end up in such a state?"

Magic heaved a great sigh. "Tom, I'm afraid that's too long of a story to recite today."

"I don't think I can wait any longer! When we were out there—" Tom jerked his head towards Magic's bedroom door "—we heard some talk about your eyes *lighting up!* Like, come on, now! *What is going on?*" he pressed.

"Magic, you can't be *that* tired, you've been sleeping for the past few hours," said Maria coolly. "I don't think it would hurt if you told him the story."

Magic got a strange feeling in the pit of her stomach. Surely, Maria would understand how tired and exhausted Magic was feeling? She found it odd of her to act his way.

"Maria's right, Magic, you don't need to be so dramatic," Charlie intervened, his voice also not far from anger.

Magic frowned in confusion and hurt. Why were her friends behaving this way?

"Yeah, " Chloe nodded slowly, agreeing with the others. "It's not like you'll die if you don't tell him now!" she snarled.

"What're you—?" Magic began, more hurt than ever that her friends would treat her this way, but she was cut off by Lockwood this time, who, to her horror, wore the most terrifying expression of them all.

"Magic, tell your friends what happened, right now," he commanded her, his voice so threateningly soft it was in danger of breaking.

"Guys…"

Magic tried to plead, but everyone immediately towered over her, their faces frozen in the most petrifying snarls, and she lost her voice.

"Magic, you're being ridiculous!"

"*Why're you being like this?*"

"For God's sake, are you that much of a show-off that you're *pretending* to be tired?"

"Chloe, you know she's just doing that to look cool, I bet she didn't even do most of the work!"

"*How—did—you—even—survive—it?*"

"RIGHT? With brains like hers—"

Magic cowered into her pillows. She didn't know how to react to this turn of events—all she could do was panic as the faces of the people she thought she could trust towered over her with their petrifying snarls, their angry voices clogging her thought process…

She cowered lower into her pillow…the fabric was engulfing her…she sunk down, down, down, deeper…

And then there was silence.

Epilogue
Illusion

Magic's eyes flew open.

First, she tried to steady her breathing. She was breathing so hard and fast that her breaths came out in sharp, loud gusts, her chest rising and falling too rapidly.

She felt round her bed; it was drenched to the core with hot, suffocating dampness. Magic sat up straight and realised that the middle of her pillow was covered in a shapeless, dark shadow. She had sweated up a tsunami.

The front of her pyjamas stuck to her as if she had just been dunked in water. The side of her face was sticky with sweat, and her hair was swept back, as if glued to her head.

Magic ripped away the covers and hopped over to the alarm clock on her desk, rubbing her eyes. The bold, red digits told her that it was six twenty-three in the morning. The room was as grumpy as the sky outside—a dark, inky grey.

Magic rinsed off her face in the bathroom and ran her wet fingers through her hair—there were dark shades pressed in under her eyes, and she was abnormally pale, almost snow-white—she felt slightly queasy, almost sick.

It had all been so vivid.

What silly little game was her mind playing at? Putting her through a night like that? She definitely didn't need to be more shaken than she already was, especially not today.

Magic stumbled silently back down the dim corridors of her house towards her dark bedroom, exhausted and sleep deprived.

She did not know what to make of all the events that had just occurred…all in her mind.

Although she knew she was being paranoid, Magic darted to her bedroom window and scanned the early morning streets, forcing her resisting eyes as wide as she possibly could. So far, no sign of anything suspicious roaming the deserted streets of Krington. The whole neighbourhood seemed to be as calm as ever, in deep, deep slumber. The whole city, even, seemed to be in a unified, peaceful sleep.

Well, the whole city except Magic. She felt like she was the only person awake...alive, on the face of the earth who knew exactly of the bizarre things that occurred during the night.

Or maybe she wasn't the only one...she could only guess what others, right now, were dreaming about, however horrible or lovely, sickening or delightful. Magic contemplated this for a second.

She began pacing blindly, still trying to shake off the creeping feeling that dream had given her, and wondering why she'd had it.

Maybe it was something she'd eaten yesterday? Watched? Done? But that still would not explain how her mind had created that whole universe...nothing she'd ever seen before, except for her uncle, Mickey, and Katie, whom she'd met yesterday...that was the only thing that felt real.

It felt like the whole thing had happened over days, months, years, yet it had all been condensed into the short span of a few hours. Yet she had so many questions.

Who were all those people? Ridiculous for her mind to invent people with names like Slay! What was her brain playing at?

Although Magic was well aware that he did not exist, she still shuddered as she remembered, very vividly, how angry he had made her feel.

And then she felt a twinge of pain in the pit of her stomach that caused her to wrap her arms round her waist in agony.

They hadn't been real.

Those five wonderful, beautiful, sweet, kind, amazing souls did not exist.

She had created everlasting friendships with mere illusions of her mind.

How could she live the rest of her life knowing that Charlie, Chloe, Maria, William, and Thomas did not really exist? She had never met anybody like them in reality...they really were the subject of every person's dream.

She couldn't bare the agony. Her face scrunched up in pain. She missed them so much, and knew she'd never ever meet anybody like them in real life.

Magic thought that she'd definitely catch herself sleeping more often just to try and see them again.

And then there was Lockwood.

Lockwood had been great, an amazing teacher, who, in the dream, had been her father's best friend.

Magic made a mental note to ask her father when he woke up if he had heard of anybody by the name of Remy Lockwood.

Everybody—Ross, Spencer, Glant, Mills, Primrose, Slay, Lockwood, Brownlow, Clark, Sherry, Charlie, Chloe, Maria, Will, Tom, Mrs Stocklin, Ian, Michelle, Phillipa, Mark, Debbie, Vandalarukk, Aurora…

They had all been a figment of her imagination.

Wow. Just wow.

Her brain was going to pay for this.

Now, going into today, she did not know what she should expect. Who would she meet? Where would she end up? Would it be like her dream? Would the people be like the ones she had met in her slumber? Would her school look the same? Would her school *year* be as chaotic? Or would it all be different? Katie had been real, after all. She guessed that was a sign. Did she even have a grandfather named Magnus—?

Magic shook herself off, untangling her arms from round her waist, and allowed her mind a second to pause before her thoughts got too hectic. After all, the fantasy parts like the sorcerer, Vandalarukk, and the diamond, had felt like a dream in the moment, almost similar to the dreams Magic usually had every other night—wild and inventive. She wouldn't really miss *that*, if she was honest with herself. It had been too hectic for her liking. She would miss the adventure, though.

She stumbled over to her window in the half-darkness and heaved open the window, the very window, in fact, that Lockwood had clambered through in her dream. She shuddered at the memory.

Magic leaned out the window and let the dark morning breeze ruffle her damp hair and brush against her face. What a night it had been, but, after all, she couldn't dwell on it forever. She had reality to get through, and couldn't spend most of her time focusing on what happened while she was *asleep*.

Like her uncle Mickey had said in her dream, she could not let the strange behaviour of her brain rattle her for the rest of the day.

Stay in your own lane, and don't allow obstacles to cause traffic on the road you're driving on.

So, instead of just sitting round aimlessly, Magic finally decided that her time would be much better spent preparing to take on the year, starting with getting ready for her first day at school.

CPSIA information can be obtained
at www.ICGtesting.com
Printed in the USA
BVHW051152020323
659559BV00006B/282

9 789948 803133